THE FAMILY BUSINESS

THE FAMILY BUSINESS

ALISON BROWNSTONE™ BOOK FOUR

JUDITH BERENS   MARTHA CARR   MICHAEL ANDERLE

THE FAMILY BUSINESS TEAM

A special thanks to Debi Sateren, Kathleen Fettig and Mike Robbins for being amazing early readers for this book.

Thanks to the JIT Readers

Daniel Weigert
John Ashmore
Misty Roa
Nicole Emens
Peter Manis
Diane L. Smith
Keith Verret
Angel LaVey
Larry Omans
Paul Westman

If we've missed anyone, please let us know!

Editor
SkyHunter Editing Team

DEDICATIONS

From Martha

To everyone who still believes in magic
and all the possibilities that holds.
To all the readers who make this
entire ride so much fun.
And to my son, Louie and so many wonderful friends who
remind me all the time of what
really matters and how wonderful
life can be in any given moment.

From Michael

To Family, Friends and
Those Who Love
To Read.
May We All Enjoy Grace
To Live The Life We Are
Called.

CHAPTER ONE

Oh, this is good. Maybe even better than sex.

Alison glanced at Mason beside her at the table and he responded with a curious look.

He's already learned to read my face. I had better be more careful.

Hints of lemongrass, sriracha, and honey played over Alison's tongue. She savored every second of the flavor of Café Artemis' special Thai wings as she chewed slowly. Across the table, Hana gobbled wings with Tahir, while the handsome life wizard to Alison's side focused on polishing off his bacon cheeseburger.

"You don't know what you're missing," she moaned.

"The way you sound, I'm afraid of those wings." Mason took another huge bite of his burger.

"Are you trying to finish that off before the cow comes back to life?" Hana asked after she swallowed and sipped her drink. "She's coming for you. Ghost cow will punish you." She grinned.

"It's a good burger. What can I say?" Mason returned her grin.

Alison smiled. It was nice to sit with her friends and boyfriend without the worry of some grand conspiracy or when the next batch of assassins might show up to use their latest experimental railgun or anti-magic bullet on her. What good was it being the Dark Princess if she never had any downtime?

I give these wings the royal seal of approval.

The last month had been a series of easy jobs and money. Even if she hadn't done much to advance her reputation or expand the Brownstone Effect around Seattle, she hadn't been forced to deal with a single power armor squad in a month, let alone any scheming billionaires with delusions of controlling magic on Earth.

Is this what it's like to actually have a fun and relaxing life again? Sure, occasionally, I have to slam a guy or two into a wall and shoot an asshole, but the guys we've dealt with lately haven't been worth worrying about.

Alison's gaze drifted around the table and she studied her best friends and boyfriend without making it obvious. Her new life seemed extraordinarily full when she considered it. Mason's existence as an actual boyfriend still shocked her at times. He wasn't merely some guy she'd gone out with occasionally.

Sometimes, it was still hard to wrap her mind around even having these kinds of connections. After leaving the School of Necessary Magic, it had seemed that she would never have this kind of close friendship again. What had happened to Tanner made it even more difficult for her to enter into new relationships. It was easy to throw herself into school and work and as easy to pretend that she couldn't be a normal person. She'd somehow modeled herself on her parents' early lives, even though they now slipped into an increasingly domestic lifestyle that would have been bizarre ten years prior.

If the Scourge of Harriken can relax, his daughter should be able to. It still feels weird to be on a double-date with Hana and Tahir but also nice. I need a good word for weird but nice. Weirce?

Tahir glanced around with slight discomfort on his face despite the beautiful nine-tailed fox who hung off him. When they'd first sat down, Alison wondered if he was worried about the Grand-Canyon-deep neckline of Hana's jade dress, but a few minutes after arrival, she realized that the reason for the hacker's tension was being around so many people. His general confidence could mislead her at times.

Even if he can rock a nice pair of khakis and a button-up and fight off an entire team of hackers himself, this is a man who spends most of his time either alone or only around a few select people. This double-date might be a bigger deal than I thought and not only for me.

Light chatter from other tables and syncopated jazz from the stage filled the air. A saxophone floated in the air beside a double bass. Bright, glowing white lines held them up while they played themselves. The lines also led to floating drumsticks and down to a self-pushing pedal, both of which played enthusiastically on an otherwise empty drum kit.

The original source of the magic was a wand in a stand atop a gleaming black Korg keyboard. A dark-haired witch in a slinky black evening gown sat behind the keyboard and her fingers danced across the keys as she swayed back and forth.

"I can't play an instrument," Alison began with a nod toward the stage, "and she's playing four. Even with magic, that's impressive. I could manipulate multiple instruments easily with my magic, but that kind of coordinated playing? I very much doubt I could pull it off even if I knew how to play. I suppose that's why I'm sitting here in the audience and not on the stage."

"We all have our talents." Hana sipped her wine and her eyes twinkled. "I'm sure jazz witch over there can't take on a mercenary company by herself."

"You never know. Maybe she does concerts at night and raids mercenary camps during the day.

Mason and Tahir chuckled.

"Anyway, I was thinking about how things have calmed down somewhat," Alison continued. "Not only with Scott and his conspiracy or Chesterton and his assassin of the week, but even moving to Seattle and establishing the business. I finally feel like I can relax. It's been a while."

"That's not a bad thing." Hana took another sip of wine.

"No, I'm not saying it is, but it makes me think about self-improvement and not only ass-kicking. I mean creative stuff. Like what's on the stage."

Hana eyed her warily. "You want to learn to play jazz?"

"No, not jazz." Alison laughed. "But back when I was in school—not only high school but college—I did more cool things simply for fun." She frowned at the wings on her plate as if they were responsible for her predicament. "Then I let hunting dark wizards and work slowly take over until...it's like I forgot how to have fun. Ugh. I'm so boring."

"You can always join me in fashionista land. It's fun here, and you look so damned good all the time." Hana winked and gestured to her dress.

Mason patted her arm. "A, you're a lot of things but you're not boring."

"My mom kicks a lot of ass, and she didn't let herself disappear into her job," Alison replied, a thoughtful expression on her face. "And Dad's always had barbecue even when he basically had no life." She nodded firmly. "That's it. I've made up my mind. A proper Brownstone is a balanced Brownstone. I need to train my creative side. The Dark Princess needs more hobbies."

Hana giggled. "Sure. I won't ever complain about you having more fun. What about what you did in college?"

"That was mostly acting, but I set it aside because it took up a lot of time and I wanted to concentrate on other things. Even if I want to be more creative, time's still a factor." She shrugged. "I guess I need a balanced Brownstone activity that isn't super time intensive. Sure, jobs have become more manageable and involved fewer conspiracies this last month, but I'm still a security contractor. I can't commit to daily rehearsals."

"Dating me doesn't count as fun?" Mason asked with a smirk. "I guess I need to up my game."

Alison rolled her eyes. "You're fun but don't really feed my creative side."

"I'm hurt, A." He grinned. "I thought we were doing all sorts of creative...things."

Alison gave him her best death glare and he threw a hand up in surrender.

Tahir's face scrunched and he exhaled a long, weary sigh. "I can sing."

The heads of his companions at the table swiveled toward him, shock on their faces as if he had revealed that he was secretly a dragon. That might even have been less surprising.

Hana stared at him and her mouth quirked into a smile. "You can sing? Since when?"

"Since I was a teenager." The hacker averted his gaze. "You might think it's mere braggadocio, but I'm actually a skilled vocalist with powerful range and volume."

"You son of a bitch." Hana punched him lightly on the arm. "You've held out on me. Haven't you ever heard that chicks dig musicians? Even bassists, but especially singers."

"I'm not a musician, even if I once harbored dreams of —" Tahir sighed again and shook his head. "I shouldn't have brought it up. It was a mistake."

Alison leaned back and watched him with a slight smile. It was so rare for the hacker to open up about himself. Much of her life had been the subject of books and movies due to her family, so true privacy was something she'd given up on a long time ago. Most people still had that option, and she let herself forget it far too often.

"Dreams of what?" Hana prodded. "You can't leave us hanging after saying something like that. It's cruel *and* unusual."

"I wanted to be a rock star, all right?" Tahir stared at the ceiling. "I had this idea that somehow, if I practiced enough, I'd be a great rock star. It was a foolish idea that entered my head on my thirteenth birthday and stayed stubbornly lodged there for far too many years."

"No damned way." Hana all but bounced out of her seat. "So not only do you sing, but you sing rock? You *really* have held out on me. My own personal rock star boyfriend. I never thought I could be so lucky."

"You have to understand. I've never been good around people."

"Maybe you've simply never been around the right people," Hana cooed. "Don't worry about it, babe."

Tahir cleared his throat and now looked even more nervous. "Perhaps I should have taken that into account more when I first came up with my dream. After a few years, I gave up on the possibility of being a rock star. That said…" He managed to bring himself to look his girlfriend in the eye. "A skill once gained does need regular mainte- nance, and I don't commit to any activity I don't intend to at least maintain some proficiency in. It's wasteful to live your life in any other way."

Hana clapped. "I now expect serenades, just so you know. Daily and nightly. Glorious serenades about my beauty and charm."

He winced. "Perhaps it wasn't wise to admit all that."

The other couple laughed.

Alison turned to Mason and peered at him. "And are you a secret rock star on the side? I wouldn't expect daily and nightly serenades if you were, but maybe weekly."

Tahir groaned.

Mason shook his head. "I do have a little artistic secret, but nothing like that. I wanted it to be a surprise, though."

"I think I've dealt with an entire lifetime of surprises

these last few months," Alison pointed out. She folded her hands in front of her and leaned forward to hold his gaze. "If this doesn't involve a conspiracy to assassinate me, I'm sure I'll be happy."

"Here's the thing…" Mason took a deep breath. "I can paint and I've painted a portrait of you."

"That's so romantic!" Hana clapped. "Not rock ballad romantic, but a close second. At least a third."

A little heat suffused Alison's cheeks. "Oh, that is a nice surprise, although I'm sure you can find something more beautiful than me to paint."

"No," Mason replied flatly, "I can't."

She looked away, her cheeks now on fire. "Well, I'm behind the power curve. You all have your creative outlets, and all I do is consider new and creative ways to kill people or deflect rockets."

"Maybe you should ask Myna," Hana suggested. "She's been around for a while. She probably knows a thing or two about work-life balance for a Drow."

"She's been pretty scarce lately. We spent a couple of days working on the defensive glyphs for the condo and the building, but otherwise, it's almost like she's trying to avoid me. I don't get it."

"She's an ancient Drow," Mason commented. "Think about it. It'd be like one of us hanging out with toddlers all day. She probably can't spend more than a few hours around one of us without wanting to kick us off her lawn."

"Little kids are cute," Hana interjected. "With their innocent, squishy little faces."

Tahir eyed her with a faint look of panic in his face.

"Setting that aside, I don't think Oriceran Drow maintain lawns."

Hana chuckled. "Probably not. But didn't you finally convince her to accept a phone, Alison?"

"Yeah. But it's not like we text each other cute messages with emojis. She wants to help me out, but she prefers very specific and brief messages and, to be honest, she seems somewhat cold when I have to talk to her on the phone. I've checked on her a few times and she made it clear to me that I didn't need to do that. It's not like she's my employee, and she's centuries older than me and more powerful, so I can't exactly tell her what to do."

"You're not thinking about this the right way." Hana clucked her tongue. "You're the Princess of the Shadow Forged. It doesn't matter that she's way older than you. She's pledged to serve you as royalty. Work your royal privilege here."

"The last thing I want to do is pull the royalty card. If anything, I try to get her to stop constantly thinking of me as a Drow princess. I don't want to be pulled into their crap, especially since they haven't figured things out yet. Fortunately, they're Drow, so they don't mind spending a few decades doing it." Alison picked her wine glass up and took a sip. "I don't know what I expected, to be honest. It's not like we would be best friends. Like Mason said, to her, I'm barely an infant, and even if she has invested all this effort into me, it's because she's about to die. Still, I... I don't feel that she understands how grateful I am for her help in the past. I simply wish I could make her fully understand."

"I'm sure she does," Mason replied. "But I'm also sure

that it's hard for her to relate to modern Earth, especially since she didn't visit all that often. It's probably over-whelming for her, and she needs a break from the full blast experience of modern life."

Alison nodded. "You're right. I'm probably overthinking things and there's no reason to look for problems. I should simply be satisfied and grateful for her friendship. I guess I feel a little guilty that I can't do more to repay her."

Hana shook her head. "Don't worry about something freely given. Trust me. I spent enough years conning people to know the difference."

The witch finished her jazz concert and the room erupted in claps and whistles of approval. Alison and her friends joined in. The applause continued for a good minute until the witch moved toward the back of the stage with her wand in hand and all the instruments except the piano floated behind her.

"That was fun," Hana commented. "I'm not all that hot on jazz, but she still put on a great show." She nudged Tahir. "Not exactly as fun as my man serenading me, though. Am I right?"

He shook his head. "A mistake. A total mistake."

Alison stared at the empty stage for a moment and her thoughts continued to linger on Myna and her magical glyph training. Preparation for the dark eventuality of attack, as the old Drow had called it.

"Training," Alison blurted. "We need more training."

Hana looked away from Tahir as confusion settled over her face. "What are you talking about? We train all the time."

"Not only you." Alison nodded at Tahir. "Him, too. After

what happened, it wouldn't hurt for him to be a little better equipped in hand-to-hand combat or with a gun. We have the firing range and gym in decent shape now, and even if we don't have the obstacle course finished yet, there are plenty of obstacle training gyms in Seattle we can use."

Tahir scoffed. "I'll admit I was taken somewhat by surprise during that unfortunate incident, but I'm dubious that the confluence of events—which included a billionaire sending his elite men at me—will occur all that often."

"Maybe, but a little additional training never hurts even though I have other skills I can fall back on. We all need to make sure that we're as good as we can be, with or without magic." Alison pointed toward a speaker in a corner. "You never know when we might walk into a building and find out that it has some weird suppression spell or anti-magic emitter. If there's one thing that Myna has reinforced it's that I've coasted too long on raw power. I need more refined technique for both my magic and non-magic skills." She grinned. "And as my friends *and* employees, I'll force that life lesson onto you as well."

Tahir folded his arms in obvious disagreement. "I doubt that a few punches or bullets would have enabled me to escape."

Hana waggled her eyebrows. "It's your decision, but I'll say here that even though you're already reasonably fit, it wouldn't exactly hurt you in the attraction department if you were a little fitter and trained up. It'd be interesting to…explore certain things together, babe."

"I see." His face twitched before he turned to Alison. "I suppose a little additional training wouldn't hurt, after all."

CHAPTER TWO

A lison finished her stretch routine with a few toe-touches. She gestured to the obstacle course in front of her with a huge smile. "The rules are simple. No magic. And that includes foxing out."

She pointed to Hana, who was hard to take seriously in her bright pink Lycra bodysuit. Although, judging by the way Tahir constantly stared at her, he appreciated it. Or, at least, how tight it was.

"That's fine by me," Hana responded after she'd stuck her bottom lip out for a few seconds in a pout. "If it was only pure magic, you'd win anyway. This is fairer."

Mason cracked his knuckles. "So how do we want to do this? Take turns and go with times?"

"No, that's too easy." Alison shook her head. "We have to have some sense of danger and direct competition. The training transfers to tactical situations far easier that way. How about if you fall, you're out? Not simply a stumble, but actually fall off the obstacle. We'll all go at the same time, so it's a true race, but no messing with each other. Does that sound good?"

"Agreed," Mason responded.

Tahir shrugged. "Fine."

Hana bobbed her head eagerly and bounced a few times on the balls of her feet.

The quartet wandered toward the first obstacle, a series of large tires.

"Okay," Alison called. "On three, two, one, start!"

Everyone rushed into the tires but their awkward movement destroyed their attempts at real speed. Alison jerked her legs in and out and resisted the urge to try to run on top of the tires. Even if they'd not set down any rules against that sort of bypass maneuver, she was at greater risk of falling if she tried the move.

She continued to pump her legs as she closed on the next obstacle, a steep ramp. This ended with several loose ropes that would take the team across to a rope wall that led to another platform. She arrived at the ramp at the same time as Mason, but Tahir and Hana were only a few feet behind.

I'm doing well but I need to keep my focus.

Years of obstacle training—first on her mother's course and later in gyms like the current one—had instilled an important lesson in Alison: pacing. Rushing through an obstacle could easily lead to a mistake or early lactic acid build-up.

She wasn't sure about Mason, but she doubted Tahir had over a decade of obstacle course experience. Even though she'd trained Hana, they'd focused more on combat and general fitness with only the occasional obstacle course.

Alison jogged up the ramp as Hana and Tahir raced past but Mason kept pace with her. They both reached the top of the ramp as the other couple leapt onto a rope.

A few seconds passed before Mason and Alison grabbed their own ropes. Their friends arrived at the rope wall and scrambled up. Hana's face was locked in determination.

She's taking this seriously.

Alison jumped from her rope onto the meshed wall and rushed upward. Her heart had finally begun to pound.

Did I take the beginning too easily?

Tahir cleared the top of the wall first, followed by Hana, then Mason, and Alison brought up the rear. They all snatched hold of a zip line with two abrupt jerking height changes during the course.

Alison enjoyed the temporary breeze as she sailed downward. The first jerk didn't challenge her hands. She let her mind drift for a second, which made the second jerk more of a surprise, but she still arrived at the bottom of a new ramp with little trouble, as did the others.

Tahir hesitated when confronted by the latest obstacle in front of him—a staggered series of wide, flat poles.

Good instincts, Tahir. Balance obstacles are always the worst. If you rush through those, you'll fall, and even though you won't be hurt with all those mats, you'll be out of this race. Come on, though, be cocky. Charge through and take yourself out.

She had never been one to deny her competitive streak.

Humming loudly, Hana bounced onto the first pole and the next and took the lead from her man. He frowned and

continued. Alison and Mason settled into a more deliberate pace, but both began to catch up with their friends.

"I'm the Fox Queen of the Gym," Hana declared. She
even turned to jump back over the last few poles before she
raced toward the climbing wall. "And queens outrank
princesses." She rushed down the outgoing ramp. "Fear my
harsh but fashionable rule!"

"Win first, your highness," Alison replied. "Then worry
about policy."

Tahir grunted as his foot slipped off the final pole and
he fell backward. He made no effort to flail for balance and
simply wore a resigned look on his face as he crashed into
the mat below with a loud grunt.

There we go.

Alison didn't dare look at him until she cleared her last
pole. "One down, three to go."

Mason ran past her and gave her a salute. "I could say
the same thing, A."

"We've barely started. Don't get cocky."

Judging by Hana's furrowed brow and narrowed eyes,
her concentration might be responsible for her lack of
witty response. Her hands and feet attacked the small holds
of the climbing wall that blocked her path.

Alison did her best to ignore Mason although he
remained visible out of the corner of her eye and she
pulled on the first set of handholds to lift her body. She
trusted her grip strength as she continued to move up the
wall and gradually drew closer to the bright pink leader of
the race. Careful movement and pacing helped her gain on
Hana, and Alison arrived at the top of the wall at the same
time as her friend.

"Damn it," Hana muttered. She surged forward.

The course bottlenecked at this point with only two salmon ladders available. Alison was still ahead of Mason, so he'd be the one at a disadvantage.

Sorry, but not sorry.

Hana jumped from the small ledge at the top of the climbing wall to sprint along the last few yards of the platform that led to the right-side salmon ladder. A quick bound launched her forward with ease, and she caught the bar with her slender fingers.

Yeah, we've done upper body work, but nothing like this. It isn't only about raw strength. Let's see how you do.

Alison charged toward the left obstacle and soon, she had taken a firm grip. With a jerk, she yanked the bar from its resting spot and set it over the next set of rungs. A few moves later, she was ahead of Hana.

The nine-tailed fox looked Alison's way and panic began to set in on her face as her victory seemed set to slide away. She pulled her bar out and attempted to skip two rungs. Her placement failed, and her hands slipped.

The automated obstacle whirred and the bar retracted to the starting position, which gave Mason his opportunity.

Hana tumbled to the ground and shook her fist at Alison until she finally collided with the mat.

"The queen is dead," Alison shouted. "Long live the princess!" With several additional quick clacks of the equipment, she finished her ascension of the salmon ladder. Her arms and shoulders burned when she arrived at a small metal platform.

A series of small overhead handholds offered another

grueling gauntlet to test her grip and upper body strength. After she'd rubbed her hands together, she grabbed the first handhold and swung toward the next.

Mason had finished his ascent and was now only yards behind her. His ragged breathing was a loud reminder of that fact. Longer reach helped him on the obstacle, and both dropped onto the exit platform at almost the same time.

Alison's heart pounded and sweat dripped down her face. She didn't waste time to even glance at Mason as she sprinted toward the last two obstacles.

The first was a dangerous lattice dome, the main hand- and footholds all free-to-rotate rounded cubes. The last was easy in concept if difficult in execution after the rest of the course—a thirty-foot free rope climb. Whatever speed either of them achieved would be destroyed by the penultimate obstacle. Even if it theoretically allowed them some respite, it presented numerous opportunities to fall.

A few shadow lines or wings would have been nice, Alison thought as she puffed toward the dome. *Should I simply try to use the corners? It doesn't look like I can really get my foot in that tight space. Damn it.*

She grabbed at a lattice juncture with her hand and used her other one to steady the handhold. As she continued up and over the dome, she realized her earlier analysis was wrong. The constant muscle control required didn't make the dome a place for rest, but instead, another source of strain and challenge.

"You're almost at the end!" Hana shouted from the base of the dome. "Show that wizard how it's done."

A number of other cheers arose, and Alison blinked.

How did she do that? She doesn't have general magic.

She spared a quick look in Hana's direction. Her friend stood surrounded by about a dozen other people from the gym, all of whom watched intently, excitement on their faces, with the exception of Tahir. His gaze was calculating as if he studied the obstacles and the racers.

Oh, I guess most people don't attack this course in a group so aggressively.

Alison crossed the dome and leapt the last couple of yards to the ground. She landed and rolled easily to her feet. Mason copied her move, and both sprinted toward the ropes at the end of the course.

Step after step, foot after foot, they mirrored each other until they arrived at their ropes. She scrambled up without a jump, whereas he bounded up and risked slight rope burn at the beginning of his ascent.

Alison's lungs burned. Her arms and legs ached. With quick movements, she shimmied upward and focused on nothing but the completion of the course.

Thirty feet. Twenty feet. Ten feet. Five feet.

She looked to her side as she grasped the edge of the platform. Mason's hands had also found purchase and he stared at her, red-faced from exertion.

They both pulled up and over at the same time.

Alison fell on her back and dragged in several deep breaths. She wiped the sweat off her brow and sat up.

The makeshift crowd below cheered and clapped. Hana gave a thumbs-up.

"It looks like we tied," she managed hoarsely.

Mason took a few more ragged breaths. "I underestimated you, A. I figured that without the magic, I'd win. Not easily, but still."

"I've done obstacle courses like this since I was fifteen. My mom insisted."

"And I thought my parents were overbearing."

About thirty minutes later, after showers and comfortable banter, Alison, Hana, Mason, and Tahir made their way toward the entrance. The front of the building formed a conventional weight-training and cardio area, and if the facilities at the Brownstone Building weren't mostly complete, Alison might have considered switching to this gym full-time, given its challenging obstacle course.

She glanced at one of the TVs on the wall. They all played the same channel and the sound issued from speakers in the corners.

A gray-haired male newscaster looked at the camera and the chyron below him read, **TWILIGHT OF THE TOP TECHNOMAGIC BILLIONAIRES**.

"Continued investigations by the FBI and PDA into the activities of technomagic billionaires Scott Carlyle and Derek Chesterton have led to a series of coordinated raids at several of their offices," the newscaster reported. "Both Carlyle and Chesterton are currently held without bail pending trial. In addition to several public statements from Oriceran governments, including several by King Oriceran himself, there have been massive and continuing public demonstrations concerning the anti-magic conspiracies and anti-magic biological agent Scott

Carlyle has been accused of developing by the US government."

The video cut to a huge mixed-species crowd outside the White House. Witches and wizards held their wands and chins up with proud defiance on their faces. Alison hadn't seen so many elves in one place since she'd visited the Drow on Oriceran. Giant species stood out among the crowd, and the skies were filled with winged races that circled overhead.

Hundreds of National Guard in power armor lined the front of the fence, along with the Secret Service, both regular and magical, with wands ready inside the fence and spread out among the White House lawn.

Glowing and changing messages floated in the air in several different languages. Some struck Alison more than others.

MAGIC IS HERE TO STAY. GET USED TO IT.

I MIGHT BE A WITCH BUT I WAS BORN IN MILWAUKEE.

OPEN THE GATES WIDER AND QUICKER!

HATE WON'T WIN.

Magic makes protest easy, huh?

"Scenes like this one outside the White House two weeks ago," the newscaster explained, "have been seen all over the world, while authorities continue to urge calm. Religious leaders have issued statements of condemnation concerning Scott Carlyle's actions, including the most recent statement from the Vatican, but not all groups see a problem. Representatives of the Humanity Defense League have criticized Carlyle's methods but suggested his underlying concern is worth discussion. Other groups have been more openly enthusiastic, such as in this statement released a few days ago by the New Veil."

The image changed to a stylized multi-colored spiral inscribed in a circle. Alison's stomach tightened.

"In a war, the only true consideration is that of victory," the newscaster read. "Quibbles over tactics and short-term morality obscure the fact that once entered into, the goal of a war should be nothing less than the annihilation of the enemy until the point where they no longer represent an existential threat. We of the New Veil do not recognize Oricerans or other magical beings as our enemy, but we do recognize magic itself as a direct threat to our existence and way of life.

"What Scott Carlyle has done should be accepted and evaluated in the context of the war for reality—a war that, thus far, humanity is willingly losing because of the Siren song of the potential aid of magic. Indeed, Mr. Carlyle's actions represent, to date, one of the most merciful attempts to win the war against magic with minimal casualties. His virus, regardless of some of the sacrifices involved in its creation, didn't take the lives of its later targets. Instead, it only limited their magic, and he should be congratulated and praised for his efforts. We of the New Veil fully support Scott Carlyle and condemn, without restriction, any government or authority that seeks to punish him for his actions."

The televisions all switched to a baseball game.

"Hey," yelled a man doing curls on a bench. "I was watching that."

Alison slowed as she approached the door and looked at him.

"I prefer the game, man," protested another man doing crunches. "Let the politicians figure out all that shit. That's why we pay them the big bucks."

Mr. Curls set his weights down. "I think New Veil's got the right idea, you know?" He surveyed the room with a frown and his eyes narrowed as if he looked for an obvious magical to harass. "We let all these magic freaks do whatever they want like it's no big deal. Shit, at least you can tell the average Ori from a human, but it's not like you can see a witch and know unless they wave their wands around."

Most of the nearby patrons turned to watch the exchange.

Alison had raised her hand to push the door open and stopped with a frown.

"Maybe you should let it go," Hana whispered. "He's not worth it."

You could tell what I was thinking, huh?

Alison turned toward Mr. Curls.

Mason stepped to her side. "Whatever we do, please don't use magic," he murmured. "But I have your back."

"I don't need magic for this asshole," she replied.

"Screw New Veil," shouted the man doing crunches. He stood and marched to the bench where the other man sat. Mr. Crunches towered over Mr. Curls and his muscles bulged under his Western Washington University tank top. "Fucking terrorist douchebags." He grunted. "First of all, they kill people all the time. Like that shit in D.C. They could have killed thousands of people."

The other man grimaced. "I'm simply saying they have a point."

"Magic's part of the world, man. Some magicals are

assholes. Most aren't, much like the rest of us. We have AET and the PDA to keep the assholes in check." Mr. Crunches sneered. "And it wasn't a magical who had a secret lab and made biological weapons now, was it?" He pointed to the door. "If you want to join some terrorist hate group, then get the hell out of here. I can't work out next to a load of crap."

The other man stood and glared but he was a head shorter and probably sixty pounds lighter than the other man. Without another word, Mr. Curls stormed toward the hallway that led to the locker room.

Alison opened the front door and stepped outside as other people returned to their workouts. They had walked several yards before she spoke. "Huh. I'm pleasantly surprised."

Mason shrugged. "There are assholes on every side."

"True enough."

Tahir looked over his shoulder at the gym receding in the distance. "That being said, I'll be happy when we have our own place for obstacle training."

"Our obstacle course will be better," Alison suggested. "And—"

Her phone buzzed and she pulled it from her pocket to look at the message.

"Problem?" Mason asked.

She furrowed her brow. "I'm not sure. It's from one of the Death Knight informants. They want to meet. Apparently, there might be some trouble in the neighborhood." She picked up the pace. "I suppose there's no better training than real-world practice."

CHAPTER THREE

Yay. A seedy alley. It reminds me of when I met Dad, although two Harriken wouldn't be much of a match for me anymore, even without my magic.

Alison opened the door to her Fiat Spider and stepped onto the street that ran in front of the narrow alleyway. Mason exited on the opposite side and soon, Hana appeared as well, a spring in her step. Apparently, visiting ex-gang member informants in alleyways was another bright spot in her day. Still, since meeting the woman, Alison continued to be impressed by her friend's ability to wring joy out of almost any situation despite her dark past.

I could learn a lot from her.

A nervous man in torn jeans leaned against a wall. He rubbed his hands together and looked both ways as if power armor might drop from the sky at any second to kill him. Given Alison's life since she moved to Seattle, she wasn't sure that the idea was necessarily outlandish.

Maybe I should try to schedule a pay-per-view like Dad did that one time. Although ten years later, Mom still bitches at him about that. If I tried it, she'd probably show up with an anti-magic emitter, tie me up, and ship me back to Los Angeles.

With a quiet chuckle, Alison marched toward the man with her hands shoved into the pockets of her red denim jacket. "Hey, Jeff. You said it was urgent." She shrugged. "I'm here."

"Hey, ma'am," the informant replied. "Yeah. Urgent and shit. I figured it was better to do this face-to-face. You never know who is listening, and…well, I mean, it's not like bodies will hit the floor right away. But it is important." He sucked in a breath. "Still, we wanted to make sure before we wasted your time. We know you're busy doing shit." His shoulders sagged.

As a former member of the Elliot Bay Death Knights, he'd once roamed the streets with complete confidence. Even after Alison forcefully disbanded the gang and recruited several of them as informants, the average member still walked with confidence. After all, they had the Dark Princess on their side.

Seeing him nervous and fidgeting didn't do much to brighten Alison's day. On the other hand, if she finished the day without a new evil billionaire targeting her, she'd still do okay by the standards of the year.

"What's up?" Alison nodded toward Mason. "By the way, I know you've met Hana already, but this is Mason."

"Oh, yeah. I know about him." Jeff grinned at Mason. "It takes a brave man to date the Dark Princess."

Mason shrugged. "I'm doing okay so far."

Jeff grimaced at her raised eyebrow and raised his hands defensively. "Anyway, I wanted to let you know about some shit we've seen lately. Shit you should know about. The boys have been spread out, keeping an eye on things in case trouble comes in. Trouble for you means trouble for us, you know?"

"I can't disagree," Alison replied. "And what sort of trouble have you seen?"

Could Carlyle have reached out somehow? He bought several buildings around here before I took him down. Maybe he's sent a few mercs in to try to finish what he started.

"Suspicious dudes. Shitty suspicious." Jeff's eyes darted back and forth. "These assholes rolled in a few days ago. Nice cars. Nice suits. But we've never seen their asses around here before. So, it makes you wonder—who the hell are they, you know?"

Mason chuckled. "Nice suits make someone suspicious? I must be the most suspicious man in all of Seattle."

"I rock a sexy librarian look," Hana interjected, "but maybe not a full suit. I don't know if it'd be considered suspicious or not."

"Yeah. Suspicious." Jeff gestured toward Alison's jacket, a worried look still on his face. "It's all about the background, you know. That's how the camo works. Miss Brownstone is cleaning shit up, but it still takes time, and this was a shitty neighborhood for a long time before she showed up. So when you see a bunch of guys in suits and they don't drive a hearse, it makes you want to pay attention, right?" He licked his lips. "And so we paid attention, real close-like, but we're smart-like, see? You don't want to look like you're paying attention because then the assholes came after you, you know?"

"It sounds like a good plan," Alison replied. "And good tactics."

A little smile crept across Jeff's face.

I didn't exactly spin these guys up like Trey's gang but showing a little restraint has still worked out well for me.

Hana leaned against a brick wall with an increasingly bored look and her arms folded.

Jeff rubbed his hands together again. "But we got close to the place and checked around. These guys took over an old office building only six blocks down from yours, Miss Brownstone." He rattled off the address. "I don't know what they're doing in there because they have a bunch of renovation signs up. You know, 'pardon our dust,' and shit like that, but nothing about the kind of business." He shrugged. "One of our boys went to ask what was up, and a huge-ass dickhead in a suit ran him off. He didn't flash his gun but it was obvious he had one. We don't know who they are straight up, but they smell way connected. I thought you should know. You said you didn't want us to kick people out ourselves. I've told you so you can go and give them the meet and greet and let them know who the royalty is around here and shit."

Alison frowned. "Yeah. I'll double-check on these guys and if they are trouble, I'll have a little corrective chat with them. Thanks for the information, Jeff. We'll take it from here. You guys stay away from these people, okay?"

The informant gave her a little salute. "You keep doing what you're doing, Miss Brownstone. The rest of us live to serve." After one last quick glance up and down the alley, he jogged off. As he moved, sunlight glinted off the revolver tucked into the waistband at the small of his back.

Alison groaned. "If these guys turn out to be Eastern

Union, I swear I will blow their entire damned building up. I wonder if Ava can get me some explosives by tomorrow."

Mason laughed. "They might simply be accountants who like low rents and high security. Dial it down before you go all Scourge of Harriken on them, A."

"They could be PDA spies watching you," Hana suggested.

"Latherby wouldn't try that crap on me. He knows how I might react." Alison looked from one to the other. "And that situation would be easy to deal with, but my guess is it's something a little more annoying than that. The Death Knight guys might not have been tough enough to take me on, but they were a decent enough gang. They have a good nose for trouble."

"What's our move, then?" Mason asked

"If our new friends are at a particular building, they have to have some sort of online presence." She allowed a wicked smile to take over her face. "And if Tahir can help expose Carlyle's dirty secrets, I doubt these guys' systems can stand up to him. It's time to give him a call and let him do his thing. I'm sure that by tomorrow, we'll know everything we need to come up with a game plan."

It didn't even take a day. Alison was still twenty minutes away from where she would drop Mason off at his place when Tahir called her back. She answered on speakerphone, confused.

"Did you need more to go on, Tahir?" she asked. "I didn't plan to introduce myself yet, but I can poke around some more if you need it—or plant something if you need it, too."

He scoffed. "There's no need. The poor level of defenses these people have makes me almost embarrassed for their entire criminal organization. It speaks to a lack of professionalism, in my opinion."

Hana perked up in the back of the car and leaned forward. A slight frown crossed Mason's face.

"And what criminal organization is it?" Alison didn't hide the disappointment in her voice.

"Russian Mafia," the hacker replied.

The life wizard's face darkened but he remained silent.

Alison slowed as the upcoming light turned to red. "Wait. Only the Russian Mafia? Not the Eastern Union?"

"No. The Russian Mafia. This particular group is nasty but small, and they have no ties with the Eastern Union based on my initial searches. Admittedly, we're talking only fifteen minutes of research, but on the other hand, they've done the cyber equivalent of all but hang a sign out saying, 'Hello, we're an arrogant criminal gang with little concern about getting caught by any computer specialist of real ability.'"

Hana snickered.

Alison stopped the car at the light. "Why has the Russian Mafia set up shop in this neighborhood? I assume they didn't pick the address at random."

"No, they didn't," Tahir replied. "It was purposeful, and your building's presence was a major reason."

The light changed, and Alison accelerated through the busy intersection. "How so?"

"I found an email in Russian and ran it through a translator. Much of it concerns target areas for drug dealing and prostitution, if I interpret this correctly, but that's not the interesting part."

"So what is, then?"

Tahir cleared his throat. "Mind you, this is translated, but I otherwise quote, 'The difficulties with the police shouldn't be ignored. The best plan is to hide in the shadow of the Dark Princess. No one will look for us there. That elf whore will be our shield. If we don't cause trouble near her, she won't come looking.'"

Hana's face scrunched into a frown. "Elf whore?"

Alison shrugged. "I've been called worse. Usually by guys I kill shortly thereafter, though."

"If Tahir is in their systems, can't we simply send this along to the police and have them clean up?"

"I'd need more time to scrub some of my digital fingerprints from the retrieved information," Tahir replied. "But it's possible."

"No." Alison shook her head. "No police."

"I agree," Mason concurred.

"Why not?" Hana asked. "This isn't some billionaire's personal mercenary squad. I'm sure the police can handle them fine. They probably don't even need the AET."

Mason glared out the window. "They'll take too long. They have restrictions and procedures, and you heard the email. These assholes will do their best not to do anything obviously illegal at the location. That means the police will merely set up observation and wait. Even if Tahir hands them everything, they might spend weeks—if not months —trying to collect evidence and hunting around for bigger fish."

Alison nodded. "Exactly. These assholes specifically want to use my rep to protect them. If I let them sit there for a while, it'll make me look weak or stupid to the entire Seattle underworld. No, I need to handle them and quickly before word gets out beyond my informants."

Hana sighed. "And I just finished getting the stains out of my last favorite ass-kicking outfit."

"You don't need to get involved," Mason barked, his face tight and his shoulders stiff.

Alison raised an eyebrow and glanced quickly at him. It wasn't like him to be rude to Hana. The fox stared at him, more confusion than irritation on her face.

"Did you have a suggestion?" Tahir inquired over the phone. "One that doesn't involve Alison or Hana?"

"Yeah." After a few seconds, Mason visibly relaxed. "That is, neither of you needs to handle this. I've dealt with the Russian Mafia several times in Seattle. I owe them for a few clients, too. Let me clear them out, Alison, as a favor to you and me."

She turned at an intersection and made a quick mirror check. If Russian mobsters had moved into her neighborhood, they might follow her, too. "Wouldn't it make more sense for Hana and I to come? Not that you couldn't handle them, but maybe a bigger show of force will solve more problems in the future."

"Sure, if the Dark Princess shows up, everyone knows you'll be able to clear them out, but if only one of her employees shows up by himself and takes them down, that'll also send a message." Mason's jaw clenched. "It'll help avoid shit like what happened with Hana and Tahir."

Hana's face reddened. "I'm still sorry about that, by the way."

The hacker muttered something under his breath.

Alison's hands tightened around the wheel. "You have nothing to be sorry about, and you were almost out of there before I even showed up." She let a few moments of tense silence tick by before saying, "I understand having history with groups, Mason. I'm sure that half of this is about vengeance but considering the kind of crap I pulled when I first showed up in Seattle, I won't judge. You promise me you can take these guys?"

He nodded curtly. "Yes. They won't be much of a problem. Trust me."

"Fine. Do it then. But don't kill anyone." Alison shook a finger at him. "Yes, I'm being a hypocrite, but this is about protecting the business. If we don't kill them, we don't give them an excuse for vengeance. At the same time, a show of force makes it clear they won't be tolerated in this neighborhood."

"But I can break bones?" Mason arched an eyebrow.

"Sure. Knock yourself out. Them, too."

CHAPTER FOUR

T his ought to be worth a few relationship points along with a few vengeance points, Mason thought as he approached the office building in the evening. He adjusted his tie and marched resolutely toward the front door.

Faces carved with fear flashed into his head, men and women. He'd seen too many over the years.

My screw-up. I let those assholes kill my client, and that's on me. All that poor bastard wanted to do was leave the criminal lifestyle behind, but they wouldn't let him, just like they wouldn't release those girls they brought over.

I bet every one of you deserves to die, but Alison's giving you a chance. So play it smart if you want to live.

Jeff was right. A huge **PARDON OUR DUST** sign hung over the front door with a number for a construction company along the bottom. Tahir's digging had already confirmed the company was controlled by the Russian Mafia.

I'll give them a little extra work.

Mason withdrew his wand smoothly from his jacket. A

little preparation would lead to a lot less pain later. At least for him, but a lot more for the men he was about to confront.

Several intricate movements and incantations later, warmth swept over his body and his heart did its best machine gun imitation. Without his support spells, he would have had a heart attack. If the mobsters had any magicals, he'd be a damned inferno of obvious magic, but it wasn't like he intended to hide his identity. There would be no mysteries tonight, only mobsters in pain or leaving.

Mason slipped his wand into the holster inside his jacket and stepped in front of the door. He frowned as he searched for any obvious cameras. None. Either the Russians were very confident or very stupid. Or both.

It didn't matter. These kinds of criminals understood the language of violence, and that was one language Mason maintained with perfect fluency.

Time to see how much they value their lives.

He pushed the door open into a dust-covered lobby with several chairs embedded along the wall and a tall counter. A hallway led to a series of doors and a corner at the end. It reminded him of a hotel. Perhaps the building had been that in another time or life.

A huge man sat alone behind the counter, a deep scowl on his ugly face.

"Who the hell are you?" he demanded. He had no accent, but the Russian Mafia had long since ceased to rely on imported manpower in the area, especially since so many of these local groups had fused with Yakuza to form Eastern Union operations.

I don't know if I should respect their ability to hold out against the times or simply dismiss them as stubborn idiots. I'll find out here soon enough.

"Mason Lind." The life wizard gave the man a winning smile. "Now you know who I am, so I have an easy question for you. Are you authorized to speak on behalf of your organization?"

The mobster rose to his full height—easily seven feet—and glared at his visitor. "This is private property. You better get the fuck out of here or I'll call the cops."

Mason waited exactly three seconds before he responded. "You should do that. Exactly that. I'd love it if you did."

"Huh?" The man frowned. "Do what? You're the one who needs to get the fuck out of here, asshole."

Enforcers who are big but stupid are never a good play, boys. Too bad. This will be satisfying but not as much fun as I hoped.

He took a few deep breaths. His heart still raced and his body had grown uncomfortably warm as a side-effect of his enhancement spells. "Call the cops, dipshit. I want you to explain to them why a bunch of Russian Mafia think they can set up shop here. I'm sure if they toss the place, they'll find something interesting. I'm sure it'll be easy to find an excuse to hold all you assholes for a few days."

The mobster stomped around the desk and veins bulged in his forehead. "If you know who we are, then maybe you shouldn't come in here and fuck with us. At least not if you want to continue breathing, because right now, I think you really have something against breathing or even want to have every bone in your body broken."

A door in the hallway opened and three other men filed out with frowns. They weren't as huge as the lobby guard but they still looked as though they enjoyed their daily servings of beef. There was no sign of any magic, though.

You poor bastards don't have a chance. Do you even remotely sense that?

"Yeah, that's the thing," Mason replied. "My boss—and my girlfriend, by the way—is Alison Brownstone. You might have heard of her. Dark Princess and all that jazz. Well, she doesn't want scum in this neighborhood. She went through all the trouble to personally clean up the gangs." He shook a finger and his head. "But then you assholes creep in here and think you can hide in her shadow. Things don't work like that. Not in this neighborhood. Not anymore."

The three new arrivals moved into position behind the lobby guard. They all slipped brass knuckles on in a deliberate show of force.

Ballsy bunch, aren't you? But you have to ask yourself, "Doesn't this guy seem unconcerned that he's outnumbered? Shouldn't we be worried about that? What could that possibly mean?"

"Did you hear that shit?" the lobby guard asked and pointed at Mason. "The fucker says he's doing Brownstone. I bet she's frigid. All cold and shit with that white hair. The Dark Princess is probably the fucking Ice Queen."

Mason's face twitched.

No killing, but broken bones allowed. There are many bones to break in the human body. Over two hundred.

He gritted his teeth. "Okay, now you've really pissed me off by being disrespectful toward Alison. She likes warnings, so here's one for you—and consider it a bonus as I should break your fucking jaw for what you just said. If you agree to leave right here and now, tonight, you get to walk away free. Hell, if you even simply start the process of leaving, that's enough. I'll go back to Alison, and she'll agree to look the other way. But if you don't agree, then I'll have demonstrated to you why you don't fuck with Brownstone Security, and that will definitely involve a hell of a lot of pain."

He clenched his hands into fists and sweat trailed down the side of his face from the intense activity of his magically enhanced body. If these assholes had responded with anti-magic bullets right away, they might have stood a chance, but they hadn't even reached for guns. Again, the intersection of arrogance and stupidity created opportunities for an enterprising life wizard Dark Princess boyfriend.

The lobby guard stepped forward and reached slowly and deliberately into his jacket. He drew a switchblade out and pressed the button. The blade extended with a loud click.

He pointed the knife at Mason. "You don't get it, do you, you stupid piece of shit? Because you work for Brownstone, we're showing our respect. It's why you're not already dead. It's one thing if she comes in here and tells us to leave, but we won't run off simply because some piece of shit like you shows up."

Mason laughed. "You know what? This shit isn't even about what she wants anymore. I'm trying to resist the urge to kill every last one of you bastards. You're trash mobster scum, and you disrespected Alison by coming to this building, to begin with." He stepped toward the lobby guard and locked gazes with him. "But go ahead. Show me what you've got. You have one chance to kill me, so make it count. I promised not to kill you, but accidents happen, and I really do think the world would be better off without some of you in it."

The huge man sneered. "I won't kill you, but only because you're doing her and she might get pissed about that. But she can't complain too much as long as if we keep your face pretty, am I right?" He thrust the knife at Mason's shoulder.

The blade pierced the suit and bounced off the wizard's hardened skin with the faintest hint of a prick. The mobster stumbled back and his face contorted in confusion.

"Oh, did I forget to mention I'm a wizard?" Mason grinned in the split second before he thrust forward and slammed a fist into the other man's face.

The huge mobster sprawled back and crashed hard against the wall. He crumpled to the floor unconscious and left a huge indentation in the new plaster.

Mason shook his hand out and turned his baleful gaze on the other men. "That was a weak-ass opening move. Let's say, gentlemen, that I'm not fucking impressed."

The three other men reached into their jackets as one. The wizard rushed toward them and covered the distance before they could draw their guns. He smashed a hardened shoulder into the closest and a crunch brought more than a little satisfaction. With a shriek of pain, the man collapsed and clutched his shoulder as he writhed on the floor.

Shouts sounded from down the hallway, along with thudding footsteps above. A few other doors in the corridor opened and more men poured out with their pistols in hand.

Damn it. If I could simply kill these assholes, it'd be a lot easier, but her wish is my command.

Mason snapped a kick into another man. The poor bastard's lower leg bent at an unnatural angle, and he crumbled with a loud groan.

His friend managed to fire a shot and the bullet bounced off his target's armored skin but stung slightly and left a thin trail of blood.

The wizard responded instantly. He closed on the shooter and backhanded him. The blow lifted the mobster off his feet and he spun several times before he smacked to the floor, unconscious and his nose a bloody mess.

Mason didn't hesitate as the reinforcements approached purposefully, their weapons at the ready. He charged forward, his movement a near blur. A few men managed to fire and the bullets stung the wizard and fatally wounded his jacket and shirt but left only a few minor cuts on the body underneath.

Now close, he launched a flurry of punches and kicks, careful not to put his full amplified strength into them. It took only seconds to scatter the broken men. Many moaned in pain while others were still unconscious. All were still alive, if in need of a few weeks in the hospital.

Another half-dozen new arrivals hurtled around the corner at the far end of the hallway with their weapons drawn. They all held guns except for one gray-haired man in the back.

"Stop!" he shouted. Unlike the lobby guard, the man possessed a distinct Russian accent.

Finally, someone with half a brain?

The other mobsters aimed their guns deliberately at Mason but didn't fire.

The wizard took a few deep breaths. "Are you in charge here?"

"Yes, I am." The man stepped forward with a frown on his face as he surveyed the fallen thugs. "You killed my men."

Mason shook his head. "I knocked them around a little, but none of them are dead. I was given explicit instructions by Alison Brownstone not to kill anyone."

The mobster's face tightened. "The Dark Princess?"

"Yes. She doesn't like you hiding in her shadow and asked me to tell you to leave, but your men tried to kill me." Mason shook his hands out. "And then we agreed to disagree. So, we have a few options here. First, we can continue this dance." He pointed toward a bullet hole in his shirt. "But your guys already upped their game and they're the ones on the floor. But if you all want to go down fighting, I'm happy to oblige. Second, we can end this damned farce and you can agree to get the hell out of this neighborhood before somebody ends up dead—and it won't be me. That's for damned sure."

"You expect us to leave Seattle?" The mobster snorted. "Give up everything here?"

"No, no, no. That'd be stupid. I didn't say anything about leaving Seattle, and neither did Alison, but you do have to leave this neighborhood. That's non-negotiable." Mason slammed his fist into the wall and broke through with ease. He withdrew his fist and opened it to waggle his fingers. "But let me also make it clear—that's not my choice. That's her choice. The mercy of the princess, if you will. If I had my way, I would have come in here and killed every one of you assholes for even daring to think you could fucking get away with this shit."

The mobster's face tightened. His gaze traveled from Mason to his downed men over several seconds. "And Brownstone won't come after us if we leave?"

"If you start to leave tonight and are gone by tomorrow, she won't. No games. No bullshit. You simply take your shit and men and get the hell out of here. If you try anything else, though, then maybe she'll tell me to finish what I should have started, or even worse, she'll come herself."

"You do know who you're fucking with, don't you? We're not defenseless."

Mason snorted. "Please. I haven't even *tried* that hard and I've knocked your guys down like bowling pins. But please, tell me how you think you'll win. Remember, Scott Carlyle—even with his billions of dollars and technomagic —did not do so well against Brownstone Security." He laughed and slapped his leg. "Seriously? 'We're not defenseless.'" He offered the last phrase in a high-pitched voice before he dropped his mirthful façade abruptly. "Do we have an understanding or not? I'd like to spend the rest of my evening doing something other than kicking your asses."

"Yes. We have an understanding. We'll...relocate. This site was poorly chosen." The mobster nodded slowly to his men. "Put your guns down."

They all lowered their weapons with real uncertainty on their faces.

Mason smiled. "See? Go with the flow and everyone's happy in the end." He turned and strutted to the front door. "Better get your guys to the hospital. There are many broken bones. They could use some painkillers, too. And next time you have a smart idea that involves Alison Brownstone, save everyone some pain and trouble and simply drop it." He stopped at the door and stared at it. A quick kick with his empowered leg tore it off its hinges and it catapulted to the hard pavement outside. "Enjoy the rest of your evening."

Alison's clapping was audible over the phone after Mason finished explaining his success.

"Good job, Mason," she replied. "And you even managed to do it without killing anyone. I'm extra impressed."

"I wasn't exactly gentle."

"I didn't say anything about being gentle, but I'm glad you cleared all this up because I received a call from our favorite PDA agent. He didn't give me any details but wanted to check on my schedule. I think we'll be busy soon with something more important than corner mobsters, not to mention the big delivery."

"The delivery. Oh, yeah. I almost forgot." Mason chuckled sheepishly. "That's not good, considering I'm the one picking it up."

CHAPTER FIVE

Ava halted at the top of the stairs in front of the roof access door. Alison stopped behind her. Ever since the woman's performance on the night of Carlyle's take-down, Alison hadn't been able to look at her the same way. Her administrative assistant had played coy when she'd talked about her background, and even Tahir's efforts failed to reveal much more than that she'd had some "tactical experience" before she worked for the PDA in an administrative capacity.

It doesn't hurt to have a badass administrative assistant, especially when she's on your side. She's like Mary Poppins crossed with the Equalizer.

Ava stared at Alison for a moment. She pursed her lips and adjusted her glasses. "Is something wrong, Miss Brownstone?"

"Wrong? No. Why would you say that?"

The other woman leaned forward with a knowing suspicion in her eyes. "You made an odd face."

"Just thinking about stuff." Alison nodded toward the door. "But I should focus on the delivery."

With a curt nod, Ava opened the door and they stepped onto the roof. A white and black helicopter sat atop Alison's week-old helipad. A logo of two dark crossed swords decorated the side of the aircraft with Brownstone Security in large, stylized letters below.

"You didn't ask me about a logo," Alison observed.

Ava responded with a slight shrug. "I assumed you'd defer to me in such matters."

"I have to admit it does look pretty cool."

They continued toward the aircraft. It wasn't huge although it could hold a pilot, one person to his left, and six people in the back in two rows of seats. But the craft provided the quick mobility Alison had sorely lacked. Her Drow magic could get her into the air, but she wasn't that fast compared to even a reasonable car. Tahir's kidnapping and her friends' arrival at the Carlyle mansion had convinced her that she needed a helicopter or dropship sooner rather than later. Given that her boyfriend was already a helicopter pilot, the immediate choice seemed obvious.

Mason poked his head around the front and waved, his pilot helmet still on. "I delivered your package, A."

Ava gave him a flat look as if laughing would cause her to self-destruct. "Did you need anything else, Miss Brownstone?"

Alison shook her head. "I'm good for now. Thanks for taking point on this. I appreciate it, Ava."

"My pleasure. Also, to let you know, I'm still working

on the licenses for heavier weapons. They have taken longer than I anticipated because of how recently you renewed your bounty hunting licenses—although in any event, we'd need a larger helicopter to mount them on." Ava pushed her glasses up her nose with her finger. "So I suppose there's no hurry, then."

"I'm fine with this for now. I don't plan on more assaults against billionaires with mercenary armies anytime soon." Alison sneaked another glance at Mason. "At least not this month."

"I'll keep that in mind." Ava gave her a final nod and headed back into the building.

With her assistant gone, Alison moved toward the helicopter.

Mason hurried around the side and gestured along the length of the vehicle. "Your own personal helicopter. You don't even need a drone to deliver your pizza now."

She laughed. "It's not like I'll fly it to Costco or anything. I merely wanted a little better mobility for at least a small team. All these assholes constantly show up with dropships. It really drove home the point that having an aircraft or two might help." She surveyed the roof. "We have plenty of space left over. Maybe I'll still get a dropship or a VTOL or something. You can be the helicopter guy, and I can get someone else for the other. We'll see."

He patted the side of the helicopter. "Do you want to take her up? If we maintain low altitude but stay out of the drone stream, we'll be fine. We don't even need a flight plan." He winked. "But I filed one anyway to be thorough."

Alison shrugged. "Sure. Why not? Latherby hasn't sent

me an update on when he wants to talk to me, so I think we're okay for a few hours."

Mason led her to the front door and opened it. He bowed and motioned to the seat. "Your sky chariot awaits, my princess."

She laughed and climbed aboard. A helmet with a built-in mic already sat beside the front passenger seat. She grabbed the helmet and slipped it on while her pilot boyfriend walked around the nose of the aircraft to the pilot-side door and entered.

Once they had secured their harnesses, Mason performed the elaborate ritual of preflight checks and flipped various buttons and switches. The huge array of choices reminded Alison of when she'd first started serious magic study at the School of Necessary Magic. There was obviously order and logic to everything in front of her, but the overwhelming amount of information made it impossible to understand at first glance.

Yeah, I don't think I'll learn to fly a helicopter anytime soon.

The rotors came to life, not nearly as deafening as Alison expected, but she was still grateful for her helmet mic and receiver.

"During the assault on the mansion, it might have helped to have some shield spells around the helicopter," she commented.

With a faint lurch, the aircraft lifted off the roof and its skids cleared the surface edge. Mason smiled and his hands and feet rested on the flight controls with practiced ease. The 'copter continued to rise.

"You have to be careful with magic and aircraft," he

replied after a short moment. "I don't tend to mess with it because I'm a life magic specialist, but even without that, it can be tricky. Let me tell you from personal experience—and not only Carlyle's mansion—that you don't want to try to take magic on in a craft like this vs. some military-grade big-ass monster with armor and integrated anti-magic deflectors. It's merely a big target waiting to get shot down."

The helicopter pitched forward and moved away from the Brownstone Building. The gray desolation of the neighborhood spread below her in all its pitiful truth.

Damn. This really is a run-down neighborhood.

"I simply want to keep my investment from getting shot down," Alison explained. "Since the pilot has a recent history of crashing."

"Keep in mind that I crashed that helicopter in the process of helping you."

"Excuses, excuses. They won't even let me insure it." Alison continued her survey out the window. The level of vegetation and the variety of colors of buildings increased block by block as they flew away from her offices. "It's not a good actuarial risk, they say. So, if this thing gets wrecked, I'll pay the full price to replace it."

"You do have a dangerous lifestyle." Mason spoke with a relaxed voice as he divided his attention between his instruments and the front window and only rarely spared her the briefest of glances.

The helicopter continued to climb and people below became mere dots and cars a stream of fast-moving particles. The traffic and building density began to decrease and large swaths of trees became more common the farther they flew from their neighborhood.

"Dangerous lifestyle is relative," Alison countered. "At least as a security contractor, I don't purposefully go after dangerous bounties or wait for someone to come and kill a client."

"No, you take on dangerous billionaires two at a time after they've weakened you."

"Big deal. I'm all cured now, thanks to Myna, even if she seems to only want to spend a small amount of time with me during her visits." She watched a plane take off from the airport in the distance. "Not that I'm not grateful, only surprised. I'm a little worried that I've missed something. Maybe some Drow protocol thing that I've offended her with even if she knows that I don't care about that stuff."

"You worry too much, A. It's cute sometimes, but you take it too far." Mason angled the helicopter slightly to change direction. "There's no mystery here. She told you already that she's old and expects to die sooner rather than later. She probably gets tired after spending time with you or some other simple explanation—like she wants to sample all the greatest foods on Earth between training you."

"You're probably right." Alison rested her cheek against her palm. "It's still weird, though."

"Don't worry about it. For now, enjoy the flight." He nodded toward the window. "If I paid to have someone fly us around Seattle, wouldn't that count as romantic?"

"Probably not on a day as gray as this one."

"That's like half the days of the year here." Mason laughed.

"Just saying." Alison watched him for a moment. A bodyguard life wizard boyfriend who was handsome, in shape, and possessed a good sense of humor was already a nice package as is, but his flying only broadened his appeal.

I find pilots sexy. Who knew?

They hugged the edge of Elliot Bay as they flew north in the general direction of Alison's condo. Most of the coast was dominated by dense patches of trees and parks, with only a thin line of houses along the bay proper.

I don't think I've ever appreciated how many trees are in this city. Everywhere I look, there's green. For as gray and drizzly as the weather can be, it's always nice to look around and see a nice, big evergreen tree.

"Okay, I've decided," she declared and broke the comfortable silence that defined the previous few minutes of travel.

"Decided what?" Mason asked.

"It counts."

"It counts?"

Alison bobbed her head, her gaze locked on a cargo ship in the bay below them. "As a date. Even though I can fly even without a helicopter."

He chuckled. "So it's not enough to impress you? Oh, I get it. I should take on a submarine."

"I can swim, too. I've not tried any underwater breathing spells, but I'm sure I can manage some."

He lifted his hand for the moment to tap the side of his helmet. "I can teach you some. Maybe I'll fly you out to some remote island and we can practice magical free diving."

"I've had worse dates. Is that something you're into? You didn't mention it before, but then again, it took you a while to mention you could fly a helicopter, and I didn't know you could paint until the other day. Speaking of romantic things."

Mason shook his head. "Nope. I've practiced some anti-cold and anti-pressure spells, along with underwater breathing, but I'm a real fan of the land. You never know what's in the water, especially these days. Give the gates a few hundred more years to open, and we'll probably have Kraken in the ocean if we don't already."

"The Navy has to have something to do. Why not fight Kraken?"

They pulled away from the low-lying buildings in the Admiral District into Elliot Bay proper. A large ferry chugged beneath them, along with a flock of birds and a winged humanoid who soared about fifty feet down.

He decreased altitude gently over several seconds. "Does your condo building have a helipad?"

"No, it doesn't." She leaned over to try to keep the winged humanoid in her line of sight, but it soon grew distant. Still, it made her think. Even with her shadow wings, she couldn't achieve the sustained freedom many of the naturally flying Oriceran races possessed.

"It might be cool to take you home in a helicopter." Mason winked. "We can always land right in front."

"I always have too many fanboy types sniffing around me as is. The last thing I need to do is show up in a helicopter."

"Even though you can already fly?" Mason replied.

"Not as fast as I can in this thing." Alison exhaled a sigh of contentment. "I almost want to tell Latherby to stuff it."

"Huh?" Mason frowned. "What are you talking about?"

"Other than asking for statements, the PDA has left me alone this last month." Alison stared at the bay. The expanse of murky gray-blue was hypnotic at this altitude. "If he calls me in, it means it'll be something annoying."

"You're at full power again, though, so how annoying can it be?" Mason turned the craft again and headed east toward Pike Place and downtown. The modest buildings of the Admiral District were nothing compared to the tall skyscrapers that formed the steel forest of downtown Seattle.

Alison sighed and slumped in her seat. "Way more annoying than going on a semi-date in my own helicopter with my too handsome pilot boyfriend."

"I see your point. I am very handsome."

"Okay, that's enough feeling sorry for myself." She slapped her cheek. "I'll say this for Latherby, I wasn't sure after the Carlyle takedown whether he'd want to give me the time of day or not, but he's been very open and honest with me. Without his help, I don't know if Carlyle would be in jail and awaiting trial. I'm not overly fond of the government, so it's nice to know there are a few guys in it whom I can trust."

The helicopter rose and changed direction once more.

"Well, don't worry about him," Mason suggested. "We still have an aerial tour of Seattle to complete. We can't do that without buzzing the Space Needle, at least."

Alison smiled softly. "This is nice, Mason. We should do this regularly."

"Fly around aimlessly?"

"I'm the one paying for the fuel. Think of it as a couple's walk."

He grinned. "Then I'm more than happy to take you around, A."

CHAPTER SIX

The doors to the store slid open and a pit of dread burrowed itself into Alison's stomach.

This was a big mistake, even if Hana's excited about it. Why did I agree to this again?

Her companion tugged on her arm. "Come on, Alison. You promised that if Latherby didn't call, we could do this today. And everyone's favorite PDA agent hasn't called yet, has he?"

"No," she muttered. "He hasn't." She stepped inside the store as annoyed thoughts about the man filled her head.

A smiling woman in a blue shirt waved from the front register. "Welcome to Petopia. Is there a new furry, scaled, or feathered friend I can help you find today? We have a special on terrariums today—ten percent off—and a two-for-one deal on all hamsters."

"We're good for now," Alison mumbled. "Just looking around."

"All right. Just let me know if you need any help."

The woman's plastic smile unnerved her.

Hana all but skipped toward the back, humming. She knelt in front of a wall of puppies in display cases. "These are cute. Very cute. Definite contenders."

"They get bigger, you know. So does their poop." Alison folded her arms. "To be clear here, I only agreed to look at pets, not buy a pet. I don't even get why you're still so obsessed with this. Is it really only because of the Triffles?"

"They got me started, but don't you think we need a pet-slash-mascot?" Hana beamed a smile at a Corgi puppy. "Aren't you adorable? I could eat you up." The puppy wagged his tail and barked.

Several of the dogs were sleeping. Others stared at the two women through the glass. A few wrestled each other, oblivious to the human and nine-tailed fox who watched them.

Alison squatted in front of a golden retriever that snored contentedly.

Okay, he is pretty damned cute, but I'm not Dad. I don't feel like I need a pet, dog or otherwise. I have a boyfriend. Isn't that enough?

"I would have figured that as a fox, you wouldn't like dogs," she commented.

"Why? At the end of the day, I understand the glories of four legs," Hana scoffed. "I love dogs and cats and—most animals, really." She strolled toward the cats. "I always worried about having a stable enough lifestyle for a pet, but things are different these days. Things are exciting but stable in their own weird way."

I wouldn't say we have a stable lifestyle, but okay.

"Now that we're looking for a pet and mascot—" Hana began.

"You are, anyway," Alison interrupted.

"Maybe we should go for something small that we can keep at the Brownstone Building," Hana continued and nothing suggested that she even cared what her friend had said. "It makes no sense to have a mascot that no one ever sees."

Alison tilted her head at an orange tabby that stared at her. He looked a lot like Peyton's old cat Osiris. "Even ignoring the whole pet thing, I'm not sold on this mascot idea. We're a security company, not a sports team. It's not like we need a mascot. How many security companies even have mascots?"

"Not enough," Hana declared confidently. She leaned over to peer at a napping group of Calico kittens. "Maybe we can start a new trend. But it doesn't matter. I don't care about other companies. I care about ours."

"Look, Hana, I want to be honest with you. I'm not much of a pet person. I never have been." She sighed. "Sure, I helped take care of a dragon for a while, but that was a long time ago and a lot of people were involved in looking after him."

Her friend's eyes widened and she clasped her hands together. "A dragon! That would be *so badass.* It's the ultimate pet-slash-mascot, you know. We need a dragon. We can put him in ads. 'Brownstone Security will protect you like this dragon protects its pile of gold.'"

"That gold thing is a myth." Alison sighed. "And I don't plan on ads for the company." She scrubbed a hand over her face. "And do you know how many regulations there are concerning large magical creatures in the United

States? Even if we wanted a dragon, the paperwork would take years."

"But you said you had one when you were younger. There can't be that many forms and stuff."

"Yes, I had one hidden near the School of Necessary Magic. And hidden is the keyword." Alison shrugged. "We weren't supposed to have it, even there." She waved a hand. "That doesn't matter. It's a dragon. No matter how cute they are when they first hatch, they're still damned dragons, and they'll grow into trouble, not cute pet mascots. So no ifs, ands, or buts. We will not get a dragon. That's not an option."

"Fine. No dragons. Even if it would be badass. Kirin, maybe?"

"No."

Hana ran her tongue along the inside of her cheek. "Griffin?"

"No!" Alison insisted.

The fox's face brightened again, and she all but sprinted down the aisle.

What? Did you find a fifty percent off all dragons display or something?

Alison hurried after her friend, only to find Hana in front of an alcove containing various colorful birds, including a few with three or four wings and others with bright neon color schemes. She wasn't sure if they were magical, genetically engineered, or some combination. The government seemed to care far less about modifying animals that people wouldn't eat.

"I suppose a bird is like a mini-dragon with feathers," the fox observed. "Descendants of dinosaurs and all that."

She pointed toward a cage filled with small bright green birds with sharp beaks and red tails. She leaned forward to read the label. "Green-cheeked conures. Maybe some of these? They're not exactly cute, but they are pretty."

"Birds fly," Alison responded. "Like you said, descendants of dinosaurs. And they bite a lot."

"So do you. Well, the flying, not the biting. I think. I've not asked Mason about it." Hana raised an eyebrow in question.

Alison gave her a dirty look, and her friend grinned merrily in response.

"I'm just saying," she explained, "that despite what you said earlier, we still have a very busy and irregular lifestyle, so I think it's best to avoid any high-maintenance pets. We never know on a job if we'll be out for a few hours or days, and I don't want to risk any pets getting hurt at the building. I mean, I'm a Brownstone. I think I'm essentially required to kill a hundred guys and blow up a building if any animal I own gets hurt."

Hana rubbed her chin. "You do raise some good points. I don't know why I found those Triffles so cute but I did." She pointed to a large sign several aisles down. "Maybe fish? They are two-for-one—a pet *and* a decoration. Again, more pretty than cute, but it's a nice compromise."

Alison laughed. "Okay, I admit those sound low maintenance enough. Maybe we could get a nice, large tank for the Brownstone Building. Let's scope it out today and not buy anything until the renovation's complete and Ava has everything settled. We don't know how much space we'll have in the end. Does that sound okay?"

"Fine. It's a start. You can't pet fish, but at least it's

something to brighten the place up." Hana gasped. "Does this mean our mascot will be a fish? I don't know if that's badass, but it does feel strangely appropriate for Seattle."

"No. Fish, yes. Mascot, no."

———

After twenty minutes of detailed aquatic pet discussion, the two women were back in the Fiat and headed toward the condo. They'd gone over some decent possibilities, and Alison planned to ask Ava to handle the logistics of the fish tank, even if she'd promised Hana the right to handpick all the individual fish.

She's as excited about the fish as she was the idea of the dragon. I'll take my victory.

"Am I crowding you too much?" Hana asked suddenly.

Alison looked at her with a frown. They hadn't spoken in the last minute, but prior to that, they'd discussed the merits of their respective shampoo choices. Both preferred a nice strawberry scent.

"What do you mean?"

"I was thinking about it. We're shopping for pets together like we're married because I live in your place and I'm your best friend." Hana nibbled her lip. "But you have a man now, a nice, handsome, great badass boyfriend. Before, I was grateful because you gave me a nice place to live, and I felt safer after everything with the Eastern Union, and..." She shook her head. "Look, I still love living with you, and the view is too damned gorgeous to give up without it hurting, but I'm not the semi-poor con artist I was when we first met. You pay me well, and I've not paid rent, so I can afford my own place. I don't want to move, but I don't want to crowd you or be that guest who overstayed their welcome. I'm unsure, is all."

"You're overthinking it." Alison smiled. "And you know things are bad if I'm the one telling you that you're overthinking something."

"You think?"

"I know," she replied. "You have to understand, Hana, the School of Necessary Magic was a boarding school and I didn't only have a single roommate. Then, I was in college for years and I lived at home for a while after that. The point is, I spent most of the last ten years living with other people, so it's not like I feel crowded by one other woman in a huge condo. Roommates are comfortable to me. Normal."

Hana looked out the window with a wistful smile. "But what about Mason?"

"What about him? I like him and we have a good time, but I haven't dated him for very long so it's not like we'll move in together anytime soon." Alison changed lanes as a squadron of pizza drones cruised overhead in tight formation. Their bright colors stood out against the gray sky filled with swollen, rain-laden clouds.

Someone's having a nice party.

"But what if he does want to move in with you?" Hana rubbed her hands together with a little too much glee for Alison's taste. "And sooner rather than later?"

"Then we'll worry about it when the time comes. The Brownstone tradition is slow-burn relationships anyway." She snickered as she thought about the trouble her dad had gone through with his proposal and her parents' long engagement. "And I like Mason, but it's not like those kinds of thoughts are anywhere but in the distant 'possible future' stage." She gave Hana a nervous look. "Why? Is it different for you and Tahir?"

The fox's cheeks reddened. "No, we're still at the fun stage." She shrugged. "But it feels good, you know, to have a guy who actually gives a real crap about me. And to know I can be honest with him rather than always trying to figure out how I can con him for a place to stay or a new dress or something. And I know he can be a little stiff, but I feel so relaxed with him. Like I don't have to hide anything, and I think he feels relaxed with me because he doesn't have to put on any fronts. I accept him for who he is."

"That's good. It's the same way I feel about Mason. It's hard being Alison Brownstone the Dark Princess at times, let alone the daughter of James Brownstone, Scourge of Harriken. I'm lucky to have you and Mason around. You're good friends. I wasn't sure how things would work out for me when I moved to Seattle. I never did settle into D.C., and I half-wondered if things would turn out the same here."

Droplets of rain splattered on the windshield and Alison turned on the wipers.

"Thanks, girlfriend." Hana exhaled a contented sigh. "But remember, just because Lily and Izzie and your other friends aren't around doesn't mean they don't still care. It's too bad you can't convince Lily to join the company. We'd be so badass then. We could be the Terrible Trio."

She chuckled. "The Terrible Trio? You think that's a good team nickname?"

Hana shrugged. "It's a work in progress. It does have a

certain *je ne sais quoi.*"

"I'll keep that in mind. As for Lily, she's too addicted to the tomb raiding lifestyle, but I'm sure we'll be able to work together again in the future." Alison slowed slightly as the rain picked up. "If there's one thing all this crap with Carlyle and Chesterton reinforced in my mind, it's that it doesn't matter if I'm the Dark Princess. I can't predict the future. For that matter, the Seers on Oriceran could, and people still messed a lot of things up when they tried to react to their prophecies. So whether it's my relationship with Mason or what's going on with all my friends from the old days, I like to play it a day at a time. That's the only thing I can do and stay sane."

She frowned as several police drones flew overhead in tight formation in the same direction as the pizza drones.

I guess that party was a little too nice. Hana would probably have enjoyed it.

"You really don't mind then?" her friend asked. "You don't want my nine-tailed fox ass to get the hell out?"

"Nope. You stay as long as you want to. If anything, I figured you'd get tired of me first."

"Nope." Hana shook her head. "Mason's right. Whatever people might say about you, life with you is never boring."

Alison's phone buzzed and she glanced at it. "You're lucky."

"Why?"

"It's a message from Latherby. You had your chance to visit the pet store."

Hana sighed with relief. "I am lucky."

"Me, not so much," Alison replied. "I'll drop you off and head over there. I wonder what fun he has in store for me."

CHAPTER SEVEN

Alison strolled into the PDA field office and waved at the dark-haired receptionist. "It's my favorite PDA administrative assistant. Do you have more sunshine to share with me today? You know, I always miss our time apart, Helen."

The woman rolled her eyes and muttered under her breath. "Agent Latherby is waiting for you, Miss Brownstone. Please don't keep him waiting. He's a very busy man."

"That he is."

She must be a joy to work with—or the best damned administrative assistant of the two worlds. Well, second, after Ava. It could be worse, though. She could be some rude, chain-smoking pixie or something like that.

Alison continued toward Agent Latherby's office. The door was open and the PDA agent sat behind his desk. Her eyes widened at an unexpected new treasure. A chair stood in front of his desk.

Now this is a bona fide miracle right before my eyes. Dad

should call the Vatican and have them send someone to Seattle right away.

"Thank you for coming on such short notice," Agent Latherby stated with a curt nod. "Please close the door behind you and take a seat, Miss Brownstone. We have much to discuss."

Alison shut the door before she sat gingerly.

Huh. Comfy chair, too. Nice, Latherby.

"I'm glad you finally decided to dispense with the power play and buy a damned chair," she replied. "Now, it feels like a regular visit versus being called to the headmistress's office." She chuckled a little nervously. "Not that it happened all *that* much."

"Headmistress's office." Agent Latherby's mouth quirked into a smile. "You truly are a product of your schooling."

"You get the idea." Alison rolled her eyes.

"As for the lack of a chair, it was never about a power play. I might be a wizard with the PDA but in the end, that still means I'm an underpaid public servant. You'd be surprised at how much even random members of the city council think they can call the PDA and verbally abuse us. Arrogant politicians." Agent Latherby gestured around his office. "The truth is that receiving guests in this particular office is rather rare versus talking in a conference room or even a building. A chair has simply been unnecessary before. This office's relationship with you is unusual. Very unusual."

The wizard withdrew his wand from his jacket. He made a few careful motions and chanted in Latin.

The walls of the room glowed for a few seconds.

Alison arched an eyebrow. "What's the spell? I assume you're not dumb enough to try to kill me."

"Not without a huge team and probably a few explosives, no. This spell will help to keep our conversation extra private."

"You're usually not worried about that kind of thing. Not enough for a bunch of extra magic anyway. What's the deal?"

The agent slipped his wand back into his jacket holster. "The reason will become clear enough, Miss Brownstone. But we should first dive into the most important matter directly relevant to you, namely why I need your help—which you will, of course, be compensated for."

Alison rubbed her temples. "Please tell me this doesn't involve more scheming billionaires. It doesn't mean I won't handle it if that's the case, but I've enjoyed the leisurely ass-kicking pace of this past month."

Agent Latherby chuckled quietly. "No, nothing like that, at least not directly. Although who knows where the trail will end by the time this is all over." He frowned. "I wouldn't have thought Scott Carlyle would be the mastermind behind the anti-magic plot, but he was. In this case, though, the enemy is a little more obvious and familiar and even personal. I'm talking about dark wizards."

Alison perked up. "Dark wizards? Yeah, I take dark wizards very personally, billionaire or not."

Christmas came early this year. Maybe Robert's coming to town.

"I thought that would get your attention. The primary issue is that our intelligence indicates that a decently sized group of them will begin to gather in Seattle soon for an unknown purpose. Your task is simple in description, if more difficult in execution. The PDA needs these dark wizards handled."

She nodded. "I have no problem helping you deal with some dark wizards, but why do you need me? If you're already following these assholes around, I would imagine that you have enough to suspect them of magical terrorism or other crimes. Can't you push your investigation a little further and tag them when they arrive? Why not round up all the PDA agents, FBI RRAET, and Seattle AET and kick in their doors?"

The man's expression darkened, and he leaned back in his seat and folded his hands on top of his desk. "In perfect circumstances, that would be an excellent plan, Miss Brownstone. We would track them down and apprehend them exactly as you suggest. Regardless of the number of dark wizards they bring, if we mustered all our law enforcement personnel, we'd be able to overwhelm them and capture them with, dare I say, ease."

Alison made a circular gesture with her hand. "What's the big unspoken 'but' after all that?"

His face twitched a few times and he didn't respond immediately. The seconds ticked by in complete silence.

"What is it, Latherby? You called me in for a reason, and it's not because you like my jokes. You need me, I trust you, and I hate dark wizards, so I'm more than willing to help. But that doesn't mean I don't want to know what's going on."

He shook his head. "I have a strong personal reason to believe there's a dark wizard mole in one of the local PDA field offices, maybe even this one."

"Is it possibly H—"

"It's not Helen," Agent Latherby cut in. "She's not even a witch, for one thing."

Alison shrugged. "I merely wondered."

"And if it's not a mole," the agent continued, "then there is at the very least a dark-wizard sympathizer passing information along to them."

"Damn, that sucks, but I guess it's inevitable that you'll end up with corrupt cops, magical or otherwise."

"Unfortunately, yes." The wizard's face twitched again as if the thought of the mole caused him physical pain. "I've been very circumspect with how I've handled this information, but it won't be enough for this situation to be managed without trusted outside aid, namely you. Arranging a major interdepartmental operation would almost certainly mean that the information would be leaked to the dark wizards. Our raid would either end up as an ambush or a raid of an empty building. We'd waste time and resources for nothing, and whatever plot they have would continue without interference."

"And you're absolutely sure about this?" Alison clenched her jaw. "I'm the last one to tell someone they're too paranoid, but I'll toss that out there for consideration."

Just like at the school. They're always there, hiding in plain sight. We need to find them and take them down before they hurt innocent people.

"I'm sure enough to bring you in," Agent Latherby replied without hesitation. "I wish I had reason to believe otherwise, but there have been some recent incidents that make it clear that some of the local dark wizard cells knew the PDA was coming. One such incident could be written off as random chance. Two times could be dismissed as coincidence. Three times points to a traitor."

He frowned. "I will continue to do my best to see if I can flush them out, but in the meantime, I'll need your help. I'll even have to expense your assistance in a more misleading way than usual to convince any potential moles that you've been brought on to deal with rogue elves and not dark wizards. That said, it's not as if I can order you to do this. This situation will involve even more danger than usual because neither of us can freely rely on the full range of PDA resources. As it is, we still don't clearly know when the wizards will arrive or where they will gather other than the city, so I can't even help you there."

"I don't care about all that," Alison replied. "Merely knowing that dark wizards are involved is enough for me, and I have my own contacts and resources. If I get lucky, I'll be able to settle some old scores, and even if I don't, I'll help screw up whatever twisted-ass plans they have come up with. I doubt you'll have a major gathering in Seattle because they want to sit around and swap stories of their magic training or fond stories about their cousin who went to the School of Necessary Magic."

Visible relief spread over the PDA agent's face. "Indeed. These aren't any dark wizards, either. They are Galbrathians."

A vague sense of disappointment inched into Alison's mind. The one dark wizard she most wanted to find, Robert, was an evil bastard, but he wasn't a Galbrathian to the best of her knowledge.

So many species of the sons of bitches. Well, I'll have to whack away at them until they become extinct.

"I don't get why these guys are still obsessed with Galbraith," she replied. "The guy's been dead for twenty-five years now, and every scheme to bring him back has failed. Why follow someone who had his ass kicked back when everyone on Earth was still figuring out how to handle a post-gate open world?"

"Symbols and martyrs are important." Agent Latherby snorted. "Especially to the dark wizard families who love such things and need people to rally around. It doesn't matter why they care about him. It only matters that they do and that it motivates them. Unfortunately, things might be easier for us if they continued their obsession to resurrect Michael Galbraith, but that's no longer the case."

Alison frowned. "What do you mean? It's been a while since I've run into Galbraithians in particular, but I thought that was still their big thing."

Even her own mother had interfered with them about ten years prior.

"Most of the major groups we at the PDA and our counterparts in other countries are aware of have all but given up their attempts to bring him back," the wizard explained. "Whether they think it's an impossibility or not a good use of resources, who knows? But that's the current state of things." He shook his head. "At least when they were more focused on doing that, it kept the potential risk to the civilian population much lower—the kemana incident aside, of course. But now, several of the largest groups have shifted their focus from a literal resurrection to a resurrection of his vision of a world thoroughly and completely controlled by magical beings, with the dark wizard families the foremost among them. In that sense, they aren't very different from some of the other dark wizard groups, but their existing level of organization and resources make them extremely dangerous."

"It also means that taking down one of their cells will do more to screw with the dark wizards' plans than most other groups. I like to call that efficiency in ass-kicking."

Agent Latherby's brow raised. "That's one way to look at it that I admittedly hadn't considered. In addition, the recent take-down of Carlyle seems to have particularly emboldened them. Whether this is out of concern or perceived opportunity in the chaos of the current world situation remains unclear."

Alison groaned. "Perfect. I didn't want to replace anti-magic assholes with pro-magic assholes."

"I understand, but their ideology is of secondary concern to their typically brutal methods and poor regard for non-magical life." He gave her a pained look. "And although I understand your personal history with those types, we'll need at least some of them alive for interrogation purposes. We need living prisoners and not corpses. You can't simply...Brownstone or Dark Princess this situation."

"I'm a verb now?" she responded with a hint of amusement in her voice.

"Both you and your father, actually." The agent sighed. "The point is to take down the entire group, as loosely organized as it is, and not simply annihilate this particular gathering. For that, we need intelligence, and that necessitates prisoners."

Alison waved a hand dismissively. "I assume I need to capture *some* of them and not *all* of them, right?"

"Yes, that would be an accurate understanding of the situation."

"Then it'll be fine." She flexed a bicep in real anticipation. "I can stop these assholes without too much trouble, but I can't do much if they have suicide spells."

"That has been less of an issue than you'd think. There are other possibilities but concentrate on their capture and we'll worry about those during interrogation." Agent Latherby nodded. "All I ask for is your best effort."

She cracked her knuckles. "When it comes to dark wizards, I always bring it."

***

The next morning, Alison sat at the head of the table in Conference Room A in the Brownstone Building. The walls hadn't been fully painted, but the room was functional enough if she ignored the echoed sounds of power tools, hammering, and the occasional shouts from down the hallway.

Pardon our dust, huh? But I have to hand it to the contractors. They've hurtled through this renovation damned fast considering that they haven't used much in the way of magic.

Ava sat near Alison and took notes on a tablet while Hana, Tahir, and Mason sat on the other side of the table. Alison was surprised that the hacker had agreed to come to an in-person meeting until Hana mentioned that he now worked out in the morning at the gym. It wouldn't hurt him to get more used to hanging out somewhere other than his apartment.

Maybe if I gave him an office all decked out with whatever equipment he needed, he could work from here. It'd be safer than always being at his apartment, especially when I hire more staff. I don't want to ever have to rescue one of my people like that again.

"That's the summary of what Latherby told me." Alison finished her explanation. "The PDA has confirmed that an unknown number of dark wizards will come in, and we need to find them and take as many into custody as possible. I wanted to come up with a general strategy on how to approach this.

"Obviously, the first thing we need to do is find the bastards. Latherby wasn't able to give me anything more specific than soon. I figure I'll hit Vincent up and a few other people I've run into. I don't think the local informants will be much use unless the dark wizards are stupid enough to try to set up in this neighborhood. Unlike the mobsters, I think they'll want to stay well away from me."

Ava tapped her notes in competently, her face a mask of concentration.

"I'll look around the net," Tahir offered, "although I've found in the past that these types tend to be far too leery and old-fashioned about how they share information. It makes it far more difficult for people like me."

"Even the smallest clue might help. You never know." Alison shrugged.

Hana looked from him to her boss. "I think this situation calls for some old-school fox charm. Even though everyone knows I work for Alison now, that doesn't mean all the people I knew back then won't give me the time of day. If I work some of my old contacts, they might be interested and pass some useful tips along. Sure, they're all assholes who would rob you blind if you didn't pay attention, but none of them like dark wizards. No magical in Seattle will ever forget what the Galbrathians did to the kemana." She gritted her teeth and narrowed her eyes. "I know I won't."

The fox looked down for a moment and her hands fisted. Tahir patted her on the arm.

Yeah, this is personal to me because of what they did at the School of Necessary Magic and what they did to Tanner, but at least we got him out of the coma. They killed Hana's parents.

Everything dark wizards touch is destroyed. Assholes. I need to stop them.

Mason cleared his throat. "See, this is where being an ex-bodyguard makes me less useful. I don't have a huge number of contacts I can work for information, so I think the best plan for me is to go with Hana."

Tahir glanced at him with a frown. "Why?"

"Alison can take care of herself even if she has to deal with a billionaire in a technomagic-enhanced battle suit." Mason shrugged. "Hana's quick and tough, but she's not as powerful. I can be the bodyguard beast to her beauty."

The other wizard processed that for a few seconds before the suspicion and obvious jealousy finally left his face. "That makes sense." He looked at Hana. "If that's okay with you."

She nodded her head. "It's cool. I'd love to have some ass-kicking backup. I don't think I'll have trouble, but like I said, I can't exactly trust a lot of my old *friends.*" She made air quotes with the last word.

Alison let a hungry grin take over her face. "Then it sounds like it's time to start hunting some dark wizards."

CHAPTER EIGHT

Each thump of the pulsing techno beat that filled the air at the True Portal invaded Alison's body like a sonic attack. Someday, she'd have to convince Vincent to meet her somewhere quieter. It didn't matter that things would end up manageable once she made it to his table. With the way things were, she'd end up deaf if she visited the club too often.

The sacrifices I have to make in this job.

She crested the stairs to find the information broker at a table—his usual haunt, even if he mixed the table choices up on each visit. He'd unfortunately chosen to go back to his purple suit with gold chains pimp-look versus one of his darker colored and more stylish suits.

Alison paused at the top of the stairs and grabbed the railing as she looked down at the thick mass of dancers below her. With all the magic around, there was no easy way to separate wizards and witches from non-magical humans, just like there was no easy way to separate the dark wizards from others.

If it weren't for dark wizards, Izzie wouldn't have to live a life on the run.

With all those smart and capable teachers at my school, the dark wizards still slithered in there and did their thing anyway. There are always some out there, planning whatever bullshit they have in mind. And the world needs people like me to take them down.

Vincent raised his hand and gave her a quick wave from his table, a question in his eyes.

Yeah, I'm here for you. Don't get too annoying about it.

Alison sighed and shook her head. The best course of action was to find the bastards and eliminate them. She might not be able to stop every dark wizard in the world, but she could at least clean up the trash who dared to invade her city. The Brownstone Effect could be about something more than criminals.

She headed toward Vincent's table and took a seat, grateful for his silence shell that shielded her from the loud music.

His signature magical appletini was absent, to her surprise. Instead, a glass of dark liquor on the rocks sat in front of him with no sign that it was enchanted.

Huh. I wonder if that means he trusts me enough to not worry about the truth martini?

"Judging by how much you charge me," Alison said as she settled into her seat, "you could afford your own club."

"If anything, I don't charge you enough," the informant responded and flashed a smile. "But I think a mild loss of profit is worth it to stay on the good side of the Dark Princess."

"I'm glad we agree." She gestured toward the dance floor. "My point is that you don't have to meet in a place like this. You could have your own elite little club and make us all bow and scrape for information. Maybe a place with fewer people and a more intimate atmosphere."

"Until I piss off the wrong person. At least here, surrounded by so much magic and expectation, I find I'm able to have a drink without too much stress." He picked up his glass and took a sip. "I don't drink Hennessy nearly enough. Appletinis have their charms, but sometimes, a man needs a good cognac."

"I like a good sake, but otherwise, I like to keep things fruity. Why drink something that tastes bad?"

"Tasting bad is subjective, and the power of a true alcohol is in its burn." Vincent lifted his glass to his nose and inhaled deeply. He set it down with a flourish. "But you didn't come here to talk about liquor now, did you, Dark Princess?"

Alison looked over her shoulder for a moment. "No, not unless that will lead me to some Galbrathians who will soon come into town. I'm open to whatever possibilities get me to them."

The corners of Vincent's mouth twitched. "Ah, yes, the Galbrathians." His gaze dipped to the glass of cognac. "Of course you'd come to talk about them. I'd expected it, but I hoped to be wrong."

"What's that supposed to mean? I don't think it's any big secret how I feel about dark wizards and you've helped me find some before, so why do you suddenly look like I shredded your favorite pimp suit?"

"Yes, I have helped you find them in the past." He stared into his liquor. "And I find myself sometimes questioning if that was smart."

Alison snorted and nodded at his glass. "You're actually trying to get drunk, aren't you? That's why you have no magic martini. You know exactly who and what I'm asking about, and you're worried. Is that it?"

"A smart man is always worried about all possible threats to his life." Vincent gave her a condescending smile. "It helps him live longer in a city as dangerous as this one."

"I plan to end these particular threats." Alison shrugged. "I need to know where and when the dark wizards will meet. There's also a nice bonus in it for you since I take their activities personally." She began to wonder if she should have a little cognac after all. "Unless you think they're on to something and you're ready to join Team Magical Asshole."

The informant snorted and his face contorted in disgust. "A smart businessman looks for all opportunities rather than worries about unlikely possibilities. The dark wizards are fools obsessed with something they'll never achieve, no matter how wide those gates to Oriceran open. And in pursuit of their idiot dreams, they've done a lot of damage, especially in this city."

"You're preaching to the choir." Alison leaned forward and offered him her best attempt at a disarming smile. "So, why don't you make some money and help me clean up? I'll consider it a personal favor too. Maybe I'll even agree to owe you a little favor in return."

"Poor negotiation tactics. Never let the other party know how desperate you are."

She shook her head. "Not desperate. Obsessed. There is a difference."

Vincent's right hand twitched where it lay on the table as if he wanted to grab something that wasn't there. "Here's my problem. Sending you at a handful of dark wizards whom I know you will kill has little downside for me. Your very presence in this city has made them quieter, but if I'm seen to openly cooperate with you, it's only a matter of time before they come after me. And I rather like living."

Alison snorted. "So you won't help me because you're afraid of them?"

"Something like that."

"You coward." She lifted her hand, palm out. A half-dozen writhing shadow tentacles sprang forth but remained only a few inches in length. "Maybe you should be more afraid of me. I'm the Dark Princess, after all."

The informant laughed. "I know you well enough to know you won't torture and kill me for simply being stubborn. I won't even bother with the pretense of having my guards threaten you, as we both know you're too powerful for that."

A couple of men several tables away glared at her.

Bring it on, boys, if you dare.

Alison let the tentacles linger in her hand. "Maybe I'm more motivated than usual. I don't like the idea of letting dark wizards get away when they've gone through all the trouble to gather together so I can kick their asses. That's a reasonable enough position, don't you think?"

Vincent stared at her hand in silence for a long while.

If I try to manhandle him here, I'll lose him as an informant and it'll be hard to get new ones, but I can't let these bastards slip away.

She finally released the spell and lowered her hand. "I can pay more. Like I said, I can pay a bonus. Even a favor."

He gulped down the rest of his cognac and exhaled forcefully. "That'll put hair on my chest," he muttered and slammed his glass down so hard Alison expected it to shatter. "You know what I hate about dark wizards besides their poor business sense?"

"No, what?"

"They always have a damned scheme. I hate schemes. They're always too clever by far." Vincent grimaced. "And people who scheme don't ever consider all the variables. That's why the vast majority of them fail."

Alison chuckled. "You don't scheme?"

The informant shook his head a little too forcefully, his cheeks ruddy. "No. I drink and listen to people who want to tell me things. I'm useful enough to most people without being enough of a threat that this becomes precarious, but these ideological bastards, like the Galbrathians..." He sighed. "They lack a nuanced understanding of the world. Their damned schemes end up messing up opportunities for legitimate businessmen such as myself who simply try to make a buck day to day."

She narrowed her eyes. "So you admit you know the Galbrathians are coming into town?"

"I know a lot of things, Dark Princess. It's what I get paid for. But from the sound of it, you didn't need me to tell you they were coming into town, did you?" Vincent gave her a crooked smile. "Maybe you should become the information broker and I can retire to some tropical island with beautiful women and no dark wizards."

"Yes, I know some Galbrathians will come into town, but I don't know where or when, and I hope you can help with that. So help me already."

He pursed his lips and shook his head slowly. "I don't doubt for a second that you can kill every last dark wizard bastard you run into any more than I doubt a good boot heel will take out a cockroach. But there's always another roach hiding, just like there's another dark wizard, and my concern is that if I tell you too much and one of those wizards comes sniffing around me... Well, I'm pretty damned fucked, aren't I?"

"So, what? You won't help me?"

"Nope. That would be stupid long-term, but it's more that I've purposefully kept myself out of the loop. I can't tell you something I don't know, and the Galbrathians can't come after me then. But I'll give you a freebie. They're not coming. They're already in town. They arrived yesterday—at least a decent number of them. Enough that you should be worried."

"Where?" Alison barked.

Vincent wagged a finger at her. "I told you, I'm exercising my plausible deniability to keep either them or you from killing me. All I know is that they're here. You'll have to ask someone else where and why."

Alison snorted and stood as her eyes narrowed. "This is one time you should have picked a side, Vincent."

"You don't understand. I did pick a side." He pointed at himself. "I picked my side."

She stomped toward the stairs. For all the info broker's cowardice, even his revelation that the dark wizards were already in town was useful information. It also meant she was already running out of time.

I hope Tahir and Hana have better luck.

CHAPTER NINE

The fox stared at her reflection in her compact mirror and puckered her lips. She wasn't in love with the shade of lipstick she used on her little information gathering session. Despite that disappointment, it'd been a long time since she'd cracked out the lacy, low-cut, black party dress that would serve as her initial distraction for her targets that night.

The dress looked *Hot* with a capital H. All her workouts with Alison had helped, too.

Fitness has a bunch of rewards.

Mason's tiny reflection hovered in the corner of her mirror. She didn't want or need him close. There was no reason to have a bodyguard who loomed and scared everyone off.

Once she'd slipped her compact back into her purse, Hana sashayed to the front doors of the upscale Rainier and Sunder and slipped inside the bar. The din of the dense crowd talking assaulted her ears. It was as popular as she remembered.

She had loved the place back in the old days. They were fancy enough that the true scum stayed away but not too upscale that she didn't feel comfortable there as long as she wore a nice dress. A lot of lonely tech employees liked the place as well, which made it a rich well of potential marks for any busy con woman who needed a little extra cash.

The fox pushed deeper into the crowd and her gaze flitted back and forth. She wasn't the only criminal, previous or current, who liked to frequent the place. Drunk men made for easy victims.

I hope I have better luck here than I did at the last place. From what Alison said, she hasn't had great luck today either.

Hana didn't bother to look over her shoulder for Mason. The man was an ex-bodyguard. He knew a thing or two about shadowing and protecting people without being too obtrusive, and she'd learned to defend herself effectively since she last visited the bar.

She glanced into her purse and verified that the crystal shield ring was inside. It'd be easier to slip on than the pendant if trouble started, so Alison had insisted Hana take it with her. It was a little too gaudy to wear with her outfit without drawing attention, though.

A man in a suit and his tie loose grinned invitingly at her from the bar as she passed. She replied with a coquettish smile.

I might have a man and don't have to con people anymore, but damn, I've still got it—and I'm hot. It's nice to be reminded of that.

The man's smile turned to disappointment as she continued past him in search of anyone from the old days. An attractive red-haired man sat in the corner at a table and chatted up a busty blonde in a dress that made Hana's already revealing dress look like a nun's habit in comparison.

You did always like them big, Russ.

She continued to weave through the crowd and closed slowly on Russ. With her most disarming smile in place, she approached him. His eyes widened when he spotted her and something approaching mild panic slid onto his face.

Like what you see, huh?

The man recovered quickly and a sly smile replaced the other emotions. He leaned over and whispered something to the blonde. She rolled her eyes, grabbed her purse, and shot a glare at Hana as she stormed off.

The nine-tailed fox arrived at the table and sat without asking. "Long time, no see."

"Yeah, it's been months since I've seen you." His gaze traveled up and down her body with obvious hunger. "Have you been working out? Because you were pretty smoking before, but damn, you're banging hot now. I like a fit woman. What can I say?"

Hana tilted her head and fluttered her eyelashes. "You haven't heard?"

"What? That you're working for the Dark Princess now?" Russ picked up his beer and took a sip. "Yeah, I've heard that. I can't figure out if that makes you a genius or a damned idiot. Although in a dress like that, I don't know if I care much either way."

A quiet laugh escaped her. "I'm glad you appreciate things, although I should let you know that I'm with someone right now."

The man's force contorted in confusion. "With some-one? You mean, like, a boyfriend?"

Hana nodded. "I don't even know why I bothered to tell you." She patted his arm. "Maybe I didn't want to give you false hope. I always knew you wanted to get with me back in the day."

"Hey, what can I say?" Russ shrugged. "You were always smart and hot. That's a dangerous combination. Lucky bastard."

"One quick question...why would working for Alison make me an idiot?" She tucked a stray dark strand behind her ear. "She pays me well. Very well, actually, and I don't have to do anything illegal anymore so I don't have to worry about the cops."

Well, mostly not illegal.

"She makes waves. I've heard you've been involved in straight-up fights with mercenaries and the Eastern Union."

Hana nodded. "Sure, and other people."

"I'm only saying it's dangerous, is all. But whatever works for you. Say what you will about the Dark Princess, she's a Brownstone, and everyone knows Brownstone's don't stand by when people fuck with their friends." Russ punctuated his sentence with another sip of his beer.

What? No big speech about how I'm a sell-out? I'm almost disappointed, but this makes things easier.

"What about you?" Hana asked. "I've not heard anything to suggest you're any less informed than you were the last time we talked."

The man finished his beer and set the glass down. "A man has to eat and drink, and I never had the talent or the magic to pull off the con artist game like you, but I'm good at listening and hearing things. People are always willing to pay for useful shit."

Hana folded her hands in front of her on the table and leaned forward. She licked her lips. Russ' mouth twitched and he swallowed.

You want what you can't have, don't you, Russ?

"I'm willing to pay for good information," she explained quietly. "Good money."

"Are you now?"

"Yes." Hana grinned. "And not only that. In this case, you'll do a big service for the city. Indirect hero and all that."

He laughed. "I'm not all that worried about anyone thinking I'm heroic. What are you interested in?"

"A group of dark wizards recently came to town," she clarified. "I need to know where they are."

A hint of a frown appeared on the man's face but he didn't let it linger for even a second although he couldn't hide his rigid body as well. "I try to not pay attention to crap like that. I'm simply a normal guy."

Hana stared at him. "You're telling me you haven't heard anything? I find that really hard to believe, Russ."

"Nah, it's not that I haven't heard anything. I know they came into town. There is a lot of buzz about that. But I don't know shit more than that." Russ shrugged. "Sorry, Hana. I wish I could be more help."

Bullshit. He knows something. I'm glad I wore this dress. Time for plan B. Sorry, Tahir, but it doesn't mean anything.

Hana sighed and patted his hand. "It's okay, sweetie. To be honest, I came here tonight hoping to find you for another reason. I've tried to tell myself it's stupid, but the longer I sit here and look at you, the smarter it seems, and now, I don't even care about the dark wizards. I'm sure Alison will track them down eventually. That's what she does."

"Really?" The stiffness in his shoulders disappeared. "What do you care about, then?"

"I lied to you earlier. Sure, I'm with someone right now, but I think a lot about the old days." She giggled. "You know, last year?"

Russ laughed as well. "Yeah, it's not exactly that long ago."

"I had to live my life a certain way back then because I didn't have a choice but now, things are more stable for me. It's made me question why I didn't pursue certain opportunities." Hana stroked the top of his hand. "Maybe see where they went."

The man's breathing quickened. "And you're interested in me now that you have another guy? I don't know about that, Hana."

"It's only when you start to really settle down that you question things. At least for me." She kept her hand on his and leaned forward so she could speak with a quieter, breathy voice and still be heard above the crowd. "You already admitted you're into me, so don't deny that you would be interested."

"How would that even work exactly?"

Hana leaned even farther forward to give him a better view of her cleavage. "Maybe start with a little fun, a test of…let's say compatibility. No one needs to know but us, and if we're compatible, we can see where it goes from there."

She resisted the urge to take a picture of the man's face and send it to Alison with the accompanying text, **This is what 100% horny looks like.**

A broad grin broke out on Russ' face. "You know, if you didn't do something like this, you might be full of regrets later. No one wants to be full of regrets, and I think you'll find that we'll definitely be more compatible versus whatever loser the Dark Princess hooked you up with."

Her hand twitched, but she kept a smile on her face. The atmosphere was perfect to get what she needed from Russ. Tahir could handle a few insults when he wasn't there.

Do I pull the trigger? Russ looks like he's ready and he's not a wizard, but if I'm wrong... Ugh. I'm out of practice because of Alison's 'kick ass first, ask questions later' typical strategy.

Hana brushed her fingertips over the top of his hand and tilted her head. "I'm sure we'll have a great time. A night to remember if nothing else."

"Me too."

She sighed and chuckled. Her eyes turned vulpine, and she scooted forward so her charm magic settled over him. "I have a few questions first, sweetie. Will you answer them?"

Russ stared at her, his eyes unfocused and a half-smile on his face. "Sure, Hana. Are they questions about how banging hot you are?"

Hana put a hand to her mouth and giggled. "No, no, sweetie. I don't need you to tell me that. No, it's about something else."

"Anything, but hurry. I want to see you out of that dress. I've dreamed about this kind of thing since I first met you."

I bet you have.

She finally pulled her hand back and rested her cheek in her palm as she watched him. Given her position, no one else would be able to see that her eyes had changed but she'd need to be careful to cover her tracks.

"Are you working with the dark wizards?" Hana asked quietly.

Russ shook his head. "No, no. Fuck those guys. What do they have for a non-magical guy like me anyway?"

"Was that blonde I saw you with someone you met tonight, or is it someone you know?"

"I never even got her name. I planned to take her home and have a good time, but now I have you to have a great time with." He offered her a dopey smile.

"Where are the dark wizards right now?" Hana pressed.

"I don't know."

"But you do know something, don't you?"

Russ nodded. "Yeah. I know where they'll be."

Hana patted his arm. "And can you tell me where that is?"

"In three days, a little after sunset, they'll have a meeting or something like that on some big-ass cargo ship that will dock at Harbor Island, the MV *Kilimanjaro*. I don't know more than that."

She took a deep breath and exhaled slowly. "That's very helpful. Thanks, Russ. I'll need one more favor."

He took her hand in his. "Anything for you, Hana. *Anything*."

"I need you to sleep for a while and forget that we talked tonight or that you even saw me."

"Okay," Russ mumbled. He closed his eyes and his head lolled back.

Hana stood and smoothed the wrinkles from her dress. "Sorry, Russ. If you had simply told me that in the beginning, you could have made money tonight." She winked. "Better luck next time."

Another survey of the bar revealed Mason on a barstool, a drink in hand. He nodded to her and then toward the door. She returned the nod.

Both headed toward the exit.

He fell in beside her as she stepped out of the bar. "How did it go?"

"I have a date, time, and location for a little dark wizard party." Hana grinned and clapped. "Sometimes, I forget how awesome I am."

Her bodyguard glanced over his shoulder. "Alison told me about that charm thing, but I've never seen it in action before. It simply looked like he was into you from where I sat. Are you sure he won't remember?"

Hana shook her head. "Nope. He'll wake up and have no idea what happened. If someone does happen to tell him they saw him with me, he might come asking questions, but Russ isn't exactly connected. If he finds me, I'll simply lie and say we had some fun in the bathroom but I was disappointed with it, so I erased his memory so it wouldn't mess up my relationship. He'll be so embarrassed, he'll let it drop."

Mason grimaced. "Damn, you're more ruthless than Alison."

CHAPTER TEN

Alison yawned as she entered the lobby of her condo building. Even if she'd struck out with her best sources of information, Hana had come through. With a date, time and location, they could ambush the dark wizards. Tahir was already working on obtaining the layout of the ship and to ensure that there wouldn't be any other surprises.

There's nothing to do but wait, now. I capture all their asses on that ship, and this whole dark wizard threat is over before it even started. This is almost too easy.

She chuckled.

"Did you hear a good joke?" A familiar man's voice spoke behind her.

Alison stopped and pivoted toward him. Ryan stood there with a broad smile and a briefcase in hand. His suit was a little rumpled.

He must have just got off work himself.

"Hey, Ryan." Alison greeted him with a smile. She couldn't say she liked the man all that much, but she didn't dislike him either. Being annoying was a minor sin in a city filled with vicious killers and schemers.

"This is fate," he replied.

Okay, now I'm worried. He does know I'm dating someone, so that should at least keep him off me. I hope.

Alison quirked a brow. "Fate?"

"Yes, I had hoped to talk to you. This way, I don't have to go up to your place and bother you. I hate bothering people at home." He nodded toward the elevator. "You look a little tired, so it seems like you've had a long day taking down bad guys and all that."

"Something like that. What did you need?"

"The elections." Ryan nodded, solemnity on his face.

"The elections?" Alison frowned. "I'll admit I still don't pay attention to a lot of local stuff, but what elections? Are you talking about the special elections coming up in April?"

I wish I was in Luke's district so I could vote for him.

"No, no, not those elections." The man chuckled. "Elections that actually matter."

"The congressional and presidential elections next year?"

"No, no."

She stared at him for a second and waited for an elaboration that never came. "Okay, I have no idea what you're talking about."

"Oh, I'm sorry. I merely assumed you knew." Ryan rubbed the back of his neck. "The condo board elections."

"Condo board elections?" Alison repeated inanely and blinked. "Oh, yeah, we have a condo board. I don't really pay attention to that other than what they say in the newsletter."

Yeah, I'm sure they would have liked it if I asked permission before I set up defense spells on my condo and a few key spots on the building, but I don't really have time. I haven't seen any other magicals in this building, so they probably wouldn't understand.

"Well, fortunately, I do pay attention to that kind of thing," Ryan explained. He knelt and set his briefcase down, opened it, and pulled a tablet out before he stood once more. "I checked around. Did you know you're the only magical person in this entire building? I think that means your interests as a half-Drow need to be better represented. If we had a magical board member, it might even signal to other magical races that this isn't a discriminatory building, and we could get more."

"Uh, maybe. I guess. I hadn't really thought about it. No one's said anything to me since I moved here that made me think they were anti-magical. Several people even told me how disgusted they were by Scott Carlyle's actions." Alison shrugged.

He swiped at his tablet. "Of course. But I think it would be best if the board had a magical member, and who better than you?" He cleared his throat. "Now, of course, you're our only magical resident, but I'd support you even if others move in."

She shook her head. "Look, Ryan, I'm flattered, but I'm way too busy with Brownstone Security. I'm just getting my business off the ground and I'm about to go through a major hiring push."

Ryan held up the tablet. "Before you decide, take a look at these campaign posters. How about this one?"

The tablet displayed an image of a stylized red and blue stencil campaign poster with an illustration of a stern-looking Alison who looked into the sky at a slight angle. **A PRINCESS OF THE PEOPLE** was written on the bottom.

You've got to be kidding me.

"Where did you get this?" She stared at the poster in horror.

"Oh, I made this myself. I minored in graphic design in college." He swiped and brought up another picture. This one was a full-color photograph of Alison's face with a gradient disappearance into the condo building. The caption read, **GET A MAGICAL PERSPECTIVE.**

More swipes brought up a half-dozen more posters, including Alison with a halo and wings of light fighting a dragon. She didn't quite understand how that one fit the condo board election theme, especially with its puzzling caption of **A LITTLE MAGIC FOR THE BOARD.**

She chuckled nervously. "Look, these are all very impressive, and if I ever do decide to run for something, you'll be the first person I call, but I definitely won't run for the condo board. I'd miss too many meetings and people would get annoyed. There's no reason to commit to something I know I don't have enough time for."

Ryan sighed. "That's understandable." He knelt to replace his tablet in his briefcase and closed it before he stood and picked the case up. "Well, you know where to find me if you change your mind. I think I'll make another dozen or two in case." He waved and moved toward the stairs. "Maybe I need them to be less realistic. That would have more impact."

Alison waited until he entered the stairwell to head toward the elevator.

She frowned as she approached her front door. A small glyph glowed red next to the handle. She'd set up the spell with Myna's help during her last visit. It was only visible if someone was inside but Alison wasn't.

Seriously?

In all honesty, she hadn't expected to ever need the warning at her home. Resigned to what lay ahead, she pressed her keycard against the reader plate and the lock clicked open. She pocketed her card and sighed.

Alison summoned a shield and a shadow blade and opened the door with her free hand. She stepped into the condo.

"If you surrender right now, I'll call the cops and you can leave this place breathing," she shouted. "If you try to fight me, I will kill you and quickly, too, since I don't want to have to clean more than absolutely necessary."

"Such threats are unnecessary, my princess," Myna called from her living room. "Although it does please me to see you've maintained a certain level of Drow defiance to possible threats."

She released her spells and hurried into the living room. The old Drow sat on the couch in one of her high-necked dresses but this time, she also wore a wide-brimmed hat with a flower.

I'm glad to see she's adjusting to Earth fashion, even if she seems to like stuff that's about a hundred years out of date.

Alison took a seat. "I thought we'd discussed calling ahead."

"Yes, we had." Myna looked down for a moment, exhaustion on her wrinkled face. Alison had never seen her so tired. "I apologize."

"Are you okay? I haven't seen you for weeks and then you show up and you honestly don't look your best."

Myna chuckled ruefully. "When you've lived as long as I have, you stop looking your best most of the time."

"But you're not sick or anything? Maybe there's something we could do to make you more comfortable, whether Earth medicine or magic."

"The centuries make you tired, but in this case, this is nothing that human doctors or simple spells can help with," the old woman replied.

Alison frowned. The ancient Drow had never exactly been forthcoming about many things, but she now had the distinct feeling that Myna was hiding something from her.

The frown slowly faded. The Drow had been upfront about the fact that she now stared at the end of her life. If it came sooner rather than later, maybe she didn't want to dwell on it.

Okay, I'll let it go for now. I have to respect this woman. She gave me such an important gift when I'd worried I'd never be able to cure the virus.

"I know I thanked you before," Alison began, "but I want to thank you again. This last month…it's almost impossible to express how I'd gotten used to reduced magical power, and now, I feel so free again. I don't have to rely on magical artifacts and can even use magic for different spells like the glyphs without straining myself."

Myna raised her head. "Excellent. I'm pleased to hear that. In fact, your increased magical power is the reason I choose to visit you again."

"More magical training?"

I bet Mason's right and she spends all these weeks between her visits exploring Earth. I can't complain if this woman who already gave me my full magic back doesn't spend all her time holding my hand and teaching me new spells.

"Indeed. I wanted to expand on your passive glyph instruction." Myna nodded toward the front door. "I presume the intruder glyph worked considering you came in ready for battle."

"Yeah." Alison sighed. "Sometimes, I wonder if I should live in the Brownstone Building instead of this condo."

The old woman narrowed her eyes. "Why? Do the humans reject your presence?"

"No, nothing like that." She chuckled. "At least one human wants me to run for the condo board."

"Condo board?" Her companion looked puzzled.

"That's kind of like a council that helps run this building."

"Then what is the problem?"

Alison raised her hand. Sparks of multi-colored light appeared and danced in her palm. "I'm the Princess of the Shadow Forged and Alison Brownstone. I recently took down two billionaires. Criminals and shitbags hate and fear me."

Myna furrowed her brow. "If your enemies fear you it's a good thing."

"Not if they decide to attack this building. There is security here but not enough to repel a major attack. Maybe I'm irresponsible. At least if the Brownstone Building is attacked, everyone there knows the deal. But it's not like everyone in this condo agreed to face those kinds of threats."

"If you let your enemies drive you from your home, it's a sign of weakness." The Drow glowered. "If you fear their attack, make it clear that they will be punished. It's not as if Laena hid. Any Drow could have approached her at any time. For all her faults, she understood the need to keep her enemies in check."

Alison shifted in her chair, uncomfortable with the turn the conversation had taken. "Yeah, it's not like I want to take pointers from Laena of all people, and I get that she poked at my dad to get him to come."

"You should learn from your adopted father," Myna declared. "He's an excellent example of what I'm talking about."

"What do you mean?"

The old woman lifted her chin. "James Brownstone doesn't cower in his building. He lives in a house that everyone knows."

Alison sighed. "True, but his old house got blown up."

"And how long has it been since someone challenged him at his new home?" Her companion raised a white eyebrow.

"Okay, I'll give you that." She rubbed her hands together. "And you're right. All the more reason to learn more about the glyphs."

Myna carved through the air with intricate movements

of her hands. A pulsating lattice of light appeared in front of her. "Containment glyphs can be useful for enemies you can't destroy outright. Sending someone to the World in Between is always a possibility, but that's something even I can't do by myself. In either case, it doesn't matter. For all your power, you still lack the necessary technique to freely open portals, so containment glyphs are a useful skill to master. Properly prepared, they can be created and sustained with far less magical energy than it might otherwise take to defeat the relevant enemy. Even at your full power, your magic is not unlimited, and this might prove of use in the future, especially given your family history."

She blinked. "Huh? What does my family history have to do with containment glyphs?"

The Drow sniffed with a hint of disdain. "I've studied on your Great Internet Library about some of the battles your father fought in the past and I'm sure there are many more that have been hidden."

"It's only...the Internet. It's not really like the Great Library." Alison chuckled.

"I'm aware that gnomes don't organize most of the Internet." The old woman stared at her for a moment. "But that doesn't matter. It's a collection of curated information, is it not? The sum total of much of this planet's knowledge, yes?"

"Sure, I suppose. Among other things." Alison shrugged, more interested in hearing what insights Myna had to provide about her father's past fights than correcting the old woman on the true nature of the Internet. "What about my dad?"

"There are several battles where he dealt with opponents who summoned creatures from elsewhere," Myna explained. "Some from Oriceran but others from strange existences foreign even to Oriceran. His magical armor allowed him to win, but had he used containment glyphs, some of the destruction that happened in his wake would have been unnecessary."

It's not magic armor, but she doesn't need to know that right now.

"There are different types of containment," the Drow continued. The glowing lattice disappeared. An image of a man bound in chains of shadow appeared. "Physical restraint is the most common and easiest." The man disappeared. An elf woman appeared and turned slowly into a tree over several seconds. "Physical change is also useful. Rob a creature of its mind, and even if it's soul remains, it can be easy to restrain, even for years."

Alison stared at the floating image of the tree. "And you've done this to people?"

"I've done it to dangerous creatures that were too difficult to defeat without the risk that others would be harmed." Myna lowered her hand and the tree vanished. "Does it bother you?"

"I don't know, to be honest. I've killed a lot of people, so it's not like I'm that squeamish. But I try to make sure they have it coming. Something about trapping them, though, seems almost crueler." Alison frowned.

"I have no idea how long you'll live, my princess," Myna replied, a concerned look in her eyes, "but even if you only live as long as a human, you have many decades before you. Those decades will be filled with enemies, no matter how much you strive to avoid it. Every tool that is available to you can help you defeat them and save others. Isn't that your ultimate goal—to protect others who can't protect themselves?"

She nodded but with an odd sense of reluctance. "Yes, it is. You're right."

The old Drow cut through the air with her hand and dozens of complicated floating glyphs of different colors appeared in the air. "It's as I said. This won't be something I'll be able to teach you with ease, but I will continue to pass this information along until such time as I can't, together with other training. Today and tomorrow, I want to familiarize you with the types that best work with your existing magic."

"Today and tomorrow?"

"Unless you have something more important to do."

Alison shook her head. "I have some dark wizards I will have to deal with soon, but that's not for a few more days." She grinned. "Hey, do you want to come along? Double Drow ass-kicking would be fun."

A brief gleam of excitement appeared in Myna's eyes but it disappeared almost as quickly as it had arrived. The corners of her mouth turned down in a pained grimace.

"To fight alongside the Princess of the Shadow Forged would be a great honor, but it wouldn't be a good idea."

"Why?" Alison groaned. "Is this Drow political crap again? I already told you, I have no desire to be queen, so if anyone shows up to complain, I can explain the situation."

"There are other more complicated considerations in this matter. In this case, don't blame yourself. It's more about me." Myna pointed to a series of interlocking spirals among her series of glyphs. "Your servants and friends are more than sufficient to aid you but thank you for the offer. For now, let us concentrate on the study of magic."

Alison released a frustrated breath and nodded. If she couldn't even get the ancient woman to reliably text her, it wasn't like she'd be able to cajole her to join a battle that didn't involve the Drow. The ancient elf might have come to help Alison, but that wasn't the same thing as being her employee.

No, Hana. I will not go all royal on Myna. She has to want to help me.

Myna's face twitched and she hissed for a moment. The glyphs in the air disappeared.

Alison's breath caught. "Are you're sure you're okay?"

She looked away and moved her hand again to summon the glyphs. "A momentary lapse in concentration, nothing more. Let's continue with our discussion."

She watched the old woman for a few seconds before she turned her attention to the glyphs. While she might not want to use her royal status to order Myna to help her, in the future, she might need to order the old woman to look after herself.

CHAPTER ELEVEN

A thrill of excitement rippled through Alison and she smiled as she surveyed the tactical training room. Various black metal ramps, walls, and blocks formed a multi-level maze that provided numerous places to attack from and hide behind. Her integrated augmented reality gear was still on order, but the sturdy construction and high melting points of the interior construction would allow them to engage in realistic training, both conventional and magical, even without special gear.

In truth, she preferred not to use fancy gadgets for training, even if she'd gotten used to it during her summers training with the Brownstone Agency.

We'd have to really go all out to seriously damage anything in here. That's the problem with using the electronics. It's all simulation in the end. Too much fake training can make for bad habits.

Alison wasn't sure if she had the right ideas about training, but they felt right for her needs. Her father initially focused on turning non-bounty hunters into bounty hunters. It made more sense that he needed certain types of people and environments for that purpose. While she could see his reasoning, she didn't intend to grow her team in the same way.

She wasn't interested in low-level bounties and common threats for security jobs. All her people would already be elites. Hana would likely be the closest she would ever have to an amateur hire, and the woman already had incredible natural abilities.

The door opened behind her and she turned and stared as Hana entered. Her friend wasn't in a hot pink bodysuit this time, but her outfit wasn't conservative either—blindingly bright green yoga pants and tennis shoes, along with a sports bra a shade of green that managed to be even more of an assault on the eyes.

Where does she keep this stuff? I haven't seen any of this in the laundry at home. I think I would have noticed. Then again, it's not like I go through her closets at night.

"You won't exactly blend into the environment in that outfit, Hana," Alison commented. She'd not selected her gray T-shirt and sweat pants on the basis of their camouflage potential but compared to the other woman, she was practically invisible.

"Big deal." Hana interlaced her fingers and stretched her arms above her head. "Hiding's for wimps, especially during this kind of training. When I fox out, it's about speed and power, not hiding. Otherwise, I'd turn into an actual four-legged fox and go camp out in some bushes until the fighting's over."

"I agree about hiding," offered Mason as he stepped inside in black shorts and a white tank top, his wand in hand. "I doubt we'll end up in too many situations where we can hope to ambush people. If anything, when she's foxed out, the whole glowing tails thing will make it damned hard to hide. She might as well dress in neon every day for all that it matters."

"True enough," Alison replied. "And far be it from me to criticize fashion." She grinned and nodded toward the nearest ramp. "There are a few spots where they need to finish painting, but I told them not to bother since we'll scrape and burn it anyway. I think it'll be more authentic if it's a little more banged up, too." She gestured around the room. "Eventually, maybe we'll grab some anti-magic deflectors for certain walls or something, and I hope to get some drones in here, but for now, it's a good place for general tactical training with an emphasis on cover and mobility. Today, though, I wanted to focus on more pure magical training. We've done that to a degree, but not really all out in a place where we don't have to worry about anyone else getting concerned."

He nodded. "Not that I mind, but I'm a little surprised you were so insistent when you called me the other day. You never seemed to care that much about this kind of training before."

"It's not that I doubt your skills, and Hana's training has improved dramatically." She looked thoughtful. "But the dark wizards got me thinking. I know we've all fought our share of magicals, but let's face it, the average asshole we run into is more likely to sling some lead than a fireball." She shrugged. "And I'll be honest. Up until a month ago, the risk that I'd use too much magic during training was something I had to worry about, so I focused far more on how to be efficient rather than on raw power. After the training I did with Myna the other day, I was reminded that I will continue to train for my entire life if I want to be able to defeat all possible enemies. I never know who might show up and what magical skills I might need to win against them. Now that I don't have to worry so much about strain, I want to go all out more."

Hana sat and leaned forward to stretch her hamstrings. "Foxing out's always fun, and at least with you two, I know I can go full force and see what I can really do. Not that I held back against the Eastern Union." A dark grin settled onto her face. "Bastards."

Mason made a few movements with his wand and murmured incantations.

The fox sniffed at the air. "That's a lot of magic. I'm not the only one who plans to go all out."

"That's the point. You've seen me in action. You know I'm not the fireball-from-far-away kind of wizard, but the punch-you-in-the-face-through-the-window kind of wizard." He moved beside the door and set his wand down. "I might as well really make it a challenge and train with some of my baseline enhanced speed, strength, and resistance spells." He smirked at Alison. "I expect you to keep it reasonable, A."

She backed toward a ramp and lifted her hands. An orb of white light appeared in one and a dark violet orb appeared in the other. "Reasonable is relative, don't you think? The enemy won't always be reasonable."

"I don't know if I like that look on your face. Remember, the point is to train, not to kill us."

She grinned. "No one's dying. Maybe. But be careful."

Hana hopped to her feet. "Seriously, what are the rules here? If you go all out, we won't last that long, and unless you're training us to take down Drow princesses, I don't know how fun or useful that will be. I also don't know that I have a chance of taking both you and Mason on at the same time, even if you're not on the same side. Maybe we do it in rounds or something?"

"Don't worry. I'll hold back a little, and to balance this out, how about you both try to take me out together?" Alison let the orbs vanish and pointed to a small box on the wall. "I have a few healing potions in there if things get out of hand or Mason and I can't get our healing magic to work because we're knocked out or something. But maybe, don't try to rip my throat out, okay?"

"Okay, if you have to make things boring, I can do that." Nine tails of light winked into existence behind Hana. Her eyes turned yellow, and her claws extended. "How will we know if we won?" She tapped her ring three times and a red glow extended over her skin. "Do we keep at it until someone's knocked out?"

"Don't kid yourself," Mason interjected. "It won't get that far." He stepped forward. "And we're not supposed to win. We're merely supposed to practice taking on someone powerful. That's your main idea, right, A?"

Alison nodded. "Yeah, something like that."

Maybe I'm enjoying this a little too much.

She allowed herself a sly wink. "This crap's a lot easier these days. What can I say? When I trained with my dad and his people, even when we used simulators or ran team-based mud challenges, much of the time it'd be him versus everybody, or maybe the Brownstones versus everybody. As for Brownstone Security, we can bowl through the cannon fodder already. Why worry about facing them?"

"Wait. Mud challenges?" Hana replied and made a face. "Let's skip those, okay? I'm not a huge fan of mud."

"I'm simply saying that I'll try to give you guys a semi-reasonable handicap." Wings of shadow extended from her back, and she lifted off the ground. "Otherwise, I could do stuff like this, but flying takes a chunk of magical energy. It's not my most efficient magic, even if it's cool." She flew to the top of the ramp and released her wings, fell a few feet, and wrapped a shield of light magic around her. "I'll try to mix things up. I know you're probably used to magical strategy, Mason, but Hana's mostly dealt with straight-forward magical assholes, and I'd like her to get a feel for different tactics."

The fox stuck her bottom lip out in a mock pout. "You mean you simply try to shoot me? How very boring of you."

Mason shrugged. "Bring it on, Dark Princess. Let's see what you've got."

"Wait." Hana threw a hand up. "Before we start, you won't turn me into a toad, will you?" She peered at her friend with suspicion. "Some things are off limits, even during power training."

Alison laughed. "No. The reality is that in fights, it's hard—if not impossible—to pull off complicated magic like that, which is why most people rely on simpler things like fireballs or ice lances. I merely want you to be ready for some of the other possibilities. If you at least have them in the back of your mind, it might mean you'll react that much quicker." She stepped behind a wall. "Are you both ready?"

"Ready," they called back in unison.

"Then let's try to kill each other. 'Cause that's what good friends do!"

Mason laughed. "Oh, I love it when you talk murder, A."

Even with Alison's vision blocked by the wall, it was easy to sense Hana and Mason's general directions given the heavy magic that surrounded them. The fox rushed toward an opposite ramp, obviously hoping for an easy flank, while Mason approached Alison's ramp with a slow, deliberate pace.

Maybe he's trying to draw my attention, but the lack of immediate attack will give me an opportunity to demonstrate a little something to Hana.

Alison ducked and thrust her hands out as she gathered magical energy and muttered an incantation. Several seconds later, she formed an invisible wall of magic between her and the approaching nine-tailed fox.

Sorry, but not sorry.

Hana couldn't sense magic in the same way her companions could. She could only smell it. Perhaps she should have taken the time for a big sniff. She slammed into Alison's wall and bounced back to land on her rear with a hard thud atop the metal platform.

"Ow." The fox sat up and rubbed her backside.

Alison laughed. "See, that took some—" She scrambled backward as Mason cleared the wall with a sudden jump, his fist pulled back.

The wizard landed with a grunt and swung at her. She threw her arms up to block his heavy blows but staggered back at the force of the attacks. Her shield flashed with each hit.

Damn, he could easily punch through a wall with this kind of hit. Seeing him do it to someone else simply isn't the same as feeling it through my shields.

Hana shook her head and scrambled to her feet. She tapped at the invisible wall with a frown and sniffed at the air before she leapt down to the first floor and landed in a crouch. "Damn it. I can't believe I ran into an invisible wall. That's so ridiculous. I'm like some dumb bird."

That wall won't last long, but it'll last long enough for me to make my point.

Mason kept up his truck-force pummeling, but he only pushed Alison back with minimal damage, despite the sting of some of the blows. She threw a shadow line to the floor and allowed it to yank her away from the platform. Once she landed and rolled back to her feet, she thrust her palm out to blast a light orb at her boyfriend.

It struck him in the shoulder. He grunted and stumbled back. Alison followed up with another two quick blasts of light magic, but he ducked behind the half-wall extended above the platform and avoided her wrath.

"Nice shield, even if I didn't put my full power into that attack," she yelled.

Hana took the time to close on her friend as the invisible wall only extended into the air and not to the floor. With a growl, the fox leapt toward her and swung her claws. Alison's shield flashed, and she summoned a small shadow blade and stabbed at Hana, only to miss and have the woman spin around her and claw at her back.

"Nice try and good thinking, but the shield goes all around, Hana."

With Alison distracted, Mason leapt over the wall and landed hard on the floor. She jerked her arm back and ignored Hana as the fox tried to shred her shield and reach her back. With a surge of shadow magic, a massive, dark-violet tendril erupted from the floor and wrapped itself around Mason.

He grunted and strained as the tendril twined around him and pulled him down.

I bet you would have liked that one, Myna.

"You probably should have kept your wand on you for a counter-spell," she taunted. "Like I said, I want to mix things up a little. Sometimes, a girl needs an explosive ball and sometimes, she needs a creepy shadow tentacle."

Hana continued to claw at the shield. Alison maintained her focus on Mason but too much so. Her shield failed and claws ripped into her back.

She hissed and spun toward her friend, flung her arm out, and launched a thin blade of concentrated shadow energy. The attack clipped Hana, and the red nimbus around her skin dimmed. The fox fell back and a thin trail of blood ran along her side and dripped to the floor. Her teeth were gritted in pain.

Mason's footsteps thundered and forced Alison's attention back to the wizard. Even without a counter-spell, her distraction had been enough for him to escape her now dissipated shadow tendril.

Damn, I sometimes let myself forget how good he is.

She launched two quick light blasts toward him. He took them squarely in the chest. The magic burned holes through his tank top and charred the skin underneath. Despite his grimace, he continued his charge and barreled into his girlfriend shoulder first, his movement a near blur.

Training with James Brownstone had its advantages. One of which was that it taught Alison what it felt like, even with a shield, to collide with a large man. Despite that, Mason's magical speed enhanced his impact force enough to catapult her backward into a nearby wall.

The barrier announced Alison's impact with a loud, reverberating clang.

I should have layered a few more shields, but I'm glad I made sure these walls were all metal. Otherwise, they wouldn't have lasted one fight.

She dropped to the floor and layered another shield around herself. This time, she threaded in some shadow magic. Pain spread from her chest and back from the force of the impact and she took a few deep breaths.

Alison grinned. "My guess is that if I didn't have my shield up, that would probably have broken half the bones in my body, if not outright killed me. You really aren't holding back, are you?"

Mason wiped some sweat off his forehead. "Yeah, you're one of the few people I know who can take that kind of hit and barely be hurt, and I figured you wanted a challenge, A."

Hana crept forward, the wound in her side still weeping blood. "It looks like I got through too." She grinned and gave a thumbs-up. "Fear the fox."

"Yeah," Alison replied. "Those claws of yours are a little better at shredding magic shields than I realized. That's good to know."

The fox lifted her claws in front of her face and smiled. "There are always a few surprises left, huh?" Her red glow was noticeably dimmer. "I'm simply not used to fighting really tough people. I mean, you know, people who don't die so easily."

Alison pooled magic at her feet and crouched. "I have to end this now. We'll heal up, relax for a few minutes, get a drink, and start round two. I can mix it up with the spells to keep the surprises coming."

Mason laughed. "Getting a little cocky? Sure, you got a few good hits in, but we're nowhere near done."

Hana scraped her claws along the wall. "Yeah, we hurt you at least a little." She winced and glanced at her side. "Although you did the same to us."

"A little's not enough to win." Alison released her building magic and hurtled toward Mason. She flung her arm up to release a white-blue bolt. It struck him and he fell to his knees, then to his face.

He groaned.

"Sorry," she called.

Still in motion, she passed under the platform above and launched two stun bolts at Hana. The fox stumbled back and the energy arced over her body. The red illumination of her defense ring had now almost gone.

Alison summoned shadow wings to arrest her momentum and spun before she dropped to the floor and released her wings. Hana sprinted toward her and her tails fluttered as she approached her friend in a quick, jerky, zigzag advance. The fox's evasion was enough to dodge her opponent's first few attacks.

Nice.

With only seconds to react, Alison couldn't risk anything complicated. She extended her arm to throw a shadow crescent blade at Hana and followed up with two quick stun bolts. The first two attacks missed, but the last struck home and slowed the fox.

She took her opportunity and blasted her friend with stun bolts in rapid succession until the red glow vanished and Hana collapsed and skidded across the floor with a low moan.

As she leaned against the wall, Alison took a deep breath and touched her wounded back gingerly. She stood and waited until her companions stirred, both paler than before. "Are you two okay?"

Hana rose and swayed slightly. "I've been better. Damn, you really kicked our asses."

Mason stumbled toward his wand. "I didn't expect the stun bolts. I might have used a slightly different defense spell if I had."

"I figured I'd practice them," Alison responded with a lopsided smile. "Since I have to take some of the dark wizards alive. Who knew? It actually *is* harder when you don't try to kill everyone as quickly as possible."

"I'm too used to being on the opposite side of that ass-kicking." Hana groaned again and limped toward the wall. "Don't ever turn evil on us, okay?"

"Sure. I'll try."

"To turn evil?"

Alison laughed. "No, to stay good."

CHAPTER TWELVE

*I*t's a little easier to avoid attention when you're not in a red sports car.

Alison parked the vehicle and stared out the front window. People walked around the surrounding dock and no one paid any special attention to the nondescript black van.

Massive cranes lined the east side of Harbor Island. One perched over a gargantuan cargo ship docked in the distance, its name painted on the side in huge white letters —*Kilimanjaro*. Another large vessel was docked farther down.

This is the first time I've ever had to take someone down inside a cargo ship.

The *Kilimanjaro* was silhouetted by the last few struggling rays of sunlight along with a few bright dock spotlights that illuminated the deck. Rows of different colored stacked rectangular cargo containers stood beyond the cranes and separated the primary dock area from the massive white storage tanks that dominated the center of the island.

As an artificial island, the entire area was a shrine to human ingenuity and technology in a way even an advanced quantum computer wasn't. The thick, dark smoke that drifted into the air from several stacks was also a reminder of the cost of that same dominance over nature.

"Nothing's blowing up here," Alison murmured. "Whatever plan the wizards have doesn't involve the docks."

A beefy, bearded man in dark blue coveralls sighed in the seat beside her. He lifted his hand to look at his short nails with disdain. "That'll make this easier, then."

Alison snickered. "I can't get over how you look, Hana. It's not that your disguise is bad or anything, but knowing it's you under there makes it ridiculous. It's simply so…not you."

"Whatever," the fox responded, her voice deep. "You're the one who cast the spell. Couldn't you have made me more stylish? Or at least have given me a better haircut?"

The disguise spell was convincing and even conveniently hid her stun rod and holster easily because of the large frame of her fake body.

"We need to blend in with a bunch of dock workers, not the Saturday night club crowd headed to the True Portal."

Hana pointed to the rear-view mirror. "Have you seen yourself?" She chuckled. "You don't exactly look like the Dark Princess anymore."

Alison looked up and grinned at her reflection. A wrinkled and weathered dark-haired man in coveralls stared back at her from the mirror. "You still love me, don't you, Mason? No matter what I look like?"

"I don't know. Maybe Hana's right about being stylish." He grinned. "Let's say I'll be glad when you're back to normal, A."

He sat in the back seat in matching coveralls. A tall, muscular man wouldn't stand out as much on the docks as two young, beautiful women, or so their theory went. Especially when one of them was famous for defeating one of the richest men in the world and had trademark white hair.

"So shallow, Mason. I'll remember this." Alison shook her fist in mock anger. "Let's get down to business. Do you see anything we should worry about, Tahir?"

"I don't see anything," he responded through the earpiece receivers of everyone in the van. "At least, nothing unusual. One cargo container is being transferred from the ship, but it's not like I see anyone with wands or who looks like they don't belong. Although given what I find in the manifest logs, it's obvious that dark wizards boarded the ship in Vancouver and most of the cargo bays are empty. The entire crew was replaced, from what I can see. Allegedly as a result of illness, but it's painfully obvious that the dark wizards have taken over the entire thing."

"Are you sure they're still there? I'd really hate to think we all got dressed up for this and there was no one at the actual party." Alison narrowed her eyes and focused on the ship. "Vincent said they were already here, which means only some of the wizards were here and the rest came in with the ship."

"I've watched them since before they docked," Tahir replied. "No one disembarked, and if they could portal out easily, why bother to hide on the ship? Several people have walked onto the boat as well, and many of them didn't look like dock workers. I think it's a safe bet the wizards are already here and on board with the others who arrived."

"And also, some of them know how to run a ship? Or do we think an innocent crew's still on board?"

"They might have them under some sort of control or have threatened them. I wonder if they even have an info-mancer given how sloppy their attempts to cover up the change in personnel were. If my information is right and all those I saw on board are wizards, there should be about fifty people at maximum on the ship, and I've not found anything to suggest they're smuggling more. That's actually a high number for the type of ship, so probably about twenty of those are sailors and around thirty are wizards." Tahir snorted. "I'm almost insulted by how lazy they've been. I think you should reconsider my offer of active support."

"We can't be sure how sensitive they'll be to remote magic, and it'll be too difficult on our timeline if you use any. I'm sorry, Tahir, but you'll have to sit on the bench this time unless one of us contacts you."

He sighed. "If you say so."

"And you're sure they aren't in any of the containers being moved?" Alison squinted her eyes in an effort to make out the movements of the crane in the distance.

"I seriously doubt it. It's hard to get decent thermals off these containers, but I see no indication that there is anything warm and alive in there, and it seems unnecessary."

Alison clapped once. "Okay, so that leaves us with some sloppy wizards. That we can work with."

Tahir scoffed. "Yes, it does."

"I don't mind sloppy dark wizards," she replied. "It makes things easier. I'd like this to be as much of an in-out job as we can pull off given our limited information. I'm still concerned that we have no idea why they're here. These types don't get together for tea and crumpets. If they have come here in force, it's because they're here to do something nasty. There are too many different targets in Seattle."

"I'll keep the drones relatively distant. Even if there are a lot in this area, if we move in too close with our particular drones, we might tip them off." Frustration crept into Tahir's voice. "I could try something more direct like a focused scrying spell, but it's too risky. They'll sense the magic."

Several longshoremen in bright orange vests and hard hats walked past the van and barely glanced their way as they chatted and laughed among themselves.

Hana shrugged. "I don't see the big deal. Won't they sense all these disguise spells the minute we get close to them anyway?"

"Sure," Alison responded, "but we'll walk into a ship filled with dark wizards. There will be enough basic background magic that they won't find a little extra magic nearby weird. But if some concentrated scrying window opens, they'll realize something is wrong. Worse, if they figure out the kind of spell, they might be able to trace it back." She shrugged. "At least this way, we'll be able to get close to them before they figure out what's up, and it's not like we'll stand out." She gestured at a Kilomea dockworker who caught up with the longshoremen. "Even with all the lights on the dock, it's still decently dark, too."

The fox shrugged. "Why not invisibility spells, then? I've come to terms with this ridiculous disguise, but I don't understand why, if we can use a disguise spell, we can't use an invisibility spell? Wouldn't it be easier?"

Alison shook her head. "If they see someone who looks like they belong, they won't have any reason to question the magic, but if they see nothing, they'll know they're in trouble. This isn't like using a stealth spell to sneak past some professors so you can get to the kemana under your school and have some fun. These assholes are paranoid. Even if they don't expect me or the PDA, they are still probably worried about trouble."

Her companions both stared at her.

"What?"

Mason chuckled. "Sneaking past your teachers to get to the kemana?"

"Maybe that was only me," Alison replied. "The point is, we can take advantage of the situation, but only so far. I don't want to risk spooking the assholes too much. If they get away, we might not be able to track them again. If it were as simple as using tracking spells, they would have been caught a long time ago. We have to grab a few of these guys so Latherby can figure out what they're up to."

Hana frowned. "Do you really think there's a dark wizard traitor in the local PDA?"

"I don't know. If Latherby thinks there is, there probably is." Alison sighed. "I learned firsthand at the School of Necessary Magic how those bastards can crawl into the shadows and jump out when you least expect it. Even if there isn't a traitor, it doesn't matter, as Latherby's suspicions mean that in this case, we can't rely on the PDA, so it's up to us to grab these guys." She stared at the ship in the distance. "I know it's unlikely, but for all we know, they have access to portal magic. If we're too obvious, they might run before we take anyone down, but once we're on that ship, we can hopefully deal with them easily—knock them out and take their wands. The goal should be to take them all down, but as long as we manage a few survivors, we should be in good shape."

Tahir cleared his throat. "I know this will sound odd coming from me of all people, and I should have mentioned it before, but after hearing all this, I have to ask —have you considered a more direct strategy?"

"More direct?" Alison glanced at her companions. They both looked confused. "What do you mean? This is about as direct as it gets. We're not watching. We'll board their ship and kick their ass like magical pirates."

"Between the artifact loadout and abilities among the three of you, I'm dubious that the dark wizards will pose much of a threat. A quick and brutal frontal assault might take them off-guard in a way the infiltration won't. Even if they can portal, you should be able to secure at least some prisoners with your initial attack. And they might not even have such magic. Again, if they did, why bother with the ship?"

"They might have a single-use artifact," she replied. "Something for emergencies."

"A surprise attack worked on Carlyle's guys," Hana pointed out. "Those assholes never thought we'd show up, and I could almost smell their panic from the helicopter."

Alison rolled her eyes. "They shot you down, too. The shock of surprise maybe didn't work as well as you hoped." She followed it up with a smile. "That said, you did help save my ass, so maybe I shouldn't bitch too much."

"Besides, we defeated them in the end." Hana winked. "Even if you took down Scott and his biceps."

Mason frowned. "Scott and his biceps?"

Alison shot a glare at Hana, and her friend only grinned slyly in response.

The fox's mannerisms attached to her current large, bearded male shape simply didn't fit. Alison's brain had trouble processing what she was seeing and hearing.

Oh, well. She only has to look like she belongs for a few minutes. It's not like she'll go through an interview.

"Whatever." He shrugged. "I don't care either way about what tactics we use. We have to fight them in the end. This is one group of guys who won't back down simply because Alison gives them a big speech."

She leaned back in her seat as she considered the strategy. "If we go in too hot and we don't win right away, even if they don't all portal out, the AET's will show up too soon. We'll lose time trying to explain what is going on and some of the roaches could escape. Maybe too many." She sighed. "Before, I had either Carlyle or Agent Latherby to back me up officially, but this time, I have neither. We need to play this carefully. Yeah, I know. That's so not Brownstone of me, but that's the best plan."

Hana grinned. "You're saying we have to be sneaky?"

"Yeah, sneaky. If we're deep in the ship, especially split into two teams, we'll be able to nail most of them before they even know what's going on—if we're lucky."

"I like sneaky." The fox chuckled darkly. "The big entrance is fun, but there'll always be a soft spot in my heart for creeping around and surprising people when they least expect it."

"I'll keep that in mind the next time you spend the night," Tahir responded. "All that decided, keep in mind that I'll have to terminate the comm links once you get out there. Given their partially magical and unusual nature, they might draw unnecessary attention. Does everyone still have the ship layout downloaded on their phones with the points of interest highlighted?"

"I do," Alison replied.

Hana and Mason nodded their agreement.

"They do, too," she told the hacker as she looked into the mirror again and squinted at the unfamiliar face. "Remember our goal here and the target areas Tahir highlighted, but also keep in mind that anyone we run into on that ship might be a dark wizard. Try to take as many as alive as you can, but I don't think Latherby will cry if we eliminate a few. That said, we also can't be sure that everyone on that ship is a dark wizard. Verify before you take anyone down, and keep in mind that they might have the crew somewhere." She grinned hungrily. "But with all that said, let's go kick some dark wizard ass."

CHAPTER THIRTEEN

They exited the van and made their way down the dock, now without Tahir in their ears. Alison resisted the urge to summon a shadow blade and shield. Everything she'd said about surprise was logical, but it was hard to not want to arm up when she knew that potentially dozens of dark wizards could be inside the ship, ready to kill anyone who might stumble upon their secret.

I have to keep reminding myself that this isn't about revenge. This is about capturing some assholes and figuring out what their real plan is. There are other dark wizards in Seattle, too. I have to rein it in.

Hana leaned closer to her companions. "To be clear, we still go with the same teams that we planned before driving over here, right? Because I thought of something awesome if that's the case."

"Yeah." Alison nodded. "What are you talking about?"

"Okay, Team Boy Toy-Hot Fox will work our way from one side of the ship," Hana replied, "and Team Dark

Princess will work their—well, her—way in from the other side of the ship."

Mason raised an eyebrow. "Team Boy Toy-Hot Fox? When did we come up with these team names?"

"Right now." Hana beamed. "Spur of the moment. Like I said. Awesome."

Alison chuckled. "Remember, we don't have active backup, but if you get in trouble, contact Tahir so he can go live and get hold of me. You'll probably have to do it from the top deck. I don't think we'll get any decent signal inside."

"The same applies to you, A." Mason gave her a pointed look. "Just because you're feeling stronger doesn't mean you're immortal."

"Don't worry about me. I know how to handle dark wizards. I've fought them since I was a teenager," she scoffed.

Damned dark wizard families. Won't you assholes ever give up?

He frowned slightly. "If there's one thing I learned as a bodyguard, it's that you're in the most danger when you take things for granted."

"I'll keep that in mind."

They continued toward the ship and the density of dock workers increased. The crane moved another container from the deck of the ship and added it to the huge container wall already present. Cranes on the ship itself were also moved to pick up containers.

Hana stared at the massive vessel as they approached the white gangway that led from the dock to the ship's deck. "I've lived in Seattle all my life, and I still can never get over how huge these things can be. Magic's neat, but technology's cool, too."

"Keep in mind that size also means a lot of area to cover. Still, we'll stick with the general plan to head to the cargo hold Tahir marked on our maps, given that it's our best bet to locate a lot of dark wizards." Alison turned to Mason. "I don't know if they have an alarm rigged, and without active support from Tahir, we have no one to block it. If they try something not obvious, it'll probably be magical, so pay attention, Mason, in case Hana doesn't smell anything. Otherwise, take people out as you run into them."

As they arrived at the angled white gangway, she was surprised to see no guards. She'd worried that they might have to fight their way onto the ship, but she'd also banked on being able to join a few longshoremen on the deck as they worked to secure the cargo.

Tahir's checks didn't suggest that it would be a problem, and she suspected the dark wizards wouldn't worry about a few dock workers on the top near the containers. According to the manifest and customs documents, they didn't intend to offload any internal cargo, only several abovedeck containers. Even dark wizards couldn't dock a massive cargo ship at a port for no reason without raising suspicion.

No one spoke as the trio tromped up the narrow gangway in single-file. The sun had fully set, but the bright port lights meant they didn't have to walk in complete darkness, even if the artificial lighting didn't do much for the water. The soothing blue and white ocean of daytime was now an inky black pool of doom below them, one that could easily conceal three bodies.

They arrived at the top deck.

"Team Boy Toy-Hot Fox is on the job," Hana murmured.

Mason chuckled and leaned toward Alison to whisper in her ear. "Seriously, be careful, A."

"You too." She nodded to the others before she headed toward a door. The other two circled in the opposite direction.

I now realize how much use having a few extra teams might be. But the good news is if Tahir's right, there isn't exactly an army in there and they won't all be together. I merely have to make sure I stow people where I can find them later—or Latherby can, at least. I guess it doesn't matter if there's a PDA traitor if I've already knocked all their asses out when I call him.

Alison sighed and layered a thin shield around herself. It wouldn't be too obvious given the disguise spell already in place, but all it took was one suspicious wizard to create a loud, unwanted catastrophe. Despite all her magic, she still had a lot to learn. She'd seen Drow on Oriceran regenerate from massive wounds that would have killed her instantly.

I guess I need a few more centuries of practice.

She grabbed the latch that secured the door and glanced around. No one lingered in the vicinity but there were a few cameras.

Do I look suspicious? Even if I do, all they see is some random guy.

Alison pushed the thought out of her head and opened the door. She took the time to gently close it behind her before proceeding down the narrow passageway, alert for any trouble. There wasn't much room to maneuver, let alone run along the wall or use shadow lines or wings. Any fight would depend on her taking maximum advantage of her defenses, but she was confident in her ability to win one-on-one against any single dark wizard. Or three or four.

The passageway continued for a long distance before it ended at an angled ladder. Several closed doors lined the bulkheads. It would take a while to work systematically through the ship but she suspected that once the action began, the enemy would mostly come to her. She simply wanted to make sure she secured at least a few of them before things got serious.

Her spell disguised the bundle of zip ties attached to her belt. The wizards who surrendered would have a little time to sleep while tied up. Those who didn't would get the crap kicked out of them and then the same treatment.

Alison slowed when she sensed a moderate level of magic nearby and behind a door to her left.

Huh. This is easier than I thought. It looks like we have our first contestant.

The door swung open and a lanky blond man with a bushy, unkempt beard stepped out—a longshoreman judging by his vest and hard hat. He was out of place and should have been on deck helping with cargo removal, not inside the ship in some random room.

At least she assumed so. Alison wasn't an expert on shipping, but despite that, it was highly unlikely that the average dockworker radiated that kind of magic. It wasn't impossible, but it was improbable.

I doubt he's here to check in with the crew.

She flexed her hands a few times. Her basic shield was up, so she wouldn't be taken down by any quick attacks. If he was a wizard, he didn't have a wand out, which meant she held the advantage. She could easily throw off a few attack spells, lethal or otherwise, by the time he snatched his wand from a pocket or hidden holster, but she needed to follow her own advice and verify who she was dealing with. As he wasn't an obvious member of the crew, though, that at least lowered the chance of him being some sort of prisoner.

I hope you're simply a wizard who really loves ships.

The longshoreman stopped and his eyes narrowed. "Who are you?" he rumbled.

"I'm here to inspect some cargo," Alison lied. "A specific container in a cargo hold."

"Since when?" He studied her with open suspicion. "You don't look like a customs agent."

"It's more a dock safety thing." Alison decided to turn things around. "Shouldn't you be out helping unload cargo or something?" She gestured toward the door outside. "Rather than messing around in here?"

The man's nostrils flared. "Yes, probably." His face tightened, and he nodded toward the door. "They have this little lounge in there. Let's talk in there. That's probably smarter."

"I'm not here to talk to anyone. I told you. I'm here for a cargo inspection."

"I'm trying not to make any mistakes here." The man's mouth twitched. "And there's something off here. So let's go talk in the damned lounge, or you can throw a spell at me right now and we can get this started."

Okay, so he's definitely a magical. Let's channel my inner actress and figure out what I can before I put him down.

Alison grinned. "Why would I do that? I was sent to help you. Didn't they tell you when you changed crew in Vancouver? They didn't tell me the deal, though. Did you bring in a crew loyal to us, or do you have the poor bastards stashed somewhere?"

Her stomach tightened. It was a gamble, but she needed to figure out if the crew was in on whatever the wizards planned.

The man stared at her for a moment as if he tried to figure something out before he nodded toward the lounge doorway. "Something's very off here, and I want to be damned sure. So, in there, or we fight right here. You might be what I think, or this might be a trick. But maybe I simply don't want to get a lot of blood in a passageway that I'll have to explain away. I also wonder if you don't want to have to explain that either. Win-win, right?"

Huh. He has a point. If I had to stun him or take him down, it will be less obvious if he's in a room.

"You first." She gestured toward the doorway.

"Fine." The longshoreman backed into the room and made a few quick motions with his hand. A shimmering nimbus surrounded his body.

Alison approached the room slowly and stepped inside as the man continued to back up. A few chairs surrounded a small table in the corner connected to the back wall.

She closed the door behind her but focused her attention on the man. He stood in front of the table and still glowed from his shield spell.

Wait a second. How did he do that without his wand? Damn it. Did I miss something?

The man locked eyes with her. "I have one question because I'm confused about something, and I think maybe we don't have to have some nasty little fight in this tiny room. The question is a big deal, though, but I'm not going to tell you to think about it. Just be honest."

"Ask your question." Alison layered another shield around herself and threaded some shadow magic into it. The man's eyebrows rose but he didn't do anything.

"Are you with the dark wizards on this ship or not?"

She slowed her breathing. Her initial assumption had been that he used a shield spell, but perhaps it was a truth detection spell. Without knowing more about the exact magic, she couldn't hope to counter it.

Does he expect me to lie? If he's not using a spell, he'd expect me to freak out and attack him or something. Does he have some quick way to warn the others?

"What if I am?" Alison replied, her voice ice calm. "What happens then?"

The man shook his head quickly. "The problem is that it doesn't make sense. The dark wizard families wouldn't work with someone like you. Why would they want to work with a Drow, of all things?"

"Maybe they had need of a—" She stepped back and took a deep breath. She'd almost missed something important but obvious.

Shit. He knows I'm a Drow? Is that what the damned spell was? He senses my shadow magic somehow?

"Need of a what?" the man pressed. "Are you some sort of mercenary for them?"

"Maybe I am."

"I don't know if you buy into what they sell or not, but these wizards will get a lot of people killed, including elves. They don't care if they hurt people when it comes to their plans. So what are you doing here, Drow, and do you really think it's worth it?" He shook his head. "No, that's not right. Most of it seems like Drow, but it doesn't feel like what I've seen of them."

Alison gritted her teeth. The man was right. Something didn't seem right, and it wasn't only that the man was able to use magic without a wand. His power was all obvious light magic. She doubted a dark wizard would worry to hide his more powerful and dangerous tricks, and the speech he gave didn't sound like some dark wizard deception.

So, he's not here to help the dark wizards. Then who the hell is he? Whoever he is, I need him to get out of here. Some other freelance guy rushing around to stir up trouble on the ship wasn't part of the plan.

"Look, here's the deal," she said crisply. "I don't know who you are and I don't think you're involved with what's going on here, but you need to understand something. This shit ends tonight. If you're not a dark wizard, good. Get the hell out of here before things get rough. If you are, surrender right now because you have no chance of winning against me." She extended a shadow blade. "Lucky for you, I'm explicitly supposed to make sure there are survivors for the PDA, even if I really, really want to make sure there are fewer dark wizards in the world by tomorrow morning."

The man folded his arms. "The PDA? You're a PDA agent? There are no Drow PDA agents."

"Consider me more of a subcontractor."

Alison blinked and released her shadow blade as a realization blitzed her mind. "No, it couldn't be."

The man arched a brow, now completely composed. "Is there a problem, Mr. PDA?"

"You knew I was Drow and you use light magic. You can't simply look at someone and know what kind of magical they are that easily, unless..." Alison shook her head and released her disguise spell. The false image faded around her to reveal the young woman underneath.

The man laughed. "You have to be kidding me. There are millions of people in this city, and I run into Alison Brownstone? I should have known you'd be where the dark wizards were. Luckily, I got here before you killed them all."

"What can I say? They get under my skin, but at least they aren't chasing me all around the world and trying to get to my family."

"No, they aren't." The man's body began to fade and a dark-haired woman around Alison's age reverse-faded into existence. It had been a year since they'd last seen each other but the woman hadn't changed.

Well, almost.

"Did you get a haircut, Izzie?" Alison asked.

CHAPTER FOURTEEN

Izzie laughed and patted her hair. "Yeah, I decided losing a few inches wouldn't hurt. I think it looks sporty."

"Yeah, I guess." Alison pointed to her own hair. "I still keep mine fairly long." She waved a hand. "Okay, what are we even talking about? What are you doing here? And what was with your last few letters not mentioning anywhere I could send you a reply?"

"Whoa, slow down. That's too many questions, but as for the last question, my situation got even more tricky than usual and I didn't know if it was safe. I wanted to let you know that I was okay, but I couldn't risk any pickups for a while."

"I see." Alison gestured to the obvious gun bulge in her jacket. "Is this a bounty thing or more personal?"

The other woman pulled her jacket aside to reveal her gun and knife sheath. "Both. I was following up on a bounty in London and some info fell into my lap about a group of Galbrathians trying some bullshit in Seattle.

There's a particular guy I'm interested in, though. He wasn't a Galbrathian until recently, and he has ties to some of the dark wizard families that are after me and my family."

"Why didn't you contact me? I would have helped. Well, I am helping anyway, but I would have helped even if I didn't know about it beforehand."

Izzie sighed. "I know you would, Alison, but I also know you have a lot on your plate judging by everything I've read in the news. You shouldn't have to deal with my crap, too."

She frowned. "I can't believe you still have to hide after all these years. Your mom's the original magic bounty hunter and your dad is the Fixer. You shouldn't have to be on the run like some sort of criminal. It's not fair."

Her friend sighed. "It's because my parents are who they are that I need to keep moving. Look, if the dark wizards get their hands on me, they might be able to use me against my father, let alone gain access to all the power of my mother's line." She shrugged. "It is what it is. Part of the reason I'm here right now is that I want to send a message to these assholes that just because I'm on the run doesn't mean I'm powerless. Now that you're here, that'll be easier than ever. It's my lucky day."

"It'll be exactly like the old days, then." Alison smiled. "Fighting side-by-side against dark wizards."

"Speaking of reasons, why are you here, exactly?" Izzie nodded toward the door. "I thought you were concentrating on the security game. Did these guys threaten a client? Or is this a little payback for me, Tanner, and everyone else?" She smirked. "I'm surprised you have time since you're so busy taking down billionaires."

"I can always make time to kick dark wizard ass."

"You also mentioned something about the PDA?"

"I have a local PDA contact. He's worried that the dark wizards have infiltrated the PDA so he's afraid to make a move himself, but he's the one who pointed me in their general direction."

Izzie's expression darkened. "They are always there waiting, aren't they?"

"Exactly. He's the one who tipped me off that they were coming into town, and then my people followed up and found out about this ship. My team and I showed up for the raid. I want to capture as many as I can to help figure out what they're up to. Worst-case scenario, some get away, but we still take down a decent number."

"You mentioned your team. How many do you have with you? A half-dozen? A dozen? All magicals?"

Alison looked up and to the side, a sheepish smile on her face. "Two. But they are both magicals."

"Two?" Izzie laughed. "We had more people than that when we did things at the school. You planned to take this entire ship on with only three people?"

"You're alone." She raised an eyebrow. "Last time I checked, one is less than three."

"I don't need to take on the whole ship. I only need one guy." Her friend shook her head. "Anyway, what about your friends?"

"One's a nine-tailed fox," Alison explained. "Her name's Hana."

"Nine-tailed fox?" Izzie furrowed her brow. "Is that like a kitsune?"

"Different, even though some are called kitsunes in Japan, and based off some stuff I've read, they've mixed a lot in the past. Essentially, she's a fox shifter, but don't call her one. She has charm magic, moves fast, and gets claws, that sort of thing, but she doesn't have the general trickster magic of a kitsune."

"Huh. You learn something new every day. Who else you got?"

Alison cleared her throat and scraped her boot against the floor. "Uh, well, my boyfriend Mason. He's a badass life wizard."

Izzie's eyes widened. "An actual real-life boyfriend? Not some guy you go out with a few times?"

"Yeah, we met at the gym and hit it off. He helped me take down an evil billionaire. Literally flew in to save me. You know, typical dating stuff. What about you? You haven't mentioned anyone."

"The whole hiding from dark wizards thing kind of puts a damper on my love life." The woman shrugged.

Alison snorted. "I can imagine."

"Well, now that you're here, there's no reason for me to sneak around by myself. What's the plan? Did you want to hook up with Mason and Hana?"

"They're walking through the opposite side of the ship. We have some information that suggests some of the wizards might be holed up in what's listed as an empty cargo hold, so we'll approach it from opposite sides and take people down as we go." Alison patted her zip ties. "Like I said, I need to take prisoners. At least some."

"Sounds good. You don't have a problem if I grab my guy and go, do you? No offense to your PDA contact, but if he's the one who claims they've been infiltrated, the last thing I want to do is stick around and wait for more dark wizards to show up while I interrogate their buddy."

"You do what you need to, Izzie. I only need a few of them. The more the better, but I'm sure losing one won't hurt." Alison smiled warmly. "It's damned good to see you again, and only a month after seeing Lily, too."

"Lily? Alison Brownstone old friend tour, huh?" Izzie shook her hands out before she layered another shield spell over herself. "Did you know that Luke's in congress now?"

"Yeah, I saw that. He always was a leader. It's not that surprising."

Izzie glanced toward a porthole. "I always half-thought he would try to go pro in Louper since the pro leagues had only started up when he was in college."

"After everything we went through at that school, I don't think he would have been satisfied as simply an athlete." Alison turned toward the door. "Okay, I figure we search each room as we proceed—or maybe check the bridge out first. We might as well secure that in case they have some clever plan to pull away. Not that this boat's exactly fast."

"It sounds like a plan."

Alison recast her disguise spell. "There are plenty of cameras."

Her companion took a moment to transform back into a male longshoreman. "Judging by these last few years, you aren't the type to worry about going loud anymore. What's with all the sneaking around?"

"I want to make sure they don't run. I need prisoners or even a few corpses, but I don't want to waste my time."

"Good point."

Alison opened the door and peeked back and forth in the passageway. She didn't sense any nearby magic but Izzie's. "I haven't heard anything that sounds like Hana and Mason have run into trouble. Let's make our way up to the bridge and see who we can find. If there's an alarm system, they'll probably control it from there."

The trip up the angled ladders took them to the display- and controlled-filled bridge, one that was noticeably empty. There wasn't any residual magic that either woman could sense.

"Huh, I didn't expect this," Alison commented.

Izzie frowned as they stepped inside. "I don't know a lot about big ships, but my guess would be that you prob-ably want at least some little cockney kid in a weathered peacoat or something to sit here in case someone calls or something starts beeping and smoking."

"They are docked. Maybe the crew doesn't care."

"Or the crew are being held somewhere."

Alison nodded. "Yeah. That's what I'm worried about."

Her companion sighed. "I should have known this would get complicated. You mentioned a cargo hold. Maybe we should simply head down to that. They might have the crew there."

"Fair enough. Let's do it."

Their boots echoed through the empty, narrow metal passageway as they approached the door to the cargo hold.

Alison's stomach refused to untie itself. Since boarding the ship, she'd not seen anyone but Izzie. They'd heard some distant knocking that sounded like it might have come from the opposite side of the ship, but nothing else. The empty bridge refused to leave her mind.

"Damn it," she muttered.

Izzie looked her way. "What's wrong?"

"What if they already ran?"

"We have no reason to think that. It's not like this ship docked itself, and someone had to communicate with people over the cargo."

"You're right. One of my people watching the ship didn't see anyone leave. But they could have portaled." Alison's hand curled into a fist. "I'm so tired of dark wizards getting away. What if they were never even here? Maybe the crew's all running around worrying about cargo stuff."

"No, they're here. Your info and my info both brought us here. And why would they run if they didn't know we were onto them?"

Alison released a long, weary sigh. "Because they somehow found out the Dark Princess was coming for them?"

"Dark Princess?" Izzie's face scrunched up in confusion. "Who is that? I thought you said your friend and boyfriend were here."

"The Dark Princess is me."

Her companion stopped and stared at her. "You're the Dark Princess?" The corners of her mouth turned up in a tight smile. "Seriously?"

"That's the name the underworld gave me." She shrugged. "I've kind of run with it. It helps when I try to intimidate people out of fighting. It sounds feminine but spooky and powerful, right?"

Izzie slapped a hand over her mouth to stifle her laughter. She averted her eyes for a few seconds before she removed her hand. "So you're the Dark Princess now? I don't know why I find that so much funnier than Princess of the Shadow Forged."

Alison chuckled. "Well, my other friends like it, too. Hana even declared me a member of Team Dark Princess for this job."

"And does she have a nickname?"

"Not normally, but she decided that she was on Team Boy Toy-Hot Fox for this job. Uh, the boy toy's Mason."

"I kind of figured." Izzie snickered. "Hana seems like fun."

"She is," Alison admitted.

"It's good to have someone fun in your life. I know how much everything that happened at school and the dark wizard hunting after that has weighed you down." She licked her lips. "Maybe I need a cool nickname. Fixer's Daughter? Nah. It doesn't have that zip I want."

"You go from town to town doing bounties and disappear as quickly." Alison grinned cheekily. "You're the Woman with No Name."

"I like that." Izzie halted. Her smile vanished, and she narrowed her eyes. "Do you feel that?"

Alison's heart kicked up. The modest level of background magic had given way to something stronger ahead of them. "Yeah, I feel it."

"I think your info about them hiding in the cargo hold was spot on."

Magic pulsed behind them. The two women spun immediately so they were back to back, their hands raised. Alison faced the cargo hold door and Izzie stared down the passageway.

The large metal hold door creaked open as several men with wands appeared around a corner farther down. A few seconds later, more men with wands emerged from the now open door and frowned.

Alison appreciated their casual appearance. Some wore jeans and T-shirts and others chose khakis and button-ups. A few were even in suits. There was nothing more obnoxious than a dark wizard who traveled around the non-magical world in robes.

"Excuse us, gentleman," Alison ventured, her voice still low from the disguise spell. "We needed to inspect the hold. Sorry, orders from my boss."

One of the wizards who emerged from the cargo hold sneered. "Don't insult us. Do you think we can't tell you're using a disguise spell?"

Okay, then.

"Plan?" Alison whispered.

"Let's drop the act," Izzie whispered. "Try to do your Dark Princess thing."

"If it doesn't work, don't kill everyone, remember?"

"I know. I'm here for a specific guy, after all."

Huh. I wonder where Hana and Mason are. I hope they

didn't run into trouble.

The woman both sighed at the same time and dropped their disguise spells.

The wizard narrowed his eyes. "That's better. And who exactly are you? Some PDA fools who have come sniffing around?"

Alison scoffed. "Seriously? You don't know who we are? Neither of us? I'm almost insulted."

Izzie glanced his way for a moment and waved before she refocused on the men in the opposite direction.

"Why should I?" the wizard replied. "You don't have wands so you're not even witches. That means you're not from a proper dark magic family. I bear no ill-will against Oricerans—at least they are proper magical beings—but Earth belongs to the dark wizard families, not whatever creatures you two women are. Probably half-breeds." His lips curled in disgust.

Thank you for one hundred percent confirming who you are, asshole.

Alison chuckled. "Half-breed? I guess that's fairly accurate." She pointed at Izzie with her thumb. "Her situation's a little more complicated, but at least I'm a normal old half-elf. But you seriously don't recognize me? Not even a little?"

She wasn't sure why it bothered her so much.

"Spare me your arrogance, half-elf," the wizard replied. "The only reason we haven't already killed you is because we need to find out who sent you and how you knew we were here. Perhaps if you cooperate fully, we won't kill you, but if you don't, the pain you feel will be exquisite before you die."

Alison rolled her eyes. "Damn. I wonder if people think I sound like that? Hey, Izzie, do you see your guy?"

"Not yet," she responded. "Maybe he's in the hold."

"Izzie?" the wizard repeated. "Izzie Berens?" He laughed. "This is too perfect. You spend so much time hiding and then you deliver yourself straight to us? It's almost as if fate herself has smiled on our cause."

"Don't get full of yourself, asshole." Izzie chuckled with dark menace. "I can take you by myself, and I have help."

"You're powerful, but there are dozens of us and only two of you. Some losses for the cause are always inevitable. Don't think we're not prepared for that."

"Only two of us? Sure, but are you really so confident, asshole, that you can take me and Alison Brownstone out by yourselves?" Izzie continued to watch the wizard in front of her. "You're so outmatched it's almost sad."

The arrogance drained off his face and fear entered his eyes. "You're powerful, but you're simply mortals in the end. Two non-pure beings such as you can't win against so many pure wizards."

They don't know that I'm supposed to take them alive. I can use that.

Alison cleared her throat. "Keep telling yourself that up until the moment you die. So, *we'll* give you one chance to surrender. Drop your wands, get on your hands and knees, and we'll secure you. Then, some friendly police types will come to whisk you off. Or you can try to take Izzie and me on. You'll probably die or get horribly maimed or whatever, but you know, your choice. Free will and all that."

"Enough of this farce," the wizard shouted. "Kill Brownstone but make sure Berens lives."

CHAPTER FIFTEEN

Alison leapt toward the bulkhead and her magic anchored her to its surface as she ran along it and summoned a shadow blade. Izzie threw two light blasts down the passageway. They knocked a wizard back, and he slammed into the two men behind him with a yelp.

Team Dark Princess-Woman with No Name: One, Team Assholes: zero.

The passageway filled with fireballs, ice lances, and dark orbs. Most missed Alison because of her odd angle of approach and her shield absorbed the remainder. A few blows stung, but her defenses remained strong.

Izzie's continued bombardment incapacitated the smaller group of men down the passageway and several groaned in pain.

Goody, prisoners.

Alison launched from the wall and impaled the lead wizard through the heart before she fired a stun bolt directly into the head of his closest companion. Her target jerked back. His shield held but her follow-up magic sent him to the floor drooling.

She released the blade and let the dead wizard drop. The mundane magic of a good boot to the head knocked out the next man. His body slammed into the hard metal bulkhead with a resounding thud.

Now that Alison was in the hold, she could see two dozen dark wizards spread out in the empty chamber. All surrounded a large and intricate sigil inscribed in the center of the deck that glowed and burned. She had no idea what its purpose was, but she doubted it was to roast marshmallows.

A barrage of ice, fire, darkness, and electricity struck her and strained her shield to its limit. She rocketed upward with the help of a quick pulse of magic and threw out a few shadow crescent blades. One dark wizard collapsed and blood leaked from a gash in his chest. Another couple of the men stumbled back, their shields weakened but not defeated.

Good for you. You should be proud you didn't die right away. Oh, wait, yeah...

Alison landed behind another and jerked his head back as she lifted her knee to meet it. His eyes rolled up in the back of his head and he fell without a sound. Another few attacks struck her and the force of the magic pushed her back and stung a little.

The dark wizards maintained their assault. The constant explosions against her shields blinded her and she stumbled back as she fed more and more magic into her defenses.

White bolts blasted into the hold and struck several

men in the legs to disrupt their attacks on Alison. Izzie rushed in a second later and fired more bolts from her palms.

The remaining adversaries formed a line and backed away slowly.

"I see my guy!" Izzie shouted with excitement. "Hey, Neville! Ready to get your ass kicked?"

The wizard flinched at the mention of his name.

Alison took a few deep breaths. She was a little scorched in a few places, but the concentrated attacks hadn't accomplished much more than minor injuries.

Mason and Hana should have gotten here first since I stopped and talked to Izzie. Did the wizards ambush them? If so, where do they have them? Is that why they knew to ambush us?

Alison elevated once more and focused her magic to form two glowing blue-white stun batons of light.

Izzie raised her hands and a made a few quick movements as she chanted.

I need to give her time for whatever she's planning.

Alison crashed into the wizard line and swung her batons at the nearest man. His shields held against the first several strikes, but the furious Drow blows made it through his defenses and he fell and twitched at her feet.

A blob of acid shot from a wizard's wand and bounced off her shield. It hissed on the floor as it splattered and ate away at the metal. She ducked as more attacks came and used the time to restore her shields. Her defenses held for the most part, but a few holes and some charred skin stung to prove that she hadn't escaped the full wrath of their attack.

Damn, that was smart. Nothing I can't handle if I focus.

Alison continued her brutal dance and mixed kicks and her stun magic as she downed wizard after wizard.

Izzie shouted her final incantation. Sparkles appeared around several of the wizards, and everything but their eyes stopped moving. Their wands fell and clattered against the hard metal.

"Nice, Izzie!" Alison shouted as she crunched her boot against the chest of another enemy.

One of the wizards rushed toward the sigil, stopped, and chanted as he pointed his wand.

Alison slung a shadow crescent at the wand. The shadow magic sliced it in half, and the man grimaced and looked at her.

The entire ship rumbled for a moment. Everyone stumbled and focused on not falling.

The sigil brightened and hummed loudly. A few seconds later, it vanished in a puff of thick, dark smoke, and the ship stopped shaking. Fear and disappointment filled the dark wizards' faces.

"Not the plan, huh?" Alison asked. She flung a stun spell at the wandless man and he dropped to the floor.

Alison and Izzie continued to fling spell after spell at the remaining adversaries and their satisfaction built as each collapsed.

With the roars and buzzes of the enemy spells now absent, the only sounds left in the room were the heavy breathing of the two old friends and the occasional groan from a downed wizard. All the victims of Izzie's paralysis spelled remained rigid but their eyes darted nervously back and forth.

Her heart pounded and Alison dragged in a few deep

breaths and wiped the sweat from her face. "That was a nice workout." She pulled a zip tie from the bundle on her belt. "Let's tie these guys up." She frowned. "Oh, crap. I didn't accidentally kill Neville, did I?"

Izzie pointed to a wizard among the paralyzed men. "No, he didn't even get banged up."

"Alison!" Tahir shouted in her ear. "Can you hear me?"

She held a finger up and pointed to her ear. "One sec, Izzie. One of my people's contacting me."

"Izzie?" Tahir responded. "Your friend from school? No, this is Tahir. Are you okay? Have they hit you with something that has affected your perception?"

Alison chuckled. "I'm fine. I found what I think is most of the dark wizards. I ran into my old friend Izzie, and she helped me clean up."

Tahir exhaled a sigh of relief. "I've tried to contact you for several minutes now, but something interfered with the signal—powerful magic."

Alison's heart had begun to calm after the fight but kicked up at the news. "Are Hana and Mason okay?"

Izzie walked over to Alison and held out her hand. She yanked the zip ties free and handed them to her friend.

"They're fine," Tahir replied. "They found the crew magically sealed in a room, safe but terrified. Mason broke the spell, and they decided to evacuate them and come back for you. When they tried to re-enter the ship, a powerful spell blocked them, just as it blocked my attempts at communication."

"The wizards were feeding some sort of special glyph here," Alison explained. She glanced at the deck. The outline of the symbol remained etched in the metal, even if the flames and magic had gone. "It's probably how they avoided PDA detection, among other things."

Izzie moved among the men and whistled cheerfully as she tied their hands together.

"The moment the crew stepped outside, they called the police," Tahir explained. "AET is already en route, and they are coming in force."

Alison blew out a breath. "That works now that I've taken them down. I would have needed to call them or Latherby eventually." She waved to get Izzie's attention. "AET is inbound. Will you stick around?"

She shook her head. "Too many questions." She hurried to her target and bound his hands. After a quick flick of her wrist, the paralysis spell vanished and he fell to his knees. She hauled him up roughly. "I think I'll make a quick exit with my friend Neville here."

The dark wizard looked at the ground, dejected.

She sighed. "You really can't stick around? We usually go out for victory sushi at this place Maneki. It's great. You'd love it."

Izzie gave her an apologetic look. "Sorry, Alison. I wish I could, but the last thing I need is a lot of attention right now, especially when there might be dark wizards in the local PDA." She smiled and shoved Neville toward the door. "I hope to see you sooner than a year the next time."

"Same. Take care of yourself, Woman with No Name."

Izzie grinned. "You too, Dark Princess."

Alison secured the surviving wizards and shoved them against a wall for easy collection. The few who regained consciousness seemed resigned to their fate and stared at the floor rather than offering any snarling resistance.

Yeah, all that arrogance lasted only a few minutes.

The sound of heavy footfalls thudded above and drew closer and closer until the source was directly overhead. A hiss filled the air and a moment later, a bright flash filled the room. Alison winced and stepped back. Her vision swam and she flinched instinctively. The deafening thud of metal hitting metal echoed in the hold seconds later and the entire area shook.

"Seattle AET," shouted a man. His voice sounded hollow through the filter of his helmet mic.

When Alison's vision cleared, she spotted a huge circular piece of metal still smoking in the corner of the room and a half-dozen AET officers in power armor with anti-magic deflectors aimed their rifles at the dark wizards. She lifted her head. The piece of metal was from the ceiling. They'd somehow blasted straight through.

Damn. Impressive.

None of the police aimed any weapons at her. That was always a good sign.

"I received a tip," Alison explained, unsure how much Latherby wanted passed along. She gestured to the wizards. "I haven't swept the ship, but these are all those still alive from this batch. I assume you know that two of my people freed the crew, but they didn't run into anyone on the way out."

"Don't worry, Miss Brownstone," the cop replied. "We have other teams searching deck by deck. And PDA will be here soon. It's a good thing you got a tip." He marched to the sigil, his armored feet clanking against the metal, and looked down. "Who knows what they would have done to the crew. Some sort of ritual, maybe?"

"Yeah, who knows?" Alison managed to keep a smile on her face. Even if a dark wizard sympathizer helped some of his friends escape, she'd still captured more than enough for Latherby to interrogate. "Just so you know, there's at least one guy missing. I'm sure one of these assholes will mention that eventually. Some bounty hunter was here. I don't know her, but she showed up, helped take them down, and grabbed a guy and left."

The cop snorted. "She'll show up eventually at a station to get her bounty processed. We'll worry about her then. Next time, though, maybe you could stop her. There's no reason for her to run off and make things more complicated."

"Sorry." She shrugged.

The AET fanned out to secure the prisoners, and shouts and footsteps from above signaled more reinforcements on the way.

"We have a few questions for you, so we'll need you to stick around," the cop explained.

"No problem."

Alison smiled. The dark wizards were all dead or captured. Whatever scheme they'd intended was over. this was not merely a victory but, a decisive one.

I wish I could have spent more time with Izzie but it was nice to do a little job together.

CHAPTER SIXTEEN

Mason held the door open at Maneki and smiled at Alison. "You earned your victory sushi tonight, A."

She sighed as she stepped into the restaurant. Hana followed her, a concerned look on her face.

"What's wrong?" he asked.

"Well...I somehow finally managed to bump into one of my oldest friends, and we spent the time dealing with dark wizards. I know she had to go, but still...it sucks, is all."

A host smiled from a podium at the front of the restaurant. "Good evening, Miss Brownstone." He pointed toward the dining floor. "Some of your party are already present in the private room on the far right."

Alison blinked and looked at her companions. "Did you guys book it? I hadn't planned on a private room."

Mason shrugged. Hana shook her head.

"Oh, well. It's a nicer sushi atmosphere. I...wait one second." Alison smiled at the man. "Thanks, Shigeru. I forgot about my friend."

She all but ran forward and the others trailed behind with quizzical expressions.

Alison reached the room and slid the door open. Izzie sat on the ground at the low table. Several plates of sushi and sashimi of every type already filled the surface, along with four teacups and a pitcher. Two bottles of sake stood beside it.

Hana clapped. "Now it's a party."

"The mysterious Izzie," Mason commented.

The three filed into the room. Alison sat beside Izzie and Hana across from her.

Mason closed the door before he sat and looked at the women with a smile.

"I thought you had to go," Alison commented.

Izzie selected some tuna before she responded. "I have Neville stowed and out for the count. A few hours won't hurt, and if any dark wizards show up here...well, they have the four of us to deal with. Considering what only the two of us did, I think they'd need every dark wizard in the world to beat the four of us."

Alison grabbed her chopsticks and snatched a piece of snapper sashimi. "If those dickheads damage Maneki, I'd call Mom and Dad and get them to help me sweep the world."

Hana lifted her right hand. "Just to get this out there, I swear I won't get captured simply because I've met another cool old friend of Alison's."

Mason's phone buzzed, and he pulled it out to look at a text. "Oh, damn. A, will you hate me if I take off?"

"Is something wrong?" She plopped her fish into her mouth.

He shook his head. "No, but I needed to drop something off with an old colleague. I totally forgot about it with the dark wizard job. Damn it."

She smiled at him. "It's fine. I've got my girls."

He snatched a piece of tuna maki and tossed it into his mouth. Quickly, he chewed and swallowed before he stood and waved. "Sorry, I couldn't get to talk to you more, Izzie, but Alison's told me a lot about you from the old days."

She gave him a polite nod. "Any man who can snag Alison as a girlfriend has something going for him."

"A death wish, maybe." Mason grinned, slid the door open, and left. He closed the door behind him.

Hana filled three cups with sake and grinned. "So it ended up a girl's night. Nice. Although I wish you could have met my boyfriend Tahir, Izzie. He's our infomancer, but he tends to want to relax at home after jobs rather than go out. He's a real introvert."

"Maybe next time." Izzie lifted her cup and took a sip. She drew in a deep breath and set it down. "I'd better take it easy on the sake. I still have a dark wizard I need to chat to and get out of the city." She smiled at the fox. "And what did you mean about getting captured after meeting Alison's old friend?" She glanced at Alison. "Did Lily get her mixed up in some sort of trouble?"

"Nothing like that." Hana laughed with undisguised nervousness. "Last month, Lily stopped by and we went on a tomb raid together. I was a little intimidated and let some dumbass trick me because of it. I ended up in an Eastern Union building, and Alison had to save my admittedly gorgeous ass."

Alison snickered. "You'd carved through half the guys

161

by the time I arrived. You would have been fine without me."

"How did you two meet each other?" Izzie asked and lifted her sake cup to her mouth.

Hana's cheeks reddened. "I tried to con and charm her so I could hand her over to the Eastern Union."

The other woman spat out her drink. "What?"

"She stopped herself before she did anything," Alison explained. "They tried to force her to do it, but I found out there was a former Harriken in the Eastern Union group, so I went and cleaned things up. Problem solved."

"You can't even make friends without crazy drama these days, huh, Alison?" Izzie set her cup down and wiped the sake she'd spat out with a napkin. "But at least you met your boyfriend at the gym before you made him help you take down a billionaire."

Hana laughed. "He volunteered for that. I think he was eager to prove himself to his Dark Princess."

"I still can't get over that nickname, but I guess I should have expected it from the daughter of James Brownstone." Izzie laughed and slapped her thigh. "Did Alison ever tell you about how her dad would come to the school and glare at every single boy who even looked her way?"

"Seriously?"

"Yes. Most of them were terrified that if they ever asked her out, the Scourge of Harriken himself would appear and drag them off to the woods and feed him to some of the magical beasts we had out there."

Alison rolled her eyes. "It wasn't…that bad. Mostly. Dad's overprotective, but he always meant well and it took him a while to understand what it meant to raise a kid—and he had to start with me as a teenager."

"Sure, sure." Izzie cleared her throat. "So, there's a big change with you. You mentioned my hair, but you didn't bother to comment on something way more important concerning yourself."

Alison grabbed a few strands of her white hair and lifted them. "I haven't done anything to my hair."

Hana looked from one to the other, confusion on her face.

Izzie pointed at Alison's face. "I was so caught up in the dark wizard hunt, I almost didn't notice. The way you moved during that raid wasn't someone using magic tricks to see energies, but you don't have any glasses. Did you get magical contacts?"

Alison pointed at her eyes. "I used the wish when New Veil attacked in D.C. I lost my glasses, and I needed to see. I now have normal vision—completely normal."

"Huh." Her friend blinked a few times. "You've gone through a lot of changes. More than I realized. New city, new eyes. I read about that virus thing, too. Is that all taken care of? The news made it sound like it only went into remission or whatever for you."

"She has a nearly thousand-year-old fangirl," Hana interjected between bites of sushi. "She helped."

"Huh?"

"An ancient Drow," Alison clarified. "Myna. She's old and looking for purpose before she passes on, and she was impressed by the fact that I used the wish because I wanted to defend people. She helped me with a cure, but from what I can tell, she could only do it because I'm part-Drow.

She comes and goes, but she's helped me work on my Drow shadow magic along with some other stuff."

Izzie looked impressed. "You have been busy. It's like you're a whole different woman than the last time we actually saw each other." She nodded toward Hana. "I see you have good friends and a handsome boyfriend, but do you like it here, otherwise?"

Hana grinned around her mouthful of rice at the compliment.

"I really like it in Seattle," Alison admitted. "I have friends, a decent guy, and the cops and PDA here seem to like me for the most part. The music and restaurant scene is nice. It's starting to feel a little like home, and honestly, I like it more than L.A. There's a different vibe, and I feel that it fits me more."

"I'm glad to hear that. You can get a little too focused at times, and it's worried me in the past. Since you hadn't really ended up with anyone long-term after Tanner was cured, it also made me wonder if you were stuck in the past. Trust me, as someone who is effectively forcibly stuck in the past, it can be annoying."

Alison patted her friend's shoulder. "I'm sorry, Izzie. I wish I could do more. Maybe you could stop running. I mean if we were all together, we could take on any dark wizards who showed up."

"Sure, we could, but we also couldn't guarantee that they wouldn't hurt innocent people to get to me, and I won't take that chance. Don't worry. I'm doing okay. I don't have a studly wizard boyfriend, but I go around, clean up scum bags, and take out dark wizards. That bastard Neville will go on a little trip with me to meet

Mom, and he'll give us a few hints about some of his friends. It's not like I have to take out every dark wizard to get them off my back. I only need to find some key players and maybe take them out. I get closer each day and each month."

Hana took a large sip of sake. "Do you think you'll be able to live a normal life soon?"

Izzie snort-laughed. "A normal life? No, but at least one where dark wizards aren't always on the hunt for me. But I can go on without additional worry now that I know Alison has a good friend who has her back."

"Thanks, Izzie. That's really nice. I think Alison's helped me out a lot more than I've helped her."

Alison swallowed a mouthful of uni. "Nope. Hana, I struck out when I looked for information on the dark wizards, but because of you, we found their exact meeting place and time. It doesn't matter that I'm the Dark Princess. Your help was crucial."

"Aww, thanks, Alison." The girl's cheeks were red, but it was hard to tell if that was from embarrassment or alcohol. "I have to admit, it felt good to go out there and pour on a little of the old con-woman charm."

"Con-woman?" Izzie eyed her speculatively. "You get more interesting the more I learn about you." She raised a cup of sake. "How about a toast then? To three talented women who all contributed to kicking a lot of dark wizard ass tonight?"

Hana topped her friend's drink up and raised her cup before Alison lifted hers as well.

"To kicking dark wizard ass," they toasted.

Alison downed the sake and smiled. She might miss

Izzie while she was gone, but every time she met up with her, she was reminded of how capable her old friend was.

I might not ever be able to return to those days back at the School of Necessary Magic, but I don't need to. I can make more than enough new memories with both my old and new friends.

CHAPTER SEVENTEEN

T his is impossible, Alison thought. *I can't lose. Not to this. Not in my own damned condo.*

Alison stared at the one adversary that didn't fear her magical power—her burning rice. So many little enemies taunted her from the pan. Or traitors, depending on how she wanted to look at the situation.

"I know I put in enough water. Why is it doing that?" Alison groaned. "It shouldn't burn already. I swear there's a secret curse that randomly activates when I try to cook. Sometimes, things come out okay, but when things go bad, they go really bad. They should stick me on that show where Tilly Ramsay goes around and yells at people about their cooking."

Mason laughed from the dining room table. "Don't worry about it. We'll go grab something. It's nice that you want to cook something for me but sometimes, discretion is the better part of valor."

"Can you imagine if people saw this? The Dark Princess defeated by rice. I bet the Eastern Union would flood this building with enforcers. Call it Rice Victory Day or something."

"Over rice?"

"Yeah, over rice." Alison shook her head and grumbled.

"Would I risk annoying you, A, if I suggested you were being a tad dramatic over a failed meal?"

She glanced over her shoulder into the dining room. "Just a tad. That's all I admit to."

Irritated, she turned the stove off. She rubbed her temples before she grabbed the pan, marched to her garbage can, and pressed the pedal on the bottom. The top flipped open to reveal the results of an earlier food battle—halibut charred beyond recognition.

"Team Dark Princess is getting its ass kicked tonight." Alison emptied the burned rice into the garbage and slammed the pan back on the stove. "I used to be decent. I swear. Way better than this."

"Yeah, you've told me you could get by." Mason pointed at the stove. "I mean, you *could* eat that. It wouldn't taste very good, but you know, if the planet goes to hell and we have nothing else to eat, at least we won't starve to death with your burned rice."

Alison glared at him. "Keep talking like that and I'll throw you into the bay from this condo."

He grinned. "That sounds fun—and I can swim. Although I now understand why you're so into sushi. You don't have to cook most of it. Wait." He laughed. "You still have to cook the rice."

She glanced toward a cabinet that contained her sushi supplies. Yes, she could prepare a mean sushi roll, but that was beside the point.

"You know I can probably arrange a Kraken at the bottom of the bay to wait to eat you," she replied. "Or some sort of monster. I'll have Myna open a massive portal to some bizarre dimension no intelligent creature was ever supposed to experience, and we'll bring something out from there." She pointed to the pan. "Or I could simply hit you with that."

A merry laugh erupted from Mason. "Oh, A. I have too much fun teasing you, but seriously, don't worry about it. I think you're too used to being so good at kicking ass that it's frustrating you because you've run into something you can't brute-force your way through."

Alison stomped out of the kitchen and dropped into a chair at the dining room table. "I'm sorry, Mason. I won't claim I was ever all that great at cooking, but it's like I've actively regressed because I've focused so much on magic and ass-kicking." She slumped in her seat and her shoulders sagged. "And maybe you're right. Maybe I'm too used to be being able to do what I want when I want. To whom I want. Just not rice and halibut."

"It's really not a big deal. It's not like I started going out with you because I thought you were some great cook. Don't let it get to you. You could be the worst cook in the world, and I'd still love you."

Her breath caught. She'd made a few jokes about loving him before, but Mason, for his part, had never used that particular four-letter word in such a direct way when he talked to her.

She enjoyed spending time with him and they both stayed over at each other's places, but she hadn't yet fully wrapped her mind around what she even felt. She'd *thought* she had loved Tanner, but now she wasn't so sure if that was true love or some teenage simulacrum fueled by unstable emotions. Whatever she had with Mason, she didn't want it to end anytime soon.

Ugh. When did I turn into Dad? What's next? Will I have to call everybody I know for advice on how I feel?

For now, she'd accept the pleasant warmth that suffused her over his declaration and not press him on the implications. She'd focus on the less emotionally charged issue of her questionable cooking skills.

"It's not really about the cooking," Alison explained. "It's about what it represents. Like at Café Artemis."

Mason scrunched his brow. "What do you mean? What does cooking have to do with a jazz witch? Or are you saying you want to take up jazz?"

"Not jazz. Creative outlets." Alison sat up and smiled. "It's something I've thought about since I ran into Izzie the other night."

"Kicking ass with your old school friend who is now a bounty hunter on the run made you think about creative outlets?" He raised an eyebrow. "What? Did she creatively beat down a bunch of guys and it made you jealous? I thought you were like me and liked to do whatever works."

"No, nothing like that. But at Maneki, she talked about being glad I wasn't stuck in the past, that I had a boyfriend, and that kind of thing. She was so happy for me."

Mason furrowed his brow as confusion spread over his face. "Those all sounds like good things to me. Why would any of that bother you? Do you want Izzie to not be happy for you, or is it about missing your friend?"

"No. I have new friends and a boyfriend, a new business, and a new building." She shrugged. "But I've turned myself into more of a weapon, especially after I left college. At least there, I pretended to care about something other than kicking ass for a little while."

He nodded. "That happens to many people. I used to paint far more when I was younger but it's hard to always want to paint after a hard day of bodyguarding. Part of the reason I'm getting back into it is that working for you gives me more time, and what can I say, having a beautiful and strong girlfriend is inspirational."

Alison looked away and her cheeks heated. "You're not so bad yourself."

"But I'm not inspirational enough to help your cooking?"

She smirked. "Very funny, Mason."

"I know I am. Thanks." He winked. "Seriously, A, you're an intelligent and funny woman in addition to being gorgeous, badass, and generous. I don't think you should worry about the kind of person you are. I know I don't. I lucked into being able to go out with you."

"It's not like I'm depressed or anything. But between Café Artemis and Izzie and other stuff, I realize that I *am* stuck in the past a little. Everything that happened at the School of Necessary Magic with the dark wizards warped me in a way, even if I didn't realize it at the time. That, combined with what happened with my birth parents...it's hard to let it go." She shook her head. "If I'd simply continued bounty hunting with the guys at the Brownstone Agency, I'd probably be a little less intense, if only because of how laid back a lot of those guys are, even the newer ones."

"To be honest, your intensity is one of the things I find attractive." Mason shrugged. "But you're not Myna, staring at the end of your life. If you want to change things, you still have plenty of time to do that."

Alison gave him a soft smile. "You're right. My parents are both incredible badasses, but they decided to relax and focus on family and other outlets rather than kick ass after years of focusing so much on being badasses. Maybe a little earlier work-life balance wouldn't be a bad thing for me, and that's what the cooking represents. It's something I can at least try to reasonably do. Maybe in ten years, I'll retire and go back to acting, too, but at least it gives me a creative outlet in the meantime."

He took her hand gently in his. "Then do it. Cooking is a skill like fighting or shooting. You mastered those because you put in the time and practice. You're your own boss, so you can make time for yourself to work on it. Just because you're the Dark Princess doesn't mean you're responsible for solving all of Seattle's problems and we all have your back." He squeezed her hand and then released it. "You helped Latherby, and now, they have a pile of dark wizards to interrogate. Take your time and have your fun. Pick easy jobs one week or hard jobs the next. Cook between them."

"You're right. I'm overthinking this. It's not like I have to become the best damned chef in the world. I simply want to be able to reliably cook meals." She rubbed her chin. "I can do this."

"And you have a life wizard boyfriend." Mason clasped his hands behind his head and grinned. "A few decent anti-poisoning and vitality spells will save me in the event of any disasters."

Alison laughed. "My disasters lead to food tasting bad rather than killing people. Although the magic thing makes me think."

"Think what?"

"That I should take cooking to the next level."

"Next level?" he asked.

Alison flicked her wrist and twined lines of light and blue light extended a few inches before they disappeared. "Yeah. I have magic, so I should look into enhancing my food with it, both potion stuff and non-potion spells. I'm not saying I'll try to use that to cover up bad cooking, but there are a lot of opportunities there. I know there are many magical chefs out there, so I can see what they're doing."

Mason laughed. "You don't do anything half-assed ever, do you?"

She shook her head and grinned. "Nope."

Agent Latherby sat across from the table from the chained dark wizard, his eyes narrowed. "Why don't you stop playing around and tell us what we need to know? A deal isn't off the table. You don't have to rot in an ultramax for the rest of your life."

The man spat but it didn't reach the PDA agent. "Wizards like you are traitors to your own kind. You should work with us, not hunt us down, and for what? Assuring the dominance of those who shouldn't rule rather than the rightful rulers of this planet?"

"This is the United States of America," Agent Latherby replied. "Nobility isn't an American value. Read your Constitution."

"Fiction based on meaningless pablum and even then, influenced by the hands of wizards," the prisoner snorted. "Magic should never have been concealed, to begin with. Even when it was low, we still had power. We should have controlled things openly. That simple truth is what Galbraith promoted, but so many short-sighted wizards like you refused to see the obvious."

The agent pulled his phone out and tapped it. He flipped the device and set it down in the middle of the table. "Do you see what that is?"

The wizard's gaze dipped to look at it. "Some sort of legal document?"

"It's a warrant for both active and passive truth spells."

"So? You can't submit that as evidence in court. You'll have to do better than that to intimidate me."

Latherby folded his hands in front of him. "I don't really care about convicting any of you at the moment, even though between what we and the FBI have, it's way more than enough already. As far as I'm concerned, you're nothing but terrorists. We have sufficient evidence to send you to an ultramax based on many crimes, not the least of which was the fact that you kidnapped and threatened that crew." He nodded at the phone. "Or maybe we should turn you and your friends over to the Chinese or the Russians for some of the little fun stunts you pulled over there."

"Your attempts to frighten me have passed into the

feeble, Agent Latherby. If you have what you need for the pathetic courts of the non-magical to convict me or any other of my comrades, why this farce?"

"Because I care about stopping whatever other little plan you have. Because I know this isn't over."

"And why do you say that?"

"You're all still too smug. I've done this job for a long time and call it intuition or merely experience, but I can tell when your type knows they're beaten." His face darkened. "And even though Alison Brownstone killed several of you and captured the rest, you still act like you're in control. Like you've won."

The dark wizard shrugged. "Call it the confidence of men on the right side of history."

"You're all locked up. You haven't won."

The prisoner smirked. "Do you think we're fools? Of course you'd use spells. We knew and expected that."

Agent Latherby's mouth curled into a slight sneer. "This isn't my first dance with Galbrathians. We'll break through whatever spells you've prepared to hide your friends and you'll tell us whatever we want. Then, we'll go to the next group you spill and the next until we've rounded up and incarcerated the lot of you."

Smug superiority settled on the dark wizard's face. "And this isn't our first time dealing with the PDA. You might have had some sense of accomplishment if you'd grabbed a few of us, but Brownstone did that, and there's a reason we came here in such a large group."

"Don't try to convince me there's nothing more we can gain from you. Very soon, you'll tell us everything we need to know."

"Then do it, Agent Latherby," the wizard taunted. "Extract all that precious evidence you think is in my head. I dare you to. It won't stop us." He laughed. "At this point, even if I wanted to help you, I couldn't. I've already made the necessary sacrifices. We all have. You lose, PDA. You lose."

"Haven't you Galbrathians hurt this city enough?" He shook his head. "You're as idiotic as New Veil. Killing people and blowing things up doesn't convince anyone of the nobility of their cause."

"We don't care. This isn't about the people. It's about ensuring that the proper families rule. Magic is the future. The gates continue to open. If we're this powerful already, what happens in the coming centuries? Crack my head open, Agent Latherby, and enjoy what you find. Or despair. I don't care."

The agent stood and adjusted his tie. "Just so you know, when this is all said and done, we'll make sure you'll never be free, even if you live five hundred years."

The wizard responded with a tight smile. "You should have killed us all when you had the chance. This disgusting non-magical government will eventually fall. All of them will. For now, I'm nothing but a prisoner of war. I'd tell you to hurry and pick the right side, but I'm confident that once our plan is complete, you'll realize how pathetic your side is and beg to join us."

"Keep telling yourself that. I'll grab some of my friends and we'll start a proper interrogation. Don't worry, though. It'll be nice and magical."

CHAPTER EIGHTEEN

Myna peered around the tactical training room with a faint look of disappointment on her face. "It's so enclosed."

"It rains a lot in Seattle," Alison replied from where she leaned against the wall near the door. "Plus, if I damage anything, I own it. It's big enough that even if I tried a shadow nova or something, it shouldn't hurt the rest of the building. It's not like I have the resources to set up a louper-like environment or something."

"It'll be sufficient." The ancient Drow nodded to herself as if finally satisfied.

"Thanks for actually calling ahead this time." Alison pushed away from the wall. She removed her jacket and tossed it down beside the door. "I have a nice hole in my schedule, so it's a good time for training."

"Have you practiced some of the glyphs we worked on?"

"Yes. I've reinforced several of the defensive glyphs on the condo and the building. They aren't as good what you might have achieved, but they'll do for now. Is that what you wanted to work on the next couple of days? More glyphs?"

Myna shook her head. "No. For now, continue working on the few I showed you, and we'll do more in the future. Today, I want to discuss improvements in your shadow compression."

Alison folded her arms. "A few of the Drow mentioned that to me when I was on Oriceran, but no one seemed interested in working on it with me. Everyone there thought I was too...impatient. They wouldn't even really explain much about it, and I didn't want to cause trouble, especially since a lot of them seemed tense to even have me around at all."

"You do seem more human than Drow at times, but no matter. How did they explain the concept to you?"

"Basically, it's a technique to concentrate shadow magic energy in particular ways. It's what empowers a lot of their advanced shadow magic. From what they told me, as a Drow with royal blood, I have a lot of raw power."

Myna nodded. "Indeed. And they're right. I suspect you're as powerful if not more powerful than Laena, especially considering your access to a wider variety of magic than most Drow."

Alison sighed. "But they also said the raw strength would only take me so far. I can always channel energy and blow things up, but it's not only a matter of raw energy for things like portals."

"Exactly." The old woman gestured to Alison. "You are a Princess of the Shadow Forged. Portals are well within your potential, but without shadow compression, you'll never be able to master the spell. That said, it might take you years to achieve the compression necessary for the technique." She pointed and a mass of writhing violet shadow tendrils appeared around her and reached halfway to the high ceiling. "Even though your raw power vastly exceeds mine, because I've spent centuries mastering compression, I can easily create impressive effects with minimal use of my magic energy." She lowered her hand and the tendrils disappeared. "If you'd already mastered this technique, you would have only been minimally inconvenienced by the virus even before your cure."

"It's that useful? Huh."

Shadow wings erupted from Myna's back and she rose into the air. "Join me."

Alison funneled magic into her own wings and glided until she hovered a few yards away from her companion.

"You're like most young Drow," the old woman stated. "I'm sure that despite all your power, you have difficulty maintaining wings for long periods."

"Yeah. I realized that during a recent training session. I'd been holding back recently and I'd forgotten how draining a lot of my cooler spells can be even without the problem."

Myna circled her.

I'm so used to being the one flying. It's kind of weird to see another Drow doing it.

The shadows wings fluttered slightly but didn't move much otherwise. Despite their form, Alison had always thought of them more like thrusters than true wings, based on how the Drow on Oriceran explained things when they'd trained her. It allowed her quick movements and changes of direction, but it also demanded a large magical expenditure to maintain them.

Myna moved swiftly away from her and headed directly toward a wall. She stopped abruptly and twirled to face her before she raised her arms. A dozen dark purple orbs grew in front of her. "The Drow, in our own way, are one of the most powerful races on Oriceran."

The orbs blasted out in different directions. They struck different surfaces, exploded in purple-black clouds, and scorched the metal.

A little more battle redecoration.

"In truth," the old woman continued, "I've often wondered if it was only our small numbers that prevented us from conquering much of Oriceran. If we had the numbers of Drow as, for example, the population in even some of the smaller countries on Earth, there would be little hope for others. But existence does promote balance, and our numbers are few, which is fortunate because it's allowed us some chance to understand that there are other potential paths than strength and war."

Alison drifted under and over some of the platforms. "Such as true co-existence?"

"Yes. You're proof of that. A being inherently more powerful than most Drow by virtue of your mixed heritage."

Myna raised an arm. Misty, wavering images of different places appeared—a deep jungle scene, a high, spiraled building that rose above skyscrapers in a city Alison didn't recognize, and hundreds of people in colorful outfits dancing in sort of festival, among others. All the images appeared to be from Earth judging by the mostly human crowds.

"Are those portals?" Alison asked.

"No. Simple scrying windows."

There are probably some nervous magicals in some of these places about now.

"Why are you showing me them?"

Her companion half-closed her eyes. "The true strength of Earth is in taking the best and mixing together what you have to create something greater. It's why despite the minimal magic on the planet in the last few thousand years, you've risen from primitives to those who can touch the stars." The windows all vanished. "Magic is power, but once you're convinced you have power, it dims the desire to think you can improve, which has led to stagnation. Whether that is a good thing or a bad thing is a question that can be debated, but it also cannot be denied."

Alison floated down a few yards. "But now, Oriceran and Earth are in contact, and it's not even like the last time the gates were open. Humans fully understand, as a planet, what's going on." She chuckled darkly. "Prometheus' sacrifice wasn't wasted."

"Prometheus?" Myna tilted her head, a puzzled look on her face.

"Don't worry about it. It's an Earth myth, something someone mentioned to me recently. The point is, since everyone's aware of what's going on, there are good opportunities for both Earth and Oriceran to grow beyond what either of the planets has settled into."

"You're wise beyond your years, my princess."

She sighed. She'd gone back and forth in her attempt to

convince Myna to simply view her as Alison and not the Princess of the Shadow Forged—and even succeeded a few times, or so she thought—but nagging the old woman about titles seemed petty when Myna had already aided her so much and continued to help her.

There are worse things in the world than having to suck it up because someone wants to call you princess.

"Thanks, Myna," she responded.

"Now, back to our lesson," the old woman commanded. "Summon the orbs as I did before and fire them. Tell me how it feels. I've focused on making you talk to keep you directing magic into your wings and strain your supply."

Alison grinned. The Drow was craftier than she'd assumed.

"Okay." She raised her hands and concentrated. Her companion watched as she funneled shadow magic into a similar number of orbs while she continued to feed her wings. After a few seconds of priming, she released her own explosive barrage.

I'm glad I already told all the workers to ignore any noises they hear from this room.

She took a deep breath. "That took a lot of magic. It already feels like I've used significant power simply to remain airborne like this. I don't know if I'd be able to do that several times in a row while flying in a fight and not have to land."

Myna's wings vanished and she dropped. A shadowy disc appeared above the floor, and she landed without any visible strain or sound. "The gates might have opened, but they are far from fully open and magic doesn't completely saturate this world. Even I find that my power is more difficult to call on here." She gestured widely around the room. "But proper technique can compensate for that. The beginnings of compression involve feeling the texture of the magic, as you call it. Once you can discern the texture, you can begin to thread it for the necessary spells or merely improve your efficiency on more basic spells."

Alison flew toward her and released her own wings. She didn't bother with a landing pad, so the collision of her boots with the metal floor produced an echoing thud. "Because of a recent job, I've thought about how in most cases, my fights haven't lasted that long—at least not when I've had to go full out—but I've been lucky. If I had been forced to do much over a long period, I might have started to run out of magical energy. I was trying to supplement with weapons and artifacts till I got stronger, but that doesn't change the fundamental truth that I'm powerful but not all-powerful."

"Yes." The Drow stepped into the air and atop a flat, dark, misty rectangle that appeared. "And I'm glad you realize the implications." Another few shadow steps appeared, and she walked up to them. "Use magic when you need it, but always use it efficiently." Several more steps took her close to the ceiling. "Now, feel for your texture."

Alison drew a deep breath and pulled her shadow magic. Something about it always felt cold and rugged to her, even if it didn't actually seem to make her body or skin cold. Subtle pulses marked the flow of energy. She called a little more and tried to harmonize the pulses until the magic combined.

Myna took slow, deliberate steps as she walked down

her aerial staircase. Her breath grew ragged. "Even as a royal, this technique will take you a long time to master. Because of your unique background, I can't say if it'll take you years, decades, or centuries. I'm unsure if you'll age like a Drow now that you've come more into your power." She stepped onto the floor and the stairs vanished. "Even though I will explain more technique, practice is vital. Take time, alternate between meditation and compression training, and you'll find it'll come naturally, even more so than if you try to force it."

"Meditation, huh?" Alison mulled that over. "When I started at the School of Necessary Magic, I found it helpful when I was first learning and needed to recover magic."

"It can be useful in many contexts."

She scoffed. "Just one thing. Are you telling me Laena sat around meditating? Even when I visited the Drow on Oriceran, they didn't exactly seem the meditating types."

"Many aren't, but even on Earth, I've read about warriors who practice such techniques."

"That's true." She shrugged.

"As for Laena, no, she didn't. Perhaps if she had, she would have become so powerful that even your father couldn't have defeated her."

I think at this point, you might be able to drop a nuke on Dad and he'd survive, but there's no reason to piss her off by correcting her on that.

"It's a good thing she was as impatient as me, then, huh?" Alison responded.

A thin smile appeared on Myna's face. "Indeed." The old woman moved to a ramp and sat on the edge. She took several deep breaths and wiped the sweat off her forehead.

Alison frowned and walked toward her. "Are you okay?"

Her companion held up a hand. "I'm fine. Age takes its toll, even when I've trained as much with compression as I have."

She nodded slowly but the frown remained. "If you're wearing yourself out simply to show me stuff, you don't have to, you know. I don't—" She looked away. "I know you'll die sooner rather than later, but there's no reason to make it even sooner."

"I do what I can to help you. My own frailties are irrelevant." Myna stood and smoothed the skirt of her dark dress. "Let me make this very clear, my princess. My life is already over. Think of me as a spirit who simply lingers and dispenses advice."

"So you don't spend time touring the Earth when you're not here? If not, you really should."

The old woman's face twitched. "I'll take that under consideration."

Huh. That wasn't a yes or no. What does she do, then, when she's not training me?

"I apologize, my princess," Myna continued. "I only wish I could spend more time with you."

Alison waved her hands in front of her. "You have nothing to apologize for. You helped me to heal and you've trained me. But I worry about you, and I want to make sure that you don't spend all your time doing nothing but concentrating on me."

"It gives meaning to do what I've been doing."

"I get that..." Alison sighed. "I'm sorry. Thank you for everything you've done."

The old Drow stared at her for a moment and gave a curt nod. "You're welcome."

Who I am to tell someone centuries old how to live their life? Still, there's something there that doesn't feel quite right, but it'd be silly to say, "Hey, go get drunk in Cabo San Lucas and don't spend so much time worrying about me."

I'll let her live out the last of her time in the way she feels is worthwhile. All I can do is acknowledge what she wants to do for me.

I also need to make sure I live up to what she's doing. She's trying to make me her legacy, and that's a lot to have on my shoulders.

Alison forced a smile. "Can you give me a few other beginner hints about compression?"

"Of course, my princess."

CHAPTER NINETEEN

Alison stepped into the cold, sterile visitor's room of the jail. Three separate booths with chairs and phone receivers lined the thick center glass that separated this side of the room from the other. Two guards with stun batons stood in either corner and watched carefully. No one else sat on the visitor side.

There must be a lot of lonely prisoners in here.

Scott Carlyle sat on the other side of the glass with a smile on his face and wearing an orange jumpsuit. He offered a polite nod to Alison as if she were meeting him in a receiving room in his mansion and not in a jail where he still awaited trial.

Is this a bad idea? Probably, but it's not like he can mess with me here. I won't have to endure anything more than an arrogant rant or two.

After taking a deep breath, she sat at the booth and picked up the receiver.

Scott placed his receiver to his ear and mouth. "This is a surprise, Miss Brownstone. When they told me you were coming to visit, I'll admit I was genuinely shocked, and that's something that rarely happens. Even our previous confrontation wasn't a true shock. The only thing I don't understand is why you're here."

"I figured this was the only way we'd get to talk," Alison responded and stared at him. "And you've been on my mind since that night. I've thought a lot about legacy and that kind of thing lately, and it made me think of you. Now that you've had a month to think about what you did, I thought maybe we could have a decent talk. From everything I've read, all your fancy lawyer moves to get out prior to trial have failed, and your trial is coming up sooner rather than later. You'll be busy soon, preparing for that and your eventual trip to prison."

"Alas. Yes, bail denied. I'll admit that being wealthy with vast technological know-how and resources does make me more of a flight risk than your common office drone." Scott shrugged. "It's not unexpected, so there is no reason to complain about something that's rather logical."

"I'm surprised by something, myself."

"Oh? What's that?"

Alison pointed at Scott. "I figured that when I showed up, you'd give me another big, ranting speech about your glorious goals right away. And how just because you're in prison, you're not dead, and I'd made a mistake when I didn't kill you because eventually, you'd get out or something like that. You know, standard supervillain stuff."

"I'm not a supervillain, Miss Brownstone. If anything, I'm the opposite. You're the half-Drow princess with incredible magical power. I'm merely a man who used his keen mind and instincts to make money. I have no special powers or abilities. Even if you understood nothing of my motivation, I thought you would understand that."

"Lex Luthor is a man, too, but he's still a supervillain."

That elicited a harsh, mocking laugh. "Perhaps that explains much. When I was a child and consumed such superhero stories, I always thought he was onto something with his fear of Superman." He ran his hand through his hair. "Although I'm not bald, but if you want something approaching a rant, I'll only point out that Oriceran is technically an alien world. So, in this case, you—the half-alien from a dangerous warrior race barely held in check by an ancient treaty—is the one who acts as a superpow-ered vigilante with very little oversight. I, on the other hand—the powerless human—am the one in jail because I wanted to do something about it. We've both killed. It's simply that they've decided my killings weren't justified. It's all a matter of perspective."

"Spare me." Alison rolled her eyes. "I give everyone their chance to surrender, and I work closely with the police and PDA. You should know. You helped set that up."

"Indeed, I did. It was so I could better watch you. But even if I am, as you put it, a supervillain, the situation has changed. My position also includes my incarceration and pending trial." Scott clucked his tongue. "When one is not in a position of strength, there are times to feign the oppo-site, but this is not one of those times. It'd only make me look delusional and say what you will about me and my goals, I'm not delusional. My losses were due to tactical mistakes, not a strategic impossibility."

"I can agree with you on that, I guess. If you hadn't infected me, you might have gotten away with it for a lot longer, maybe even until it was too late. I've read about most of the other AMDS cases. All of them seem to be regular people. No one high-profile except me and thankfully, I'm past it."

He nodded. "We needed to test the virus on a variety of subjects, but a small number. After all, viruses can mutate, and I didn't want to risk releasing something into the population that might threaten everyone. My intent is to save humanity, not doom it." He sighed. "And, alas, I'm forced to agree with the ultimate foolishness of attempting to target you, despite its usefulness for testing purposes. The virus might have been refined, but now, I'm reduced in power and influence. My influence came from my intelligence and my wealth. Although I still obviously possess the former, the government's frozen almost all my assets. That said, there are setbacks in all wars. This happens to be a rather extreme one that is rather difficult to circumvent."

I can't believe this guy. He's sitting in jail looking at prison for the rest of his life and he still acts like he'll weasel his way out of things.

"Is that why you don't have lawyers?" Alison asked. "You can't afford them? I read that you haven't hired anyone, but I'm confused because I've also read that you refused to accept a public defender."

"Why waste resources, public or private, on an outcome that's inevitable?" Scott sneered. "That teeters on pathetic, and I refuse to be pathetic. I stare into the maw of the gaping legal abyss and jump into it with a smile on my face, knowing my defeat is already at hand. Like a Spartan on the final day of Thermopylae, I will go down fighting because I know that others will live and eventually defeat our mutual enemies."

Okay, not weasel out. I'll give him that, and yeah, he's not ranting exactly. But this isn't a man who seems to fully accept that he's lost thoroughly and completely. Unless he has something else in mind...

"Wait, is this where you think the people will rise up and demand you be found not-guilty? Or you think the President will pardon you? Trust me. It won't happen."

Scott shook his head. "No, no. You misunderstand completely, Miss Brownstone. It's the opposite, as I've just said. The amount of evidence already gathered by the government is overwhelming. You also have to consider the sheer volumes of crimes I've committed. It's impressive in its own way." He flicked his wrist. "You're fixated on what affected you—my virus—but even that in of itself involved numerous felonies including illegal genetic and magical engineering, financial crimes, and murders to cover up my work. The four murders you mentioned at my mansion were recorded by my own security cameras, and the authorities have that footage. Those alone are more than enough to send me to prison for the rest of my life." He chuckled. "No, Miss Brownstone, even if I were to give the most impassioned speech in defense of my actions one could imagine, it's simply inconceivable that I won't be convicted for at least a decent number of the actual crimes I've committed. The current lack of capital punishment in this state outside of dead or alive bounties means I'll live, but I'll die old and alone in prison without magical aid."

"Huh?" Alison blinked. "If you know you can't possibly win, why bother to fight the charges? Why not plead and get it all over with? I've heard Chesterton's considering pleading. I read the other day that they even offered you a deal where you might be able to avoid a supermax or ultramax if you accepted a plea. I get that prison's not fun, but a regular prison has to be less terrible than a supermax or an ultramax."

"Again, Miss Brownstone, your views on this situation are, alas, somewhat myopic and flawed by unexamined premises, which I'll only attribute to your inexperience."

"Then break it down for me, oh glorious billionaire mastermind."

"You have to understand that all causes need a few martyrs. Their blood, metaphorical or otherwise, is the fuel of the revolution." Scott gave her a grin that made Alison's skin crawl. "But a good martyr suffers first. It makes for better fuel for their cause. I might have failed, but my cause hasn't failed."

"That's what this is? You being a good martyr for the cause of anti-magic nutbaggery?"

"Partially, and this trial will be sensational, of course. The level of media coverage will approach what was devoted to your adoption hearings. Fictionalized accounts will come soon too, I'm sure, and simply by dint of population opinion distribution, some will be inherently more sympathetic to my cause than others."

"People won't turn on magic because of a few biased movies and books."

"No, but it's a beginning." Scott shifted the receiver slightly. "I won't waste the time of lawyers because I'm only interested in wasting my own. I'll use the time during my trial to expound upon my views, to let everyone hear why

I've done what I've done, and to let themselves ask the simple question. Was it so terrible for me to defend the non-magical against the magical? The public is interested in me because of the enormity of my crimes, and so they will hear what I have to say. Then, others will also speak about it, films and novels will be created to add to the current zeitgeist, and true resistance will come."

Alison scoffed. "That's your big plan? Some rant about how the ends justifies the means? Do you think the court will let you do that?"

"What can they do to stop me? Threaten to send me to prison for contempt of court?" Scott shook his head. "America is a grand and beautiful country, and a man is guaranteed his day in court—a guarantee I intend to use to the utmost for the good of this country and planet." He snorted. "No, I won't plead to their charges. Part of that would be me officially and legally admitting I've done something wrong and throwing myself on the mercy of the court." He locked eyes with her. "I refuse to do that. I will calmly and rationally present my case and let the media spread it to all corners of the world. I'll die in prison, but I'll be content, knowing that my sacrifice will have done more to spread my views than any of the internet propaganda outlets I funded."

"You really are a crazy asshole, Scott." Alison sighed. "I can't believe I ever thought you were a good guy."

"I am a good guy. It's your perspective that needs to be adjusted."

"And you don't have any regrets at all? The New Veil and HDL have given you support. Maybe the HDL aren't *all* complete psychopaths, but the New Veil would kill half this planet to make their point. In D.C., they were prepared to murder thousands of people." Alison glared at him. "And your virus almost stopped me from saving those people."

Scott sniffed disdainfully. "It brings me no pleasure that such thuggish murderers admire me, but their mere admiration doesn't invalidate my views. As for regrets? No. The only regret I have is that I was arrogant enough to underestimate you. Not your power, of course, but your ingenuity. I thought you'd be easier to control." He scratched his chin. "At first, I'd even considered trying to seduce you. Perhaps I should have. That way, your boyfriend wouldn't have brought reinforcements in a helicopter to help you. Such is life in hindsight."

"Wow. You are seriously one creepy guy." Alison shook her head in disbelief at his stubborn arrogance. "You know the sick thing? I even found you attractive at first, but it's like my gut knew there was something wrong with you and pushed me away. And even without that, Mason's more my speed than a cold, calculating billionaire. Even if you hadn't turned out to be a ruthless, scheming bastard who plotted to infect magicals with a dangerous virus, you're simply not my type."

His cool gaze made her shudder.

"Good," he replied. "If you have such wonderful instincts, never ignore them. I should point out to you, though, that for all your magical power and reputation as the Dark Princess, it was ultimately your personal connections that led to your victory against me. Finding men and women whom you can trust is perhaps the most difficult thing for anyone of true power. It was also my people skills, more than my intellect, that helped propel my own business success. Consider my end tragic or justified as you will, but no one can deny my ascent and the extent of what I accomplished."

Alison stared at him. "I think we're done here, Scott. I can't take much more of this."

"Very well then. Have a nice day, Miss Brownstone, and consider everything I've said. It's a logical fallacy to reject advice because you don't like the person giving it."

She hung up the receiver and stood, a heavy pit in her stomach as she turned toward the door.

So now, I have an evil billionaire giving me advice. That's like Supergirl taking advice from Lex Luthor.

Not that I'm a superhero. I'm simply a security contractor. With awesome magical powers and who can fly.

Alison tried to shake the lingering thoughts out of her head as she approached the door. She had another appointment that day, and she hoped it wouldn't be as unsettling as her meeting with Scott Carlyle.

CHAPTER TWENTY

H elen wasn't at the front desk when Alison pushed into the PDA office, to her relief. Sometimes, the small favors were what helped a woman through a day.

After dealing with Scott, the last thing I need is that woman to frown at me for daring to breathe around her.

A few other PDA agents sat in their personal offices and typed away at their computers. One glanced up for a moment before he returned his attention to his work. She'd never seen so many agents in the office at one time before.

Maybe they're all doing paperwork related to the dark wizard case. Could one of them be the mole? It's not like I can tell simply by looking at them.

Agent Latherby nodded to her from his office as she approached. She hurried inside and closed the door. He used his wand to cast the privacy spell he'd used previously, a weary look on his face.

She took a seat. "There are other agents here right now.

Won't they be suspicious if you crack magic out when I arrive?"

"In other circumstances, perhaps, but not applied to you. They might even believe you're responsible for the magic." He slipped his wand back into its holster. "After all, criminals aren't the only ones with fanciful and concerned beliefs regarding you."

"Are you saying I scare the PDA?"

"Of course you scare the PDA. You're one of the single most powerful magicals in this city. We only have nominal control of you because of your personal moral standards and not because you have any major reason to be concerned about us." He leaned forward. "Let's be honest, Miss Brownstone. If you decided to lay waste to a neighborhood, the PDA and AET could stop you, but the casualties would still be staggering."

Alison shook her hand. "I'm on your side, remember? At least semi on your side."

"I know. I'm merely explaining a perspective to you that you might not otherwise fully appreciate. With that said, thank you for coming on such short notice. I again want to thank you for all the help you and your people gave in this matter. I'm convinced it's helped keep the mole unaware of how much I know."

"Can't you simply go to each agent and use a spell to figure out if they are the mole?"

Agent Latherby stared at her like she was a foolish child. "Using similar logic, couldn't that have happened at your school? We can't use invasive spells on every agent willy nilly, and that's assuming they haven't set up counters or suicide spells—or even something worse."

"What's worse than a suicide spell?"

"An explosive suicide spell."

Alison grimaced. "I didn't even realize there was such a thing."

"You'd be surprised by what fanatics are willing to do."

"And you're sure?" she responded. "Not about the explosive suicide spells but that the mole doesn't know what's up? They have to be somewhat suspicious given that I skulked around here and suddenly, their guys were hit. I understand that our main goal is to stop the dark wizards but freeing up the PDA to do their job has to come a close second."

The agent shook his head. "That is where your previous reputation and predilections prove useful. You're a known hunter and hater of dark wizards. As I've kept agency resources to a minimum, it'll be difficult to confirm that you are party to any knowledge I might have about the mole." He frowned. "At least if they are aware, they've made no moves that I can detect. But I'll admit, it's not as if the dark wizard case is the only matter the local PDA has to worry about. The mole might be working on something unrelated and watching and waiting for us to make our next move."

"So why am I here exactly?" Alison crossed her legs. "I did my part. I gave you a whole pile of dark wizards. Can't you and the FBI do your thing and get what you want out of them? That's how this works. Line 'em up like pool balls and nail one until he rolls on a couple of others, and the next thing you know, you've wrapped up the entire group."

"That's the general theory, and it does work decently

enough. But in this case, there are particular issues that limit our ability to get more information from the men."

"Meaning what, exactly? I'm not saying torture the guys. Use truth spells or something." Alison shrugged. "You have so many of the guys you're bound to find out something useful."

"One problem. One major problem." Agent Latherby sighed. "You can't make a man tell you something he doesn't actually know."

"Okay, um, sure? What do you mean, though? These dark wizards were huddled together in a big group on a ship. They obviously know something evil, and they held that crew against their will, so this wasn't simply a sightseeing tour."

"Let me take a step back. Most of the dark wizards have been transferred to a special magical containment facility in Portland at my request. I've justified it by referencing some previous cases down there, but it's mostly to move them farther from the mole. Interrogations have been conducted and continue, both there and among the few we still have in Seattle."

Alison nodded. "And you've got what? A new target you want me to go after, is that it? Unless they have a whole other secret army, it has to be easier than taking on a whole group of them on that ship."

Agent Latherby's expression turned concerned. "I wish the interrogations had already yielded actionable intelligence that I could use to task you directly, but that's not the case. We've uncovered a few additional dark wizards in some other areas, and in the long-term, these captures will be helpful and undermine many Galbrathian networks.

But I'm worried that some of that information will be—if it isn't already—compromised by the mole. Even if it's not, their information also very obviously won't help with the most pressing concern."

"How so?"

"Why did they come here, Miss Brownstone?" He raised an eyebrow in question.

Alison shrugged. "I don't know. To do some asshole Galbrathian thing. What did they say about why they came here? To sell limited edition Michael Galbraith commemorative coins or something?"

"They don't know why they came."

"Huh? Did you actually say they don't know?"

"Exactly. They don't know. They have no idea why they came to Seattle. They can remember all the steps involved in getting here but not the actual mission."

"That's a pretty obvious piece of bullshit," she countered.

"No, they truly don't know," Agent Latherby explained. "I should clarify. Are you familiar with compartmentalization spells? It's a somewhat new and dangerous form of magic."

Alison shook her head. "It's not something they taught me in school or that I've heard of, even in our dark magic classes, and we learned about all sorts of nasty curses and crap."

"That's because it's not something the dark wizards developed originally, even if they've decided to make use of it," he replied. "The technique was pioneered in recent years by various magicals who worked for government intelligence agencies, both our own and those of other countries. The short version of the description is that compartmentalization allows you to store information in someone's brain that even they can't access."

"That's kind of cool, but why bother? Why not simply use an encrypted phone or computer or something and set the biometrics to something different or not give them the passwords?"

"The harsh reality is that all machines can be hacked. You should appreciate that, given how you cracked Carlyle's conspiracy partially through the use of computer hacking." Agent Latherby gestured at his keyboard. "And it's even easier now that infomancy is spreading. Yes, you can use infomancy to fight infomancy, but the truth is that if someone gets their hands on an electronic source of information, it's only a matter of when, not if, they crack it."

Alison looked down for a moment as she pondered the implications of the spell. "But wait, if someone can't even access the information, what good is that? Is it a situation where they cast it on themselves at the last moment so the enemy won't figure out what they know?"

"Not exactly, but yes, the person carrying it can't access it. That's the whole point. You could torture them to within an inch of life, heal them, and torture them again, but they can't give you what they don't know. Even if you showed them a recording, technological or magical, it'd be odd to them—a totally new memory."

"But it's a spell. All spells can be undone. Couldn't the other people who want the information undo the spell?"

"That's the elegance of compartmentalization," Agent Latherby replied. "I don't fully understand the spell techniques myself, but the summary version is that unraveling the spell itself destroys the information being stored. The only way to access it is with a separate key spell. It's rather like self-destructing computer encryption that way. The very nature of the magic is such that it won't work if the person with the compartmentalization spell on them attempts to cast the key spell."

Alison furrowed her brow as she slowly took it all in. "So people can carry information that other people can access, but even if they're captured, they can't give it up even if they want to."

"Exactly."

"Damn. I bet every spy is using this thing. It sounds perfect."

Agent Latherby shook his head. "Unfortunately—or fortunately, depending on your point of view—the spell is extremely dangerous and difficult. It's not something that can easily be cast at a moment's notice, and it can destroy a person's mind or damage their brain if it's not done correctly. Accordingly, it's been used very sparingly by intelligence agencies and only in desperate situations, but it has also unfortunately leaked to certain groups—like some of the dark wizards, who are fanatical enough to be willing to take the risk for certain high-profile agendas. It's something we've run into before, but this is one of the largest-scale operations and one of the largest uses of it we've seen."

She groaned. "You're telling me that every dark wizard prisoner you've caught is under the effects of the spell, then? They're all compartmentalized?"

"Unfortunately, yes. It doesn't mean all their information or knowledge is hidden away. As I mentioned earlier, we have received potentially useful and actionable intelligence concerning other matters. But as for their particular purpose in Seattle, it's a complete mystery to them and us. The sigil on the boat, in addition to some of its disruption effects, was part of a ritual to complete a dangerous mass compartmentalization. It's a miracle that none of them were hurt. That said, there are a few things we do know, and that's why I cling to some small sliver of hope that we will discover their purpose here."

"And what's that?"

"One of the wizards you killed had the key spell."

Alison winced. "Oh, shit. Sorry. I think I know the guy you're talking about. In my defense, though, he did try to get everyone to kill me. He didn't say anything about why they'd come either."

He'll want to kill me and Izzie.

"I'm not agitated in particular about his death." Agent Latherby shrugged. "Such things are bound to happen in fluid situations. Given how many survivors you brought it, I applaud your restraint. In this case, though, we know there's another wizard with the key spell—and, presumably, one who understands the bigger picture of what they were here to accomplish."

"Please tell me it's not a guy named Neville."

He stared at her for a moment. "Ah, the one Miss Berens took?"

"So you know it was her?"

"The wizards gave up that information. She's not a criminal, Miss Brownstone, and given who her parents are, it's not in the interests of the PDA to harass her."

Alison nodded dubiously. "I'm glad we agree, but the problem is that I have no way to track Izzie down even if I wanted to."

The agent shook his head lightly. "You don't need to. The wizard she took doesn't have the key spell. That one left from the ship shortly before you engaged the others."

"Damn it. I knew it." Alison sucked in a breath. "I hoped that if we could find the group together, we would have caught them all, but one of them still managed to crawl away at the first sign of trouble."

"Don't feel too bad. From what we can tell, he didn't leave because you were present so much as because he already had what he needed. The others were to assist in the plan once he made some other preparations, so even though he escaped, their operation has still been heavily compromised. There's only so much a single wizard can accomplish when he expected to have dozens of people to help him." Agent Latherby cleared his throat. "We've been able to learn that much from our interrogation of the others, but this is where I need your help."

He nodded toward his closed door. "I don't want to believe that any of the men and women in this office are Galbrathians—or any of the fine other agents in the area— but I can't be certain of that. Since it took us time to uncover the information I've related to you, it also means that our key wizard has had time to continue with his plan. I can hope that he decided to lie low for at least a few days to avoid your wrath, but we can't be certain of that. Instead, he might be in the middle of some dangerous plan on the scale of the destruction of the kemana."

Alison closed her eyes and took a deep breath. "So, let

me fill in the rest of this story. We have a wizard who escaped with information for a Galbrathian plot. We don't know who or where he is, and it's probably part of some major spell of mass destruction. He has a head start, and you need me to find him before it's too late and thousands of people die because some assholes have delusions of grandeur about being the new magical rulers of Earth."

"That about sums it up, yes. Don't worry. I'll push somewhat on my end. The sheer danger of this means we can't rely only on you, but I'm concerned that if we identify or track any possible suspects, they'll conveniently escape before our arrival. Whereas with you, if you can find them, there will be no one to warn them that you might be coming. If I do become aware of a strong suspect possibility, I'll try to push it to you before we move on him."

She drew another long breath in irritation. "Damn it. These dark wizards really are like roaches. There is always one more hiding somewhere."

CHAPTER TWENTY-ONE

The elevator doors opened to the parking garage. Alison's quick dinner with Mason had been exactly what she needed after her long and frustrating day. Sometimes, it was refreshing to simply spend a few hours with her man and not worry about ideological billionaires or dark wizard plots.

With every day in Seattle, she understood her parents that much more. She had thought after her experiences at the School of Necessary Magic that she knew what it was to deal with threats, but Seattle was on a whole different level.

"You can talk to me," Mason commented as they stepped off the elevator.

"About what?" Alison responded. "I talked all throughout that dinner. I barely let you get in a word edgewise." She snickered. "I can barely even remember what you said other than, 'That sounds, great, A,' over and over again."

"Exactly. You spent most of dinner talking about the

ingredients in our meal and how you might prepare them. You even took time to pull out your phone and read me several entries from a cooking website."

She shrugged. "Yeah, and? I'm trying to get into cooking now. Is thinking about ingredients so weird? Isn't the best thing to do to analyze things you like and go from there? Learn from the best and all that?"

Mason chuckled. "That's not weird. What is weird is that it's all you talked about, except for that five minutes in which you monologued about our next helicopter date."

"I don't follow why any of that is odd."

"Setting aside the dark wizard hunt, you went to visit the jailed billionaire today—the one who almost took your magic away—and he didn't come up *once* in our entire conversation. I waited for you to at least mention him, other than your 'Yeah, the visit was interesting' dodge from earlier when we were still driving here."

Alison sighed. "I tried to relax and not think about him. And there's not much I can do about the dark wizard situation right now either. Tahir and Hana are working some of their sources. Vincent's already made it clear that he won't give me more information, and other than reinforcing that I need more informants, there's not much I can do, so I refuse to worry about it. Give me a problem I can solve and I'll solve it."

Mason eyed her, clear suspicion on his face. "And Carlyle? You're the one who went to talk to him. It's not like he reached out to you. What was so interesting about the visit?"

"I don't know. We talked. He did what he always does and gave me some big philosophical justification for general assholery. But something…I don't know, got under my skin this time." She scrunched her forehead in irritation. "I was stupid. I guess I thought he might feel bad for some of the shit he pulled. Instead, he plans to use the trial as a big speech opportunity. The guy doesn't care at all. He doesn't think he did anything wrong." She snorted. "I prefer the Eastern Union to the dark wizards or Carlyle. At least the Union admits that they are criminals and thugs."

"He's a billionaire douchebag used to messing with people's heads. Don't let him live in your head without paying some rent, A."

"I know. The thing is, it's less that I'm worried about him and more about what he represents. He's sitting in jail because of an anti-magic plot, and meanwhile, I have Tahir and Hana looking into a pro-magic plot." Alison shook her head. "You'd think that thirty years after the gates reopened, we would have had some of this shit already figured out. It's annoying."

"Earth has had ten thousand years of civilization, both with and without magic, and we still haven't figured out peace between normal people. I wouldn't sweat it too much that it'll take more than a few decades to get everything else figured and—" He looked past her and whipped his wand from his jacket. "This is annoying."

Alison summoned a shadow blade and shield before she even turned toward the source of her boyfriend's distress.

A man in a ski mask and dark clothing stood near a large concrete support pillar, an obsidian sword in hand. The blade was coated with a thin layer of crystal. An anti-magic deflector hung around his neck. He took a few steps forward. "Your magic won't work, wizard. Throw your fireball. I'm ready. I welcome it."

"Fireball?" Mason snorted. "You should have done your homework, asshole." He moved his wand and spoke his incantations. The magic was obvious to her but not visible otherwise.

Baseline speed, strength, and resistance, huh?

"If you surrender, I can make it quick," the swordsman explained. "I don't take pleasure in what I must do, but that doesn't mean I won't do it."

Alison held up her shadow blade. "One man with an anti-magic deflector won't win against the two of us."

"You're right. He won't."

Several more men emerged from behind the massive pillar and another on the opposite side to bring the total number of enemies to eight, all with similar swords and anti-magic deflectors.

"I think my *tachi* is cooler-looking than your anti-magic swords." Alison gestured toward one of the blades. "I'm guessing that's what those are."

"The appropriate weapon," the assassin began, "is necessary for the appropriate target, Dark Princess."

"Oh, I get it." She snapped her fingers. "You realized after the ass-kicking I delivered on the ship that you wouldn't win with spells, so you got the swords and deflectors. Too bad. I doubt any of you assholes can get through my shields." She nodded toward Mason. "Or his."

The first man chuckled. "Each of these blades was made by a different person, but they were all made with the same purpose—to hunt those who wield the unnatural. Witch killers, if you like."

Wait. Something's off.

"Dangerous toys," Mason replied and widened his stance. "You could easily get hurt playing with something like that. Why don't you take your toys and go home before that happens?"

The swordsman pointed his blade at Alison. "We've watched him, you know, and looked for an opportunity to rescue him, but then you—the so-called Dark Princess—dares to go in there. What, to mock him for his efforts to protect our reality?"

Huh. What are they talking about?

Alison blinked. "Wait. You're talking about Scott Carlyle, aren't you?"

"Of course!" the man thundered. "Derek Chesterton isn't a believer. He's merely a petty little man, not like Scott Carlyle who took action to protect our planet from the pollution of magic. He refuses to even speak to us, but once we've punished you, he'll understand how much we're on his side."

"You're not dark wizards. You're damned New Veil." Alison rolled her eyes. "You have to be kidding me. I know this is Seattle, but it doesn't have to rain bullshit that much."

Mason shook his head. "Do you guys think that because you have some anti-magic swords and deflectors you can win against us?"

The New Veil assassins crept forward, their blades at the ready.

Alison sighed and released her shadow blade and shield. "They do have a point, Mason. With those weapons, my defenses and preferred attack aren't as effective."

"Exactly," the New Veil assassin who'd first greeted them shouted. "Good. As I said, I'll make it quick. On your knees and put your hands behind your head. With a proper strike, this will be over in an instant."

The entire group slowed.

Mason frowned at her. "A, I always have your back, but what the hell are you doing?"

She shrugged. "It's risky with all those anti-magic blades. I'm still working on my regeneration magic."

"But we can still win, especially against these assholes."

"Oh, I know." Alison ripped her Glock from her jacket holster and opened fire. Her first bullet ripped through the spokesman's head, and she swept left and planted shots into the next two men's foreheads. The stunned assassins took seconds to understand what was going on, which suggested that they were more used to surprising people than being surprised. By the time they charged, she'd already killed four of them.

The men on the left all dead, she jerked her gun to the right and fired four shots in rapid succession. Three of them struck the heads or necks of their targets to drop them, bleeding out or dead. The fourth assassin rushed forward, his sword held high. She aimed her gun and fired again but it jammed.

Mason rushed forward. Alison dropped her gun and reached into her jacket for her gnome-crafted knife. Her boyfriend's magical speed allowed him to rush past the assassin in seconds and turn on him. She'd barely pulled her knife out when the assassin spun and swung at Mason.

The attack missed, and the wizard slammed his foot into the man's knee. An audible crack and snap sounded, and the assassin fell to the ground with a shrill scream. Another quick punch knocked him out.

Alison sighed and slipped her knife back into her jacket. She picked her gun up and holstered it before she retrieved her phone. "You didn't have to do that. I was going to kill him with my knife."

Mason kicked the sword away from the unconscious man. "A man needs a few chances to show off in front of his girlfriend."

"Now, we'll have to probably spend an hour talking to the police." She nodded. "You saved one, though. Good. They can maybe smoke some others out. It's always a good thing to eliminate a few New Veil."

"Do you think Carlyle was behind this?" Her companion glared at the unconscious man.

"Nah. You heard them. This was their version of an offering to their new martyr-saint." Alison rolled her eyes. "I love how all these anti-magic assholes from Scott to these guys are totally willing to use magic when it suits their purposes. You can't make anti-magic deflectors without spells." She dialed nine-one-one. "Whatever. Let's get the cops here and clean this crap up."

***

Alison rested her head against Mason's shoulder as they lay on her couch. Hana was still out working some contacts, so they had the condo to themselves. The police had held them for an hour but hadn't made them go to the station. When eight men were found with swords and anti-magic deflectors in public, their intentions are hard to dispute, and few people had much sympathy for the indiscriminate terrorists of the New Veil.

Mason stroked her arm. "You've been quiet for almost ten minutes, A. Are you still thinking about what happened? I'm sorry those assholes ruined our night."

"Yeah. I've scared the Eastern Union into never screwing with me again. Dark wizards might attack me, but it's not like they go out of their way to come after me like they do Izzie." She frowned. "New Veil, though? They're fanatics and might come after me forever. I'm a symbol of everything they hate and famous on top of it."

"I imagine eight anti-magic deflectors and eight anti-magic swords probably weren't easy for them to come by." He ruffled her hair. "And a certain beautiful half-Drow constantly kills them and blows their shit up. Sure, there will always be terrorists, but I bet you kill them faster than they are recruited. Think about all the resources they lost in the D.C. attack."

Alison snuggled into his shoulder. "I know but it's annoying. I thought about our past and how it defines us. I make a lot of waves, which means I always have to worry that something from the past will pop up, and I'm still way younger than my dad was when that became a problem for him."

Mason shook his head. "It's not only you. I never did tell you much about my past with the Russian Mafia and why I wanted to go kick their asses for you."

"I figured you'd tell me when you were ready."

"It's nothing as spectacular as what you've done," he added with a pained chuckle. "There was a man—a client. He was with them for a while but got married and had a daughter. After her eighth birthday, he couldn't take the lifestyle anymore. Originally, he simply wanted to leave the gang but they wouldn't back off, so he had no choice but to go to the cops and agreed to testify against them. But because these bastards were more heavily armed than ever before and they'd bought some cops off, he brought me in as his personal bodyguard." His expression darkened. "It was one of my toughest jobs. They came after him constantly and we had to keep on the move. He finally managed to testify, and that gutted most of the gang. He thought it was over and allowed himself to relax. That was a mistake."

Alison looked up at his troubled face. "Some of the leftovers killed him after you finished the job?"

"Not exactly." Mason took a deep breath. "It wasn't a simple hit. They kidnapped his daughter. She'd snuck out to visit a friend, not really understanding exactly how much danger she was in. They agreed to do a handoff and he called me. The bastards, of course, had no intention to let either of them live. When shit went bad, the client made it clear what my priorities were—get his daughter out of there—so I did. He was dead by the time the cops showed up. While he might have been a piece of shit, he'd tried to leave the lifestyle behind and his last actions on this earth were about saving his daughter." He clenched his hand into a fist. "If those assholes had simply let him leave, he probably wouldn't have testified. That's the real kicker in all this."

"I'm sorry that you couldn't save him." She kissed him on the cheek.

"It doesn't haunt me like some of your dark wizard stuff

but it does make me hate the Russian Mafia. That wasn't my only run-in with them. I was involved in saving some trafficking victims from them as well. But you're right, A. Sometimes, you can't fully escape the past. I don't think it's a big deal, though. It is what it is, and in both our cases, the people we took on really had it coming."

"You're right." Alison chuckled.

"What's so funny?"

"Well, those New Veil guys thought that as long as they came at me with the swords, they'd win. It's like it never even occurred to them that I'd use a gun."

Mason shrugged. "Lately, you've mostly used your gun only at the range. They probably read some of the recent news stories about you and assumed you now used magic all the time. Like I told you before we boarded that ship, it's when you take things for granted that you're in trouble."

Alison sat up and faced him. "Next time, they might show up with guns, too, and anti-magic bullets."

"Then we'll have to kill them more quickly."

"Simple solutions are generally the best." She grinned.

CHAPTER TWENTY-TWO

Her phone rang with a call from Tahir as Alison swallowed the last bite of her scrambled eggs. Still mulling over what she'd used to season her meal, she dragged the phone out of her pocket and brought it to ear. "What's up?"

"I have information," the hacker replied. "Because of how time sensitive things are, I won't make you come to me."

"That's nice." She chucked. "I am technically your boss. We'll have to talk about getting you a custom office at the building. Some of the old ways of doing things aren't all that efficient, and the more we do jobs like this, the more we need to change things up."

Tahir snorted. "I prefer my own place."

"And I prefer not to waste time driving across town in Seattle traffic. Besides, your apartment building doesn't have a helipad. Anyway, give me the executive summary and please end this with good news or something that at least involves me being to solve it by going and punching a dark wizard through a window."

"I probed into some of the crew manifest changes, especially after the Vancouver changeover," he began. "As I told you before, these people were sloppy—so sloppy that I was able to trace back from some of their changes and gain access to other systems. Even though they kept a lot of their activity offline, they didn't keep all of it sequestered, and cross-referencing with other records and sources allowed me to find some useful information." A quiet, confident chuckle followed. "I've identified a dark wizard safehouse on Bainbridge Island. It's located on its own in the woods, so if you choose to perform a frontal assault, there's minimum risk of collateral damage. You only need to avoid too many fire spells."

A smile broke out on Alison's face. "That *is* good news. Contact Hana and Mason. Let them know to arm up and meet me at the Brownstone Building. I want tactical drone support from you this time as well. We'll move on this place as soon as possible. I'll contact Latherby and let him know. If we have everything resolved for him by the time his people arrive, the mole won't matter."

"Very well. Anything else?"

"No, and, thanks, Tahir. You came through, and I appreciate that. It makes everything easier knowing I have skilled people on my team."

Tahir scoffed. "I'd prefer a challenge, but an easy victory is satisfying in its own strange way. Let's finish these wizards off so we can move on to more interesting prey."

The Brownstone helicopter rumbled smoothly across Elliot Bay and closed on the east coast of Bainbridge Island. A ferry chugged along below them, bringing traffic to the island from Pier Fifty-Two.

It's almost over. These dark wizards dared to show up, and we'll stop them no matter where they run. The cocky bastards won't know what hit them. Compartmentalize all you want, boys. There's always a trail to follow.

"There's a clearing about two hundred yards from the house that Tahir spotted with his drones," Alison explained through her helmet mic. "So, the plan's the same. He has his toys patrolling the area from up high. Several have rockets, so if they have an aircraft or boat hidden somewhere, he can eliminate them. Mason will fly us over and I'll jump out with Hana. Mason lands the helicopter in the clearing, then reinforces us."

He frowned. "I still don't like this plan. I have to land the chopper, get out, and run there."

"With your magic, that's not exactly hard, and between Hana and me, we can clear the house easily."

Hana watched quietly from the back, a faint smile on her face.

"That's the point." Mason lowered the helicopter as they approached the island and the trees on the coast. "They won't have thirty guys this time, A. You and Hana will cut through them like nothing, and I won't even have any fun. I'll simply be the helicopter guy."

"You get to fly us there in my shiny new helicopter. This is the first time we've used it for something actually important."

He shrugged. "I thought our date was important."

The fox laughed.

"Thermal images indicate twelve humanoids inside," Tahir reported. "This is always easier when they are in a small wooden house instead of a huge metal ship in the water. They don't seem to have detected or reacted to any of the drones. It looks like you'll have a relatively good surprise advantage."

"Then it's the dream plan from before—a quick and decisive frontal assault," Alison replied. "We still need to make entry first to be sure it's dark wizards. It's not that I don't trust you, Tahir, but I also don't want to blow up a house that might be half-filled with hostages."

They reached the trees. It wouldn't be long now.

"What if it's some guy's vacation home?" Mason asked.

She shrugged. "Then I'll apologize and send him a large pile of cash for the trouble." She unbuckled her harness and shimmied into the back of the helicopter. "Are you good with all this, Hana?"

"Jumping out of a helicopter flying barely above a bunch of trees toward a house possibly filled with murderous dark wizards?" Hana gave Alison a thumbs-up. "I think this is my new favorite Saturday fun time."

Their pilot increased altitude slightly, but more than a few tall evergreens threatened the craft. "About thirty seconds before we're over the place."

Hana undid her harness. She grabbed the *tachi* sword belt from the floor and slipped it on. They weren't able to rely on the disguise spell to conceal the sword during their ship raid, but now, they didn't bother with such petty concerns as stealth.

Alison removed her helmet and slid the helicopter door

open. The sounds of rushing air and thumping rotors were now deafening. Hana removed her helmet and tapped her ring three times to summon the shield.

The trees whipped below them. They passed over a narrow dirt road that led to a house nestled alone in the sparsely populated section of the island.

She grabbed Hana's hand and shouted, "Are you ready?"

"Let's do this thing," Hana shouted back.

Alison held up three fingers, then two, then one. With her grip firm on Hana's arm, she leapt out of the helicopter. They'd only fallen about ten feet when she extended shadow wings and secured her friend with both arms, along with shadow tendrils. Gliding rather than flying, they closed rapidly on the house.

The front door burst open and four men rushed out with wands. She summoned a shield as fireballs burst from the wands.

With little effort, she spun to the side and dodged the fireballs.

"Wee," Hana yelled. "This is fun. Drop me on these guys, and I'll take them out."

A hissing sound came from above and a rocket cruised past them and slammed into the front porch. It exploded and the men careened through the air.

"You were supposed to save the rockets for vehicles, Tahir," Alison complained.

"I have more than one," he replied with a faint hint of amusement in his voice. "And I can always bring more drones if necessary."

"We might also want to keep some of them alive, just in case."

"Duly noted."

Alison dropped altitude. She was now only ten feet above the ground and released her grip, magical and physical, on Hana. The fox dropped and her tails and claws appeared.

Hana hit the ground and sprinted forward as she yanked her sword from its scabbard. "I'll stab them in the arms and legs. That'll keep them alive in theory."

Alison flew upward and headed toward a second-story window. She extended a shadow blade and grinned. "How's this for direct assault?" She released her wings and smashed through the window to send shards of glass in a wide arc. There were no wizards in the second-floor bedroom which now needed a window replacement.

Shouts and the roar and buzz of magic sounded from below.

She rushed toward the door and threw it open. A wizard stood on the other side, his wand already raised. A dark ray fired from the tip and struck her at point blank range. Her shield flashed but held. She repaid the man with her palm shoved in his face and discharged a stun bolt an inch away from him. He slumped with a brief shriek.

Another scream sounded below, along with a familiar growl—Hana's.

Alison rushed to the next closest door and kicked it open. There were no dark wizards in the second bedroom. She backed out and rushed down the hall to the master bedroom. Magic radiated off the door which revealed several glowing defensive glyphs set into it. She could sense magic building inside the room.

What are they planning? It'll take forever to try to unravel these damned glyphs. I—wait a second.

Alison moved back quickly and released her shadow blade. She spun at the sound of someone bounding up the stairs. A blood-covered Hana appeared with her sword in hand.

The fox pointed the weapon downward. "I didn't kill *everybody*, but they're all out of the fight, at least."

Alison pointed down the hallway. "They have the master bedroom locked down with spells, so I'll apply a little lateral thinking. Tahir, do you see any reinforcements?"

"No," he replied. "And judging from the thermals, there are four wizards inside the master bedroom."

"Thanks. Time to knock." Alison raised both hands and fed magic into a growing white orb. She took a few deep breaths as the orb grew inch by inch.

I need to figure out the Drow way to do this so I can apply more compression to it.

"Knock, knock, assholes," she shouted and released the spell.

The now soccer-ball-sized orb of energy rocketed through the hallway at an angle and struck the wall directly beside the enchanted door. A white-blue explosion ripped through the hallway and blasted debris and smoke in both directions.

Alison rushed forward and ignored the thick cloud of dust and burning wood as she headed toward the newly made hole. The dark wizard's glyph-filled door remained standing, with only minor burns.

I have to give them credit for that. Quality work, boys.

Hana rushed after her.

The smoke cleared to reveal the expected four wizards. One lay on the floor, bleeding from a half-dozen wood fragments embedded in him, and two others stood in front of the last remaining wizard who knelt on a king-size bed against the wall. He intoned a chant over a small crystal in his hand. The two men in front of him glowed with obvious shields.

The guards pointed their wands and shouted an incantation. The floor turned to dust beneath Alison and she immediately fell. Hana leapt over the hole and slashed with her blade. It sliced across the chest of both men in one swing, the magic penetration of the *tachi* in good form. They stumbled back and their faces contorted in pain from their deep wounds.

Alison launched upward with the aid of a quick pulse of magic.

One of the men waved his wand, and it transformed into a glowing broadsword. He rushed in front of the chanting man and parried Hana's next swing. She leapt aside as his partner raised his wand again and ended his life with a neck stab.

Alison thrust out with her arm and released a stun bolt at the other wizard. It struck him and dissipated in crawling arcs of energy over his invisible shield, but the attack distracted him long enough for the fox to stab him through the leg. He yelped and fell to one knee. A strike with the flat of her blade to his head knocked him unconscious.

The crystal in the final wizard's hand shattered, and a swirling, opaque, cerulean portal appeared behind him. He sneered and threw himself into it as Hana stabbed at him. The portal winked closed.

"Damn it," Alison shouted. "Tahir, one of the bastards used a single-use portal crystal. I doubt we'll have any luck but keep an eye out in the area. He might have tried to head for a vehicle."

"I'll find him if he's nearby," the hacker replied.

She knelt and yanked the swordsman up by his shirt, muttered a quick incantation, and placed her hand on the side of his head.

He gasped and his eyes flickered open.

Hana stepped forward and pointed her sword at his throat. "Try anything stupid and you die."

The dark wizard's gaze flicked from one woman to the other. "You think you've won but you haven't."

Alison snorted. "Yeah, I did notice the asshole who portaled away. You guys were guarding him, which means he's important. Who the hell was he? The guy with the key spell?"

The man's face contorted in surprise. "So you know that much, Dark Princess?"

"Oh, so *this* guy knows me, but the head asshole on the boat doesn't?" She scoffed. "Yeah, I know all about your compartmentalization crap. You Galbrathians are idiots to use that kind of magic. You'll fry your own brains."

"Some losses are inevitable in any endeavor worth pursuing."

Hana wrinkled her nose. "There were two guys on the couch simply sitting there drooling. They were that way when I came in."

Alison rolled her eyes. "Like I said, idiots. You assholes

have gotten lucky to have only lost two guys, but to me, it sounds like your compartmentalization luck has run out. Maybe I should simply let you keep going until you fry all your fucking brains."

He laughed. "You say that, but whatever our mission is will succeed, because he has what he needs. You lose, Alison Brownstone. He escaped, and you can torture us all you want, you'll never get the information out of us."

She slammed her fist into his face and knocked him out again. With a muttered expletive, she shook her hand out and frowned. "Damn it. Speaking of luck, I don't think we'll have more of it again soon. I doubt there's another special safehouse in the area, and we have no way to track the guy, especially if he's trying to block it."

Hana sheathed her blade. "I don't think I'd be so sure of that. You can track him as long as you have something physical—like blood, right?"

"Yeah, but I need his blood, not just any blood."

The fox pointed at the bed.

A few bloodied wood fragments lay near where the man had knelt.

Alison leaned over and picked up a fragment. "Huh. I never thought ridiculous explosive overkill would ever help me in that way."

Loud footsteps sounded from the hallway and the two women spun to meet the new challenge.

Mason rushed in and looked around. "Damn it, A. I knew it. It's all over, isn't it?"

"Not completely." She frowned and held up the wood. "I need to go after this guy now. You stay with Hana and guard the prisoners. Tahir can contact Latherby and get him and the cops over here to pick up the survivors."

"I should go with you," he insisted.

She raised her hand to silence his protest. "It's one wizard and I need to go after him. He couldn't have gone far. He has to be in Seattle somewhere."

"And how will you get to him without your helicopter and pilot?"

Alison marched into the hallway and extended shadow wings. "With these."

CHAPTER TWENTY-THREE

S he might not be as fast as a helicopter but avoiding surface traffic would still get her to her target a lot quicker. Alison soared over Elliot Bay, alert and tense. Whatever plan the Galbrathians had was about to begin—if it hadn't already—and she needed to find the wizard and put an end to it.

I wish I knew my compression a little better. I'll burn a lot of magic to simply get there, but it's worth it. I have a feeling we don't have much time left, especially with how cocky the wizard was.

"The bastard hasn't even bothered to make much effort to block tracking spells," she exclaimed. "The fact that I can follow him this easily without using a secondary source means he was in a damned hurry to get somewhere fast. Tahir, have you picked up anything unusual? Any weird lights reported?"

The hacker muttered something under his breath. "This is Seattle. Of course I pick up things that are unusual, but I can't exactly identify an individual wizard in a city of millions with only a general direction to work with. You need to narrow it down somewhat."

Alison glanced at a cargo ship and moved lower when she reached the edge of the Magnolia neighborhood and the blue water of the bay gave way to trees and houses. The building resonance from the tracking spell informed her that she was closer to the target. Judging by the sensation, she was already halfway toward the wizard, far closer than she'd expected after only a few minutes of flight.

She frowned and glanced to her right. The Space Needle and various skyscrapers cut into the air in the distance and the man was clearly ahead of her and not to the right, which meant downtown wasn't his target. Nor any of the stadiums, she reasoned, or some of the more obvious targets for terrorism. The University District still lay roughly ahead of her, and it presented another tempting target.

If I were an asshole dark wizard, what would my mission be and where I do it? What's the actual plan?

Alison gritted her teeth. The truth was, no one knew the Galbrathians' plan. They'd gone out of their way to conceal it and even fried the brains of their own men. Whatever it was, they wanted to take the authorities completely by surprise.

People will die if I don't figure this out.

She dragged in a few deep breaths and wondered if using so much magic to fly would be an issue in the coming battle before she snorted at the thought. This wouldn't be an extended siege of King Oriceran's castle. Her next fight would be a quick elimination of a single wizard. Once she found him, the battle was as good as over.

I simply need to find him and kill him. This will be easy. Finally, it'll be over.

Alison drifted over a golf course.

Tahir cleared his throat. "I've picked up some chatter about a possible illegal low-level magical flight. That's you, by the way. Although the descriptions are amusing, several people have reported a giant crow."

"A giant crow?" She snorted. "Big deal. Maybe they'll refuse to fine me after I've saved the city, and I'm not even sure that flying at this altitude is illegal." She spun to the side to avoid a high-flying drone. "Come to think of it, we'll need the AET and PDA in the end."

"What about the mole?"

"Whatever plan they have is about to go down. If the mole knows I'm on the mission, it won't make any difference. Contact the PDA and the police on my behalf. Tell them I'm on my way to stop the dark wizard and they should arm up. The second we know where this flight ends, you can pass it along to them."

"Be careful, A," Mason interrupted over the line. "For all we know, this ends with something on the scale of the kemana blowing up. You're tough, but even you can be hurt."

"All the more reason for me not to be careful," Alison retorted. "I won't allow these assholes to kill any innocent people in my city. It's time to fly fast, kick ass, and kill dark wizards."

Alison glided over a large cemetery below and then a park.

"I'm close. I can feel it. Very close. I'm about to pass over the Fremont Cut and— Shit!"

A massive flash blinded her for a few seconds. She squinted until her vision cleared. Nine pulsating spirals of energy, all different colors, flowed upward from the other side of the canal near the northern end of Aurora Bridge.

Massive waves of magical energy passed through her. Alison rocketed toward the spirals and swallowed around the sudden lump in her throat.

"No, no, no," she shouted.

"What?" Hana, Mason, and Tahir replied simultaneously.

"Tell the PDA and AET to head to the Fremont Troll. I think I know the plan. I think the bastard's trying to free the damned thing."

"Alison, you have to stop him!" Tahir shouted, uncharacteristic panic in his voice. "I don't have time to go into the details, but I've hacked some of the files about that incident. It's far more dangerous than anyone realizes."

"I'm working on it but get those reinforcements here."

She swooped over the bridge. Traffic was at a standstill with several people outside the cars either talking on their phones or taking pictures of the spirals. A few pointed her way and raised their phones to snap pictures.

The idea of a giant stone troll getting free is bad enough, and Tahir says it's even worse than that. Great. Just great.

Alison rolled and moved to the side of the bridge. She barreled over the trees and buildings only yards below. A quick tilt to the right at the last moment brought her to the side of the statue and the source of the spirals.

The dark wizard stood about ten yards away from the

Fremont Troll, his wand in the air, and a complicated series of intricate radiant glyphs spun around him. Energy crackled and arced from his wand to strike the giant. Twelve shining glyphs now covered the statue's head, arms, and body. Something looked familiar about them, but Alison didn't have time to think about it given the situation.

She released her wings and landed in a crouch. In almost the same instant, she summoned shields and her shadow blade.

I have to kill him and end this.

Now that she was close, she could see the Galbrathian speak but in the loud crackle and buzz of the magic, she couldn't make out the words. It didn't matter. She doubted that he shouted his regrets rather than chanting a complicated spell. It was time for some distraction.

Alison thrust outward with her palm and launched a blast of light magic toward the wizard. The blast changed course after a few feet and rushed toward one of the glyphs on the Fremont Troll and faded into nothingness before arrival. She followed up with a shadow crescent attack, but again, the magic flowed into a glyph on the troll.

"Tahir, do you have an ETA on the AET?" Alison asked.

There was no response.

"Tahir? Can you hear me?"

Again, no response.

"Perfect. Just damned perfect." Alison extended a shadow blade and charged the wizard. Her shield and blade drained off as she closed on him, and she slowed to a stop. "Now this is starting to really get on my nerves."

The man ceased his chant and looked at her. He gripped

his wand with both hands and multiple rays of energy now arced from the tip and danced between the glyphs on the Fremont Troll. "You understand now, don't you? There's nothing you can do. We win."

Alison drew her gun and pulled the trigger three times. The bullets turned into mist as they struck near the glyph cloud around the wizard. She sighed and holstered her weapon.

I guess the same trick won't always work.

"How does this help the cause of wizard rule, asshole?" she shouted. "If anything, it'll only make people more scared. You've played right into the hands of New Veil. Keep this shit up, and the government could pass more extreme magic control laws."

"You might be powerful, Alison Brownstone, but you're not all-knowing. What did you think? That you'd corner me and I'd tell you everything you want to know? This thing isn't simply any giant, you know." Ecstasy spread over his face. "They have different names in Oriceran languages, but Mountain Strider is the translation I like the most. They were modified by magic during the Great War to become living weapons of mass destruction. It'll be a glorious sight. You'll appreciate it, even if you are misguided. All magical beings have to appreciate the most impressive displays of magic."

Damn. I wish I had brought the tachi. I bet it could cut through his shields.

Alison shrugged. "Congrats, you'll summon some huge-ass giant and it'll wreck a city, and that accomplishes what, exactly? I feel there's something missing between the beginning and end of this plan—if the plan is supposed to end with Galbrathian rule, that is."

"For a half-elf, you're remarkably short-sighted," her adversary sneered. "But it doesn't matter. So many pieces and plans have been put into place. Years of planning and sacrifice. That's all you need to know."

"To kill people?" She launched a few more attacks but they didn't reach him. "By the time this is over, people will rush the White House and demand a pardon for Scott Carlyle."

"You can stop talking, Brownstone. You need to understand that for all your power and reputation, this time, you lost."

Alison backed away and grew shadow wings. She flew upward to check the top of the bridge that towered over the wizard. There were no cars close on either side, which wasn't a surprise given the spirals of energy that rose through it. People's self-preservation instincts made this easier.

"Time for a test, asshole," she muttered and moved farther up the road. She shoved magical energy, both shadow and light, into a ballooning and pulsating white ball streaked with violet. The seconds continued to tick by as she funneled more energy into the growing missile and the magical pressure and heat oppressed her. Strands of energy leapt from the ball and licked at her clothes to burn holes and scorch her skin. She ignored the sting of the magic's touch as she shoved more and more concentrated power into a single attack.

You'll love this.

The colors of the spirals that trailed upward from the bridge began to shift and blend into one another.

I think that means I'm running out of time. If it tries to absorb this, it'll guide the blast right where I want it, anyway.

"Eat this!" Alison screamed and released the pressurized magic.

The massive discharge roared away from her and struck the bridge. A massive explosion consumed the area. Sizzling fragments of concrete, asphalt, and half-melted steel billowed up to form a cloud. A loud, dull groan, like the water itself had bellowed, sounded as the bulk of the impact site fell and buried both the dark wizard and the troll.

She waved her hand in front of her face to clear some of the dust that choked her as she descended once more. Even though she'd collapsed the front of the bridge, it was far enough north that the rest of the bridge remained standing without too much damage. People ran toward the southern end and screamed and yelled into the sudden silence.

Alison landed beside the pile of devastation and took slow, deep breaths. Magic wasn't infinite, even for a Drow princess at the height of her power, and she'd used more than usual in a short time, but there was no ache. Her vision didn't swim.

If I wasn't working out like I've been doing, I'd probably have passed out on the flight over here.

Distant sirens wailed, and she smiled. Sure, she'd damaged a bridge, but to thwart a dark wizard plot in doing so seemed like a good trade-off to her. Her smile fell when she sensed magical energy grow once again in the rubble pile.

The ground rumbled and the debris shifted.

She scrubbed a hand down her face. "I really hate fucking dark wizards."

A stony fist punched through the pile and then another emerged. The Fremont Troll crawled forward and the glyphs glowed all over its body. The hubcap fell off its eye. A moment later, the entire gray façade cracked and shattered to fall in pieces and reveal dark green rock underneath with intricate veins of gold and silver on the surface. The eye glowed bright blue.

Alison hissed and backed away.

"Okay, I can do this. He's big, but for a so-called Mountain Strider, he's not so big. More of a Hill Strider if you ask me."

The giant cleared the rubble and stood.

So, what? The legs were there the entire time, hidden in the bridge or something?

She craned her neck upward at the giant.

The troll emitted a roar. Screams erupted from the bridge and people bolted toward the other side. Others poured out of nearby houses and ran up the street.

Good, get out of here before it's too late.

"Okay, so now, I'm fighting a giant."

CHAPTER TWENTY-FOUR

"The bigger they are, the harder they fall, right?" Alison took a few deep breaths and pushed into the air with a new pair of shadow wings. After a few seconds, she blinked as she realized she didn't seem to be any closer to the head of the monster. Bile rose in her throat.

This is now ridiculous.

She definitely moved steadily upward. That much was obvious, given the fact that the bridge grew more distant. The problem was the Fremont Troll. It continued to grow and the seconds ticked by interminably before its size stabilized.

"That's a little more Mountain Strider, I guess," Alison murmured. "Annoyingly impressive."

It towered over the bridge as it stomped through nearby houses. The monster was now easily hundreds of feet tall. Fortunately, the nearest people had already fled.

She blasted off a series of attacks and alternated between shadow and light magic. The power simply flowed into the glyphs on his body as it had before and caused no damage at all.

The troll released another roar and swatted at her. She dodged the blow but saw that the giant's single eye wasn't damaged.

At least he noticed me. If I can hold his attention on me, maybe I can keep him from destroying anything more.

Multiple AET dropships closed in the distance.

"Alison, can you hear me?" Tahir called over her receiver.

"Finally. I think the waking spell disrupted communication. Tahir, I need you to put me in contact with AET."

He snorted. "I saw what you did to the bridge on a long-range drone camera, but do you still think you can win against something like that? It's like I told you, Alison. The files I read talked about how they didn't dare try to move it in case it woke up. Even the Oricerans thought it was best to leave it there."

"I don't know if I can win, but I have to try. To leave it where it sat isn't an option anymore." Alison flung several more magical missiles but they flowed into the glyphs. "I don't know. It absorbs all my attacks somehow. If I try another big explosion, I don't think it'll accomplish anything. Patch me into the AET. Whatever I do will have to involve them."

"One moment," Tahir replied.

The dropships slowed but immediately turned away.

What the hell?

"You're connected, Alison," the hacker said.

She circled the Mountain Strider. "This is Alison Brownstone contacting the AET. Where the hell are you going? I think I have the ultimate example of an enhanced threat right in front of me, and you're headed in the wrong direction."

"This is Lieutenant Martinez, field commander, Seattle AET," replied a crisp male voice. "Brownstone, we're not equipped to take on a whatever the hell that is. We've been ordered to withdraw. The National Guard will engage the creature with heavy artillery and ground-attack aircraft. Even you can't win against something like that. Pull out now."

The Mountain Strider roared once more and looked back and forth between both sides of the bridge. It took a single step forward, swatted another house, and ripped through the upper half.

Damn it. We're running out of time. If this guy charges in one direction, it'll be like a tornado.

Alison flew behind the monster again and launched another spell. Her eyes narrowed as she noticed a glyph on its lower back. The design was slightly different, but it looked very similar to one of the containment glyphs Myna had shown her.

Another quick trip around the monster with that insight helped her better understand what she saw— different containment glyphs. They had additional elements or the pieces were laid out differently, but they weren't completely different than those she'd seen before.

No wonder they looked familiar.

She remembered what Myna had told her.

Containment glyphs can be useful for enemies you can't destroy outright.

"Yeah, this guy definitely fits in that category," she murmured under her breath.

The giant took a step forward and crushed another house.

Alison gritted her teeth. "If we wait for the military, it'll level this entire neighborhood and, damn it, if they drop bombs around here, they might kill innocent people."

"Brownstone, we can't win against that thing with what we have," Lieutenant Martinez responded. "And people are already evacuating."

"You don't have to win. You simply have to distract it. It might be huge and made of green rock, but it's still alive. The glyphs absorb my attacks, but I have an idea. The only thing is, this idea needs you to distract it because I have to concentrate to pull off what I have in mind."

"We have our orders, Brownstone," the officer insisted.

"Screw your orders," she shouted. "Lives are on the line. Come on. I trained for years with a former AET officer. I know how dedicated you guys are to saving lives. I'm not telling you to kill it or get yourselves killed. I'm simply telling you to distract it for me while I concentrate. I can hopefully end this before it causes billions of dollars of damage and kills hundreds if not thousands of people—or before the military is forced to blow up half of Seattle."

She dropped to the ground near the rubble pile and released her wings.

"All AET units deploy and engage the monster," Lieutenant Martinez called. "I repeat all AET units deploy and engage the monster. Support Brownstone. I'll switch to a tactical frequency now to better coordinate my men, Brownstone. Good luck and good hunting."

"Thanks, Lieutenant."

The dropships turned and moved toward the bridge.

Her attempt to generate a series of containment glyphs for a massive creature with anti-magic properties on her own might have been hopeless in normal circumstances, but the dark wizard's work hadn't been completed due to his unfortunate introduction to tons of burning, hot concrete, asphalt, and steel.

Alison glanced at the pile of rubble at the north end of the bridge. The crushed wizard's spell had been interrupted and the glyphs remained. Their continued presence provided an opportunity to reactivate them. That was the thin thread of hope she clung to.

This crap doesn't have to work one hundred percent. It only has to last long enough for the government to come in and reinforce them.

The Mountain Strider took another step forward and slammed its foot into another house. The poor structure collapsed in a shower of broken wood, and the monster bellowed a victorious roar.

You're simply being a dick now.

She ran toward the giant's back, her attention focused on the glyph she'd first recognized. From what Myna had told her during their training, she could chain containment glyphs, and Alison suspected that was what had been done with the Fremont Troll. She could concentrate on trying to feed energy into and reactivate the glyph in the back. That would, if she were lucky, start a chain reaction with the others. If she weren't so lucky, then the military would have their chance to test out artillery and bombs on giant Oriceran monsters.

The AET dropships hovered over the bridge. The bay doors opened, and the powered armor-wearing police deployed by dropping to the ground. All held long silver railguns. The dropships lifted back into the air with their delivery complete.

The officers' weapons came to life a moment later and the roar of half the railguns firing at once was almost as loud as the Mountain Strider.

Chunks of green rock blasted from the back of the monster and its leg. It turned toward the bridge and knocked several trees over and crushed a truck in the process.

The other set of railguns fired next to explode more chunks out of the monster. Rock—or whatever substance made up its skin—rained down on the ground. New green stone immediately began to fill in the craters made by the attacks.

I have to give those guys credit. They're holding their ground against a skyscraper-sized monster, and it's not even like they can fly away like me.

"We're not exactly making much headway, Brownstone," Lieutenant Martinez complained over his radio. "Whatever you intend to do, it needs to be fast."

Another railgun barrage blasted into the monster, and the AET teams began to back up.

A loud humming filled the air. A dozen large tactical drones flew low over the water. They all ascended and half their number released a rocket. The projectiles sped toward the Mountain Strider and exploded in its face. The monster's reverberating bellow shook Alison to her bones.

The giant halted for a moment. Its massive head shifted between the drones and the AET.

Definitely distracted.

"I thought you could use a little more help," Tahir commented, "but it took me some time to get them there."

"Great job," she responded. "Between you and the AET, you have him plenty distracted. Now, it's time for me to finish my job."

Alison sprinted toward the troll. She pushed upward and summoned her wings to glide toward the glyph in the small of its back. Beads of sweat dripped down her face as she moved her hands and pushed magic into the glyph, murmuring some of the incantations Myna taught her.

The glyph brightened.

So I was right. That's what happened with all those glyphs. They weren't defenses. They simply tried to soak in whatever magical energy they could find to repair the containment spell.

The Mountain Strider stopped and began to turn its head toward her.

Tahir's drones performed another pass and released their final payloads. The giant swiped through the air with its massive clawed hands and smacked five of the drones. They tumbled into the water below in pieces.

The AET followed up with two staggered railgun volleys to force the monster's attention back onto them as Alison continued to chant her spell and manipulate the glyph.

Again, the monster slowed and roared. It began to reach toward its back when the AET fired again. Alison continued to funnel energy into the spell and almost shouted her incantations. Visible energy rippled from the now pulsating glyph.

Two lightning bolts rocketed toward them from across the water, the distant dark forms in suits barely visible. Maybe PDA, or maybe do-gooder wizards. She ignored everything but her manipulation of the containment glyph.

The Mountain Strider's next roar shattered nearby windows in the car and houses. She hissed in pain and her ears rang. The monster spun with sudden speed. She summoned a shield a second before its hand slammed into her and barreled her into a nearby house.

Alison crashed through four walls before she rolled to a stop beside a trampoline in a lawn. She forced herself to her feet and her arm hung loosely and unnaturally. Judging by the throbbing agony she felt, she'd broken not only her arm but several ribs as well.

So I can survive a direct hit from Godzilla's cousin. Good to know.

The troll turned back toward the bridge and took several steps forward, ready to finish the AET pests off once and for all.

She fumbled in her jacket with her good hand and retrieved a healing potion, ripped the stopper out with her teeth, and downed it. There was no time to mess with healing spells. The white and red ripples of energy which spread over the Mountain Strider weren't enough, and he hadn't slowed.

Despite her pain, she launched herself back into the air before the potion healed her bones and headed directly toward the back glyph. She restarted her incantation as her bones knitted themselves back together and the pain faded.

Concentrate, concentrate, concentrate.

No fireballs and lightning from across the water intruded. No railguns. No roar of approaching planes. Her focus had narrowed to only herself and the glyph.

Almost there.

The monster marched into the water and raised its arms. It clearly intended to bring down the whole bridge and the AET with it.

Come on.

Alison finished the incantation stream and threw one last massive pulse of magic into the glyph. Her wings vanished and she tumbled toward the ground but managed to pull another pair after a few seconds. She landed and released them, fell to one knee, and wiped the sweat off her face, her breathing ragged.

The giant stopped, its arms still raised. The frequency of ripples increased, and all the light across all the glyphs intensified. Lines of different colors and arcs of magical energy danced across the surface of the monster. It roared and began to shrink.

"Yes!" She pumped her fist in the air. "Take that!"

The AET at the bridge ceased fire as a veneer of gray stone spread over the Mountain Strider and it continued to shrink. Tendrils of bright white light ripped from underneath the rubble at the north end of the bridge and wound around the troll.

It bellowed loudly as if in defiance, but that did nothing to arrest the process. The tendrils pulled the smaller monster back under the bridge. The stone soon covered its entire body. A new hubcap appeared over its eye.

A tremor shook the entire area, strong enough to knock

Alison to the ground, but when the movement stopped, the Fremont Troll had returned to its prison as a statue under Aurora Bridge once again.

She wiped the sweat off her brow and took a deep breath.

"A, are you there?" Mason broke in over the receiver, concern in his voice. "Tahir's given me a play by play on a separate frequency so I wouldn't distract you, but he said he lost all drone signal nearby."

"I'm fine," she replied. "We won. I've reactivated the containment spell and it'll hold for now. The government can handle the rest." She suddenly laughed.

"A?"

"I woke up thinking, 'Hey, I'll probably kick some dark wizard ass today,' not 'Hey, bet I'll have to take out a rock giant killing machine from the Great War."

"It keeps things interesting," Hana interjected over the line. "A great Saturday."

They all laughed.

CHAPTER TWENTY-FIVE

The next morning, Alison sat at the head of the table in the Brownstone Building conference room. She was so satisfied with her performance that she had to resist the urge to cross her ankles and put her feet up on the tabletop. There was a line between confident and cocky that she didn't want to step over in front of her friends, especially considering how critical they had been to the defeat of the dark wizards.

We've had a tough time lately, but damned if we didn't pull it off with style.

Hana and Mason sat near her. The door to the conference room opened and Tahir strolled in, a weary expression on his face.

Alison smiled at him. "Thanks for coming so early. I also wanted to apologize for being a bitch to you the other day. You were a key part of the success of this job, and you should understand how glad I am to have you on the team. Without you, a lot of people might have ended up hurt or dead."

"Yes, I am part of the team." The infomancer shrugged and walked to take a seat beside Hana. Her mere proximity seemed to lighten his mood, judging by his face. "Some of what you suggested about me being present somewhere other than my apartment as I work with you was warranted. I'm no longer a mere contractor, and the sooner I fully accept and internalize that, the more efficient I will be at helping the entire company succeed. Coming to a meeting is the least I can do."

Hana gave him a warm smile and patted him on the hand. "Well said, babe."

Alison cleared her throat and scooted her chair closer to the table. "I wanted to go over everything that happened, and I figured it'd be easier if we were all together in the same place rather than bouncing texts off each other. Ava's busy looking into some supply stuff for me, so she couldn't come, but this isn't really a meeting where we need to take too many notes."

The others all nodded.

"We have all had a chance to sleep and rest," she continued. "I also contacted Myna to ask her to come, but she wasn't interested. She only told me she was *pleased* that her training helped, as if massive Great War-era monsters attacking the city was something that happens all the time and merely a casual thing to dismiss."

Tahir gave her an appraising look. "What was your intention in asking Myna to come?"

"I don't know." She shrugged. "I half-hoped I could maybe get her to provide more direct aid."

"But she's not here because she cares about the city or even Earth. She's here because she wants to serve you as the Princess of the Shadow Forged in her dying days. Even if your motivations inspire her, it's not the same thing as them being her motivations."

"True enough. But I keep thinking that if it weren't for Myna's training, I might have not been able to stop that thing. I hope she appreciates that."

"I'm sure she does," the hacker replied.

Hana's eyes widened and she clutched her hands together in front of her, her lips parted slightly. "I wonder if we can start getting people to call you Alison the Giant Slayer. I just thought of that. It's way cooler than Dark Princess, and it sounds more badass, I think. It'll also remind people that you helped take down the Mountain Strider."

Mason grinned. "I'm sure we could get Vincent to spread it around, and your Death Knight guys."

"I didn't kill the Mountain Strider, though," Alison replied. "I simply put it back to sleep. From the little Latherby told me quickly earlier this morning, they have a major specialized PDA containment team coming in to reinforce my work. They can't actually risk moving it, but they will heavily reinforce the glyphs, along with some new spells. The dark wizards had their one chance. I don't think that thing will wake up until the next Great War."

Tahir leaned forward with a slight frown. "What I don't understand is why the dark wizards needed all the compartmentalization spells, to begin with. It seems dangerously elaborate to merely keep their plan secret."

"Oh, Latherby had the answer for that." Alison gestured toward the hacker. "All your past hacking didn't get to everything the PDA knew about the Mountain Strider. The series of containment glyphs used was complicated and unusual. He suspects that different dark wizards all had the individual knowledge of how to disable the different glyphs, and our guy collected the information from each." She sighed. "This is where things get annoying and remain unresolved. Frustrating even."

"Unresolved?"

Alison nodded. "Yeah, the problem is that the magic used was set up with several other layered security spells. That way, no random wizard could simply walk up and try to unravel the containment spell. Otherwise, some drunk asshole might have done it on a dare years ago. It's likely the other dark wizards also each had access to that security information as well."

Hana furrowed her brow. "Is it really that big a deal? I don't understand why that's frustrating. Have I missed something?"

"Yes. Because of how quickly the bastard got through the security spells, we know that he didn't reverse some spells with his basic knowledge. Instead, he knew exactly what he was doing and how to disable the spells, and the only way he'd be able to do that is if someone from the PDA or Silver Griffins supplied the information to the dark wizards, to begin with. The Griffins aren't around anymore, so that leaves the PDA."

Mason leaned back in his chair. "So this proves beyond a shadow of a doubt that there's a traitor in the local PDA. Damn. I had half-hoped that Latherby was simply overly paranoid."

"So did I." Alison sighed. "But that means the dark wizards can still pull off some crap because that bastard's still out there. I'm not all that worried about the Mountain Strider. Too many people will be watching it now, but there is a lot of other shit they can try."

Hana snorted. "Maybe the PDA should let me go and charm every one of them until I find the little snake." A hungry grin appeared. "Or maybe I should track them down one by one and do it secretly."

Alison shook her head. "There is no way they can go agent by agent without the guy running, and no matter how much Latherby trusts me, they won't bring outsiders in to figure out who the traitor is. I'm not even sure he's told anyone else in the PDA, for that matter, about this."

"So what? If the bastard runs, at least he'll be gone. Isn't it a bigger problem that some asshole is handing information out to dark wizards?"

"If he runs, they'll also lose out on a valuable source of intelligence," Tahir pointed out. "Even if he's compartmentalized some of his work, he obviously has some contacts. The more networks and cells the government can identify, the more of them they can eliminate."

"Well, there's nothing we can do about it." Alison shrugged. "We did our part. We smoked the dark wizards out and stopped their big plot, even if I'm still confused by what they hoped to accomplish with it. Merely killing people doesn't leave them in charge in the end, and it smells more like something the New Veil would do."

"A display of magical might perhaps," Tahir suggested, his brow furrowed. "Proof that they aren't to be opposed. Fear can lead to acquiescence, and unlike the New Veil, the Galbrathians have a much more practical, if unlikely goal. Short of closing the gates, magic won't go away, but it's not impossible for a certain group of magicals to theoretically control Earth."

Hana shook her head. "I don't think it's that deep."

"Oh? What do you think it is then?"

"I think they're assholes."

Tahir chuckled. "Perhaps."

"They took a lot of losses to pull this off," Mason noted. "But then again, if it wasn't for A, the plan would have worked. The military would have shown up, but who knows how much damage that thing would have had to take before it went down? It already trashed a bunch of houses as it is. It might have demolished Fremont or a good chunk of town, and it could regenerate. We don't know if the big military weapons would have even worked."

Yeah, there are a lot of moving parts that led to us winning. I don't know if that makes me lucky or good.

Alison nodded. "It's a victory, and I'll take it." She chuckled nervously. "I think I'll even manage to avoid paying for the bridge. From what I was told, the governor will talk about having the President declare a disaster so they can get some federal funds to fix the bridge. I don't think anyone is interested in putting the screws on Brownstone Security given how we helped stop that thing."

They all laughed, and she looked around the table with a smile. "And I do want to make that clear. If it had been only me, this wouldn't have worked out. I probably wouldn't have found the damned wizards, to begin with. This was a solid Brownstone Security operation, and you're not only my friends, you're the badasses who helped save this city from destruction."

Tahir chuckled. "Well, when you're as skilled as I am, such victories tend to occur more often than not."

"It's definitely a rush taking down dark wizards instead of losers like guys smuggling Triffles." Hana rubbed her hands together and licked her lips. "I think I could get addicted to saving the city and making Seattle safe for fans of high-quality sushi."

Mason offered Alison a lop-sided grin. "Will you be satisfied with dates that simply involve a quick flight in a helicopter now that you fly around by yourself?"

"All the flying is tiring, and the way Myna made it sound, it might take me decades to improve to the point where it's not. Besides…" Her cheeks heated. "We can discuss our dates at a later time without the audience."

Hana snickered.

Alison's phone rang and saved her from the embarrassing situation. She pulled it out of her pocket, not surprised to see it was from Agent Latherby. "It's my favorite PDA agent," she answered.

"And my favorite half-Drow," he replied, his tone jovial.

Huh. I've never heard him actually sound so…happy. I guess that's what comes with helping save the city from old Oriceran WMDs. Even Mr. Calm Government Agent can feel a little joy.

The other three at the table watched her expectantly.

"What did you need, Agent Latherby?" she continued.

"I wanted to call to remind you that we had a scheduled follow-up meeting on the Fremont Troll incident later this morning." He cleared his throat. "I wanted to ensure that you were still able to attend said meeting."

"Oh, yeah, I met with my people to talk about that stuff,

too. I can still come to meet with you later. I have plenty of time left."

"Would you consider coming earlier?" Agent Latherby asked. "I understand that you're a busy woman and I'm very, very appreciative of what you've done, but it'd also be extremely helpful if you could come an hour earlier. I can, of course, throw in a bonus or something for your efforts. I know how you like to spend your money on sexy dresses for your post-victory parties."

What the hell? Since when have the words sexy ever come out of his mouth? And where did he get the idea that I spend money on sexy dresses?

Alison's face contorted in confusion. She wondered if Latherby had taken to drink on the job because of the mole. She couldn't blame him.

"Um, uh…" She blinked a few times and sighed. "I guess I can come early. It's not like I had anything else planned today. This whole dark wizard job was my main focus, and we've stopped their big plan. I'll take things easy for a few days, at least, and enjoy some things I've been putting aside."

"Oh, of course. If you're too busy because of the concert you planned to go to, I understand." He laughed. "It slipped my mind in all of this. I…maybe not. The concert can't be that important, can it?"

What concert? What is he talking about? Wait. Time to test my suspicions.

Alison took a deep breath before continuing. "I get it. We have a few important things we still need to discuss. Oh, I forgot to ask you if Helen was still interested in a girl's night. She seemed really keen last time I stopped in, but you know how shy she can be around me."

Alison's gaze flicked to the others and she mouthed, "I think something's wrong."

Tahir whipped his phone and wand out. He tapped something into the device before he slid the tip of his wand into a custom slot in the back.

"Yes, Helen told me she was extremely interested," Agent Latherby responded. "In fact, if you come early, I'm sure you'll be able to talk it over with her. That's all the more reason to stop by as soon as possible."

"Yeah, I know we had our troubles when we first met, but Helen really seems like she's come around," Alison lied. "Who knew?"

"Funny how life works out. So, you'll come early then?" Agent Latherby's voice remained unnaturally friendly and upbeat. "I'd really appreciate the favor, *Alison.*"

"Sure, let me finish a few things quickly and I'll be right over," she replied.

"See you soon. We have a lot to discuss."

"Oh, I'm sure of that." He hung up and she sighed and looked at Tahir. "Did you find out anything useful?"

"The only thing I could verify is that the call came from his office," the hacker replied. "What's going on?"

Alison stared at her phone. "Latherby did not act like Latherby. The voice is right, but the behavior and some of the stuff we discussed didn't make sense. He called me Alison instead of Miss Brownstone, for example, and that's not the weirdest thing he did." She shook her head. "The way I see it, there are three possibilities." She slipped her phone into her pocket. "First, he's lost his mind for some reason. Second, he's been replaced by someone. They've used disguise or shapeshifting magic to take his place. Maybe the mole. Third, the mole has him, and they want to lure me there early to take me out, and he tried to let me know he was in trouble."

"Would that even work?" Mason asked. "Wouldn't they know how he normally talks?"

"Not if they were from a different office or didn't know him all that well. There are a few PDA field offices in the greater metro area after all." Alison stood. "I think we should pay the PDA office a visit. The only thing is that they might expect me to fly over there and showing up in a helicopter would give up the game. If Latherby is in trouble, I don't want to get him killed."

"Then don't fly." Hana scoffed. "Let's simply drive over there with basic artifacts, guns, and knives so we don't look totally suspicious. It won't be fifty guys with power armor. They probably hope to take you by surprise to win."

"Okay, then." Alison blew out a breath. "Let's pay the PDA a visit. Maybe the best bet is to walk in the front door and act casual."

Tahir rubbed his chin. "Actually, Alison, I have a suggestion."

CHAPTER TWENTY-SIX

A cold wind whipped over her head and ruffled Alison's hair. She lay, wrapped securely in an invisibility spell, on the edge of a roof across from the federal building and stared at the edifice. Unfortunately, being invisible didn't do much to keep her warm, even if she did have a clear view of the window of Agent Latherby's office window and the street below.

This is the week that keeps on giving.

Alison looked to her side and saw nothing. She only knew Hana was there because of a stray wrapper resistant to the wind and pressed down by her friend's invisible body.

Despite all the trouble it took to head onto the roof of the nearby building, their plan had already run into one annoying and basic reality.

"The blinds are still down," Alison muttered. "And I can't see crap."

A drone zoomed by, nothing unusual compared to a half-dozen other drones in the area if anyone else took note of it. They wouldn't know it was under Tahir's control.

"There are only two people in the entire PDA office right now," Tahir reported through her receiver. "They are both in Latherby's office, with one seated at the desk and the other standing. That's only thermals, though. Should I go for scrying?"

"No," Alison responded. "If this is a dark wizard, they'll know what's up the second you try that. No, we need to do something they won't expect, exactly like you suggested. Even with the blinds down, this is a good plan, Tahir."

"I'm glad you approve."

"I'm almost in position," Mason interjected. "I'm pulling up now."

This has to work. If anything, given my reputation, it has an even better chance of working.

Her red Fiat Spider drew up alongside the building and a white-haired woman in a red jacket stepped out. They were too high up to make out more detail other than that.

Hana giggled. "I know they say couples start to resemble each other after a while, but Mason disguised as you is so funny I'll laugh for weeks. Still, there's no way anyone will be able to talk to him for more than a minute before they realize he's not you."

"They don't have to talk to him," Alison responded. "They simply have to see me-slash-him on cameras or through spells. Even if they sense magic, they'll assume it's a shield or something. If they think they have the upper hand, that'll make it far easier to take them by surprise."

The disguised Mason walked up the street and turned around the corner to enter the federal building.

"I'm in," Mason whispered over the line. "Heading toward the stairs now."

"You don't think they'll be suspicious if you take the stairs, Alison?" Hana asked. "I know you suggested it when Tahir outlined the plan, but I only now realized what the implications are."

The wrapper beneath her body scooted a few inches without obvious cause, moved by her invisible body.

"Nope," Alison replied. "I've taken the stairs before. Sometimes, I want a little extra leg work, and it's a way to stall before I get to the office on days when I'm annoyed. I don't always take the stairs, and I don't always take the elevator. It won't seem odd if they've watched me at all. We now have to wait until Mason is on the sixth floor. That should give us plenty of time to make our move."

Hana sighed. "I hate to be the one to bring this up, but what if Latherby's already dead?"

"Then the least we can do for him is get revenge."

They both lapsed into silence. The princess and the fox lingered on the roof and took slow, deep breaths as they waited for Mason's signal.

Complicated plans could fail because of a number of unexpected variables, but Tahir's plan, when distilled down to its essence, wasn't complicated at all. It relied on one thing Alison could now easily deliver—quick and powerful use of magic.

I can't believe I'm about to raid a federal building, although I guess this isn't as bad as Mom breaking into a senator's home to threaten him.

"There was minor activity when Mason entered the

building," Tahir reported. "But the two people inside the office haven't moved much from their positions."

"It sounds like they at least know *I'm* coming," Alison murmured. "Which means they are watching and waiting."

He suggested hacking some of the federal building cameras, but she thought it was too risky. The last thing they needed was some government infomancer messing with Tahir while they were in the middle of a potential rescue operation. So far, she was satisfied with the decision. His drone work provided decent enough coverage for their task.

A few minutes passed before Mason cleared his throat to get their attention. "I'm at the sixth floor now, A."

"Time to make a mess," she replied, dropped the invisibility spells, and stood.

Hana tapped her ring three times and took her friend's offered hand.

"Ready?" Alison layered a few shields over herself.

They had no idea what kind of dangerous wizard they might have to deal with. Although Alison was confident she could take almost any Galbrathian one on one, if Agent Latherby was held hostage, her tactical options would be far more limited.

"This almost tops our Saturday fun." Hana winked. "I never did this kind of thing before I met you, you know. So many sporty activities."

"I'm glad I can enrich your life. Here's a free zip line trip. Kind of." She flung out a shadow line to Latherby's office window. A moment later, she and Hana hurtled directly toward the office.

Oh, crap. I never thought to ask Tahir if it was reinforced glass.

The question was answered a few seconds later as her shielded upper body collided with the window. It shattered and she passed through the blinds, pulling Hana in with her.

What is up with me and breaking through windows these last few days? Although I have to admit, it is kind of fun.

Alison released Hana's hand, and the fox's tails and claws appeared.

Agent Latherby stood in front of his desk and a blond man in a dark suit sat behind the desk, his wand pointed at the other agent. The blond jerked his head toward Alison and Hana, his eyes wide and his mouth twisted in an angry sneer.

No disguise or shapeshifting, huh? That works. It's easier that way.

She rolled to her feet and summoned a shadow blade.

The rogue agent opened his mouth and began an incantation. Agent Latherby surged forward, grasped the man's arm, and forced it upward. A green bolt discharged into the ceiling to blow a hole in it and melt some of the overhead wires.

Latherby slammed the other man's arm against his hard desk a couple of times until the traitor winced and released his wand. The previous hostage followed up with a throat punch. The blond man gasped for air and clutched his neck as his wand rolled off the desk, but his assailant didn't let up. He grabbed the man's head and smashed it into the desk several times until the traitor groaned and stopped moving.

Alison blinked and lowered her shadow blade. "Damn, Latherby. You can deliver a beatdown when you need to."

"I don't appreciate someone threatening me in my own office." The agent adjusted his tie and wiped some of the blood on his hands off on the other man's suit. "And he's still alive for interrogation purposes. I consider that efficiency."

She chuckled.

Agent Latherby walked around the desk and shoved the man out of his chair. "This is Agent Kinkaide. The bastard's worked in the Seattle area for five years. Not in my particular field office, but still. I guess that was my mistake. I assumed it had to be someone newer. I almost have to admire how he didn't make his activity obvious until recently." He reached into a drawer and retrieved his own wand. "He surprised me by mentioning he'd found some odd PDA activity and wanted to talk about it. He even went so far as to act nervous and mentioned someone might have followed him."

"It makes you appreciate the really obvious assholes on the ship or in the safehouse." Alison studied the unconscious agent. She vaguely remembered seeing him a few times, but she didn't even know his name prior to Latherby mentioning it. "Was that you on the phone, or was that him? The strange conversation was what tipped me off that something was wrong."

"It was me," Agent Latherby replied, a frown on his face. "I hoped he wouldn't see through the ridiculousness of our conversation. He doesn't really know me all that well. It was a gamble, but one that obviously paid off."

"Just to be clear, you're sure Helen—"

"She's unpleasant, Miss Brownstone—to everyone, not only you—but she's very good at her job otherwise."

I guess you can't judge a book by its cover. Or can you? I mean, she does appear to be a bitch, merely not a traitorous one.

"Oh." Alison shrugged. "I wanted to be sure since she doesn't seem to like me."

"I understand. Speaking of that sort of thing, given some of the statements from Agent Kinkaide prior to him making me call you, you've really agitated the Galbrathians. Apparently, he thought killing you would at least be some sort of victory for their pathetic faction."

"Alison," Tahir interrupted. "You have a half-dozen men closing rapidly on your position."

She held her held up toward Agent Latherby. "Where the hell did they come from, Tahir? Did they portal in?"

"No, from that floor—a room down the hallway. I saw them before but there are several groups in different offices on that floor, so I took no special notice of them."

She grimaced. "I hate it when the bad guys know enough to have backup plans." She looked at the PDA man. "My infomancer tells me someone's coming. Were you expecting anyone?"

"No," he replied flatly. "Apparently, it's as you fear. Agent Kinkaide here was smarter than I hoped." He clucked his tongue. "Keep the destruction to a minimum. We can't risk hurting anyone else on the floor."

Alison nodded.

Heavy footfalls sounded from the hallway outside the reception area. Agent Latherby flourished his wand and muttered an incantation. The main door to the field office glowed and slammed shut as a man in a bulletproof vest with a handgun and anti-magic deflector appeared in front of it.

"Nice, Latherby," Alison commented. "Anti-magic deflectors, too. They probably have anti-magic bullets considering that they need to kill a wizard and the Dark Princess."

The door shook and thudded loudly.

Hana growled. "This is a federal building. Won't some FBI agents show up to check on what's going on?"

"The FBI is in a different building down the street," Agent Latherby replied. "Most of this building isn't law enforcement or intelligence agencies. There are armed security personnel, especially in the district court, but not the kind prepared to take on a heavily armed-strike team."

Several bullets shattered the handle of the door.

The agent frowned. "I shielded the door with my earlier spell. This confirms they have anti-magic bullets."

A shrill klaxon came to life.

Hana winced at the noise. "I bet you someone pulled the fire alarm and called the cops. We could wait for them."

"They won't get here in time," Alison snorted. "Besides, a few assholes with deflectors and anti-magic bullets is simply another evening workout for me." She thrust her hand out and shadowy purple tendrils extended from the floor and wrapped around Helen's desk. They lifted the huge desk off the ground and the computer slid to the ground. The monitor cracked and sparked.

If she didn't hate me before, she'll definitely hate me now. Sorry, Helen. Nothing personal. You simply have the biggest piece of furniture I can find right now. Consider it a sacrifice in defense of the PDA.

"What are you doing?" Agent Latherby asked.

"They have vests and anti-magic deflectors." Alison stepped out of his office as another few bullets ripped through the door and its glow dimmed. "I'll have to use something that they can't absorb so easily. I let myself forget for a moment, all the different ways in which I can mess people up."

"An interesting way to look at it." He nodded, newfound respect in his eyes.

"It's not like you keep asking for my help because I'm great at making risotto."

"I can assure you I have no preconceptions about your cooking talents, Miss Brownstone."

Hana ran out of the office and rushed to the front of the reception area. She crouched a few yards away from the front door.

The agent nodded and raised his wand. "Good instincts, Miss Sugimoto." After a quick wand movement and incantation, two chairs in the reception area elevated to hover a few feet above the floor. "Save the desk for when its most opportune, Miss Brownstone."

"Will do," Alison replied. She moved her arm and the tendrils raised the desk even higher.

The gunfire had stopped. She drew a deep breath and held it in anticipation.

A man smashed through the bullet-riddled front door and knocked it off its hinges. He rushed inside, a gun in hand, and aimed it at Alison.

One of Latherby's chairs hurtled across the room and slammed into his head. He stumbled back, but the next chair smacked him even harder and he dropped. Two more men rushed inside, and Alison flung the desk at them. It crushed them to the floor and they responded with blood-curdling screams.

The remaining three men flooded into the room and leapt over the desk and their wounded comrades. Hana launched from her crouched position and her claws ripped into one man's back on the first swipe. His unwounded comrade turned when he realized they'd been ambushed, but she tore his neck open before she twirled to do the same to his friends. They collapsed and their hands flailed as they gurgled for air.

Alison drew her gun and approached the one man who still remained alive, the unconscious victim of Latherby's chair pummeling.

Hana wiped her claws off on a dead man's vest. "Should I finish the last one off?"

"No," Agent Latherby commanded as he advanced with his wand out. "I doubt these are Galbrathians. They're probably only mercenaries, which means we have a better chance to gain useful intelligence out of them—and, as they say, a dead man tells no tales."

The fox shrugged. "Not without a necromancer at least." Her cheerful grin created an odd juxtaposition with her blood-soaked claws and clothes.

Alison holstered her gun and exhaled sharply. "Whew. Problem solved. I think. Tahir, do you see anything else?"

"No," he responded, irritation in his voice. "The police are on their way. I helped facilitate that."

"Did you trip the alarm?"

"Yes. I decided it was best not to distract you during your fight."

She smiled. "Always thinking. Good job." She shook her head. "What a wild few days. When you first called me, Latherby, I couldn't even begin to guess at the stuff it would lead to."

He retrieved his phone. "With the traitor identified, this makes certain things easier. The rest of the agents from my office, along with Helen, are in another building going over some information related to the Mountain Strider containment. I think it's best I call them back. We have a lot of work ahead of us to establish what cases have been compromised."

Alison gave him a sheepish smile and pointed to the desk. "Can you tell Helen that you did that?"

"Yes." Agent Latherby chuckled quietly. "I think you've earned a few lies on your behalf, Miss Brownstone."

CHAPTER TWENTY-SEVEN

Alison stirred the rice and stock in her risotto and hummed quietly to herself. The rice dish seemed like a good practice recipe as it involved a number of steps and ingredients but lacked the complicated failure points found in dishes like soufflés. Baking, in general, seemed a danger zone that she thought it might be better to avoid until her general skills improved.

If Izzie could see me now. Recipes for potions are not the same as cooking. One day and one recipe at a time.

She inhaled deeply and enjoyed the rich smell. If the risotto ended up tasting even half as good as it smelled, she'd be more than satisfied.

The random cooking curse hasn't activated today. Nice.

Three days had passed without any dark wizard conspiracies, gigantic monsters, or much trouble at all, or at least nothing that required the active attention of the Dark Princess. Agent Latherby had told her he'd call her when he had anything useful to share.

Her skills couldn't help him much, and she doubted

they wanted Tahir to poke around their systems. That left the PDA and FBI with a lot of work to track down the pernicious influence of the traitor.

She decided to take her boyfriend's advice. Like Mason had told her, she was her own boss, so a week off to relax and practice some cooking was a reasonable reward and gift to herself.

I wonder how many cities are like Seattle and have ridiculously dangerous monsters or magical devices hidden in them. Mom has found all sorts of crazy crap in major cities, and that's when she actually looked on purpose. There is probably some ancient Oriceran Great War black-hole artifact underneath LA, for all anyone knows.

The thought pushed her mind in a different direction. Many major cities might have something like the Mountain Strider, but they didn't suffer the kind of magic trouble Seattle did.

Alison shook her head. Between the destruction of the kemana and the Mountain Strider, it was like the Galbrathians possessed some particular hatred of Seattle.

She breathed deeply and exhaled slowly. There was no reason to overthink it. Power-mad dark wizards hurt people. That was all she needed to know about the situation.

A few minutes later, her phone rang on the counter. She glanced at the caller ID before adding some more chicken stock to her risotto and answered on speaker phone.

"Is this the part where you say some uncomfortable stuff about my sexy dresses again?" she asked. "Because I really don't want to head over there to save your ass again in the middle of cooking risotto."

Agent Latherby snorted on the other end. "It's very unlikely I'll mention sexy dresses ever again to you, Miss Brownstone."

"I think we can both agree that's a good thing. What's up?"

"I felt I should give you an after-action report now that everything has settled. Given how important your efforts were in the recent incidents, you deserve that as much as the money I sent you."

"I do like hearing that the stuff I do isn't a total waste of time." Alison returned to stirring her rice. "But not letting a monster annihilate half of Seattle is nice, too. And the money. Everything's nice."

"You saved my life, Miss Brownstone," the man responded, his voice as calm and cool as ever. "Besides bait to lure you in and assassinate you, the traitor had hoped to use me to cover his tracks. That almost annoys me more than the idea he would have killed me."

"How could he use you to cover his tracks?"

"Agent Kinkaide admitted under spell that the plan was to fake my suicide and produce a false note wherein I would confess to being the Galbrathian sympathizer."

"I would have shown up and yelled about how that was crap," Alison retorted. "And you know how stubborn I can be."

"Another reason they targeted you for elimination. He also admitted that. He knew someone was onto him, but he wasn't aware how extensive or limited the investigation was. All he knew was that I was one of the people involved and figured my involvement with you also threatened their cause and that you were likely to be aware of what I knew." Agent Latherby snorted. "It was a correct summation by otherwise foolish and misguided wizards. So much magical talent and planning wasted on such pointless cruelty."

She added a little more stock to her pan. "We've taken down a significant number of dark wizards lately. Please don't tell me there are hundreds more hiding under the Space Needle. They're really starting to get on my nerves."

"No, that particular scenario is unlikely." He sighed with exasperation. "You know as well as I do how these types operate. It's difficult to clean them all out, and we can only go after the ones who have clearly committed crimes. It's not a crime to merely express admiration for their ideals, unfortunately. That said, your actions have crippled dark wizard and Galbrathian operations in the Pacific Northwest, not only Seattle. I've been in contact with other PDA offices and the FBI, and they've made it clear that the forces you destroyed represent a major investment of personnel and resources. That said, this success isn't without consequence."

"For every action, there is an equal and opposite reaction." She frowned, not sure if she was technically quoting Vincent or Newton.

"Exactly," the agent confirmed.

Alison sniffed the air. The enticing scent of the risotto made her stomach rumble. "And what consequence and/or reaction are we worried about exactly? Are you talking about the Mountain Strider? Can't the military get ready to blow it to the moon?"

"No, that creature isn't a problem. At least not anymore.

By the time the government is done with it, you will need an army of Light Elves to undo the containment spell. I will say that issue should have been handled decades ago, but everyone was too afraid of accidentally waking it up. The Galbrathians forced the issue, and now, we're finally doing what we should have done all along. Consider that an unexpected service they performed for us."

"That's not a bad thing." she chuckled. "I guess."

Her rice grew creamier but she estimated she still had another ten minutes before it reached the texture she needed for a quality risotto.

"No, it's not a bad thing," Agent Latherby agreed. "I only wish it hadn't cost massive damage to a bridge and several houses."

"Don't we all," Alison replied quietly.

"As for the consequences, I'm talking about your direct involvement. Unfortunately, flying over the city and taking on a giant monster is difficult to suppress, and the AET has been open about your assistance as well. Not to mention the fact that many people took pictures of you."

"Oh, yeah. That. Media people constantly try to contact me for interviews, but I point them at Ava and she's managed to fend them off so far." She stirred the rice a little and added more stock. "I'm already fairly famous. It's annoying, but it's not the end of the world. The news types always get bored after a few weeks. I learned that after the media circus around my adoption."

Latherby's grunt was laced with irritation. "It's less the media that I'm worried about. It's more the Galbrathians. You're already known as a dark wizard huntress, and now, you're also the woman who stopped one of their largest plans in recent memory. It's very likely that more will come seeking vengeance. No grand schemes, merely coming for the head of Alison Brownstone."

Oh, almost time for the next step.

"It sounds like a good way for us to whittle down the number of dark wizards in the world, then. Call me a dark wizard fly zapper." Alison turned on a burner, put a skillet on it, and emptied the prepared contents of a small bowl— butter, garlic, and mushrooms. "If having to deal with a few more dark wizards in the future is the price of saving this city, I'll gladly pay it, and I'll take out every one of those bastards who dares to come at me or any of my friends."

I wonder what a good spell or potion is for risotto. I should probably nail the non-magical dish before I think about magically enhancing it, though. Walk before you run.

"That's good to hear, and I appreciate your dedication to the city regardless of whether or not it involves a bounty. There was some worry when you arrived that you might be a little more hands-off, much as your father was known for early in his career."

"You probably have a whole file you've read about him and my mom, haven't you?"

A few beats of silence ticked by before he answered. "It's good to know who is coming into your city and who might have influenced them."

Alison laughed. "Of course, and by the way, my dad being hands-on typically involves buildings blowing up."

"True enough." Agent Latherby cleared his throat. "Incidentally, per your request, I did mislead Helen as to who threw her desk."

"Oh? What did she have to say about it? Was she pissed?"

"No. She seemed to feel it was a necessary sacrifice given the situation. For all her faults, she's quite loyal to the PDA and our mission."

She stirred the contents of her skillet and her main pan. "And do you think she would have reacted the same way if she knew I did it?"

"Most likely not," he admitted. "There would have been...anger."

"Then thanks for taking the bullet for me."

"Consider it a small bonus. For now, though, Miss Brownstone, consider the following. You've stopped a rampage, taken a lot of dark wizards out of circulation, and helped purge the local PDA of a traitor. As I noted earlier, you also saved my life. Don't let my calm tone mislead you as to how important that is. I remember my debts, and I appreciate your help and that of your team. You've done a personal service to me, this city, the state of Washington, and the United States of America."

"You're welcome." An acrid scent struck her nose.

How the hell is my stuff burning? It's only been a couple of minutes!

"Not to be rude, but I really have to go. I appreciate the call, though," Alison explained hastily.

"That's fine. Take a long vacation, Miss Brownstone. You've earned it. Until next time." Agent Latherby hung up the phone.

She stared at her skillet, unsure why blackened ingredients sat in the pan. Taking down an Oriceran WMD was easy. Cooking risotto was hard.

CHAPTER TWENTY-EIGHT

The next evening, Alison smiled as she served risotto onto four separate plates beside her herb-encrusted baked chicken. Her previous failures remained unexplained, but the cooking curse hadn't activated tonight during her dinner party.

I can handle a few potions just fine, but cooking... That's taking a little longer. Still, this is looking damned good if I do say so myself. Tillie Ramsay would have nothing to say but, "Hey, Alison, teach me the recipe!"

Mason, Hana, and Tahir sat at the dining room table and sipped contentedly on wine.

"It's a shame Ava wouldn't come," Alison called from the kitchen. "I asked her a few times but she insisted that it wouldn't be appropriate. Whatever that means. The woman's willing to shoot people with machine guns for me, but she won't come to my dinner parties. How does that work?"

Hana laughed. "I'm sure she has to go back to the planet of Super-Competent English People every few days to regenerate her power. Otherwise, Empress Mary Poppins will strip her of her powers and banish her permanently to the realm of merely competent mortals."

"Probably." Alison scooped some steamed broccoli onto the plates. "After what's happened lately, some things seem less unlikely than they did before."

"What did Myna say? You invited her too, right?"

"I won't be hungry."

Hana blinked. "Huh? Why aren't you hungry? You knew you'd be cooking."

Tahir and Mason both looked at her.

Alison shook her head. "Not me. Her. Myna. She said, 'I won't be hungry.'"

"Okay." The fox frowned as she considered. "She said she's not hungry or she won't be hungry?"

"She *won't* be hungry," Alison confirmed. "She followed that up by scheduling some more defensive glyph and compression lessons. I think us hanging out together isn't something that will happen in the future, but then again, it's not like we have a lot in common anyway. I'm merely grateful for her help, even if I'm a little worried about her health. She keeps blowing it off, but I think she's in rougher shape than she lets on."

"Considering how old she is and what she said, that's not all that surprising. Didn't she basically come to Earth to die?"

"True enough." Alison sighed. "Oh, well." She grabbed a towel to wipe some risotto sauce off the edge of one of the plates. "I feel like I should do more for her."

"Do you need any help with the plates, A?" Mason called. "I feel bad sitting here drinking."

"Sure." Alison smiled at him. "That would be great, and you'll do your part eating my wonderful meal."

He stood and headed toward the kitchen. She handed him two plates and picked up the others. They made their way to the table and ensured everyone had a plate before sitting.

"Dig in before it gets cold," she insisted.

The moment of truth.

Hana inhaled deeply. "It smells delicious." She scooped some risotto up with her fork and eyed it, suspicion in her dark gaze.

"Oh, come on. I taste-tested it. It's good."

"The mind can play tricks, you know." Hana winked and took a mouthful. She chewed for a few seconds before swallowing. "Wow. That's actually really good."

"Ouch." Alison laughed. "You didn't have to sound so surprised."

Tahir gathered a mouthful of his own. "You have to admit that you've had a mixed track record when it comes to the culinary arts."

She shook her fork menacingly. "I should fire you all and get new staff." She glanced at Mason. "And you?"

He smiled. "I think it tastes great, A, and you know I have faith in you."

Everyone took a few minutes to concentrate on their meal. Unlike Myna, they were hungry. The risotto, with its perfect, creamy texture, was a nice complement to the juicy chicken, but Alison still wondered about how she could have enhanced the flavor profiles and textures.

Maybe I should have staged the meal with courses. I mean, there's a reason for that in fancy places. Oh, well, the first step should be to master the actual art of cooking and then I can worry about how to do it at an elite level later.

She washed some risotto down with a sip of wine. "Speaking of Ava, she told me today that everything's solidly on schedule. The primary renovations should be completed in May. I'm half-wondering if I shouldn't have them roll onto the second- and third-floor stuff. Yeah, we don't need it right now, but considering that I'll expand the staff soon, it wouldn't hurt to be ready."

"It might be annoying for people working in the building." Hana gobbled down some chicken. "But it's pain now or pain later."

"Also, all this flying around the county stuff has me thinking, too." Alison frowned. "About the helicopter."

Mason sliced off a small piece of chicken before he spoke. "Don't you like my flying, A? Would you prefer to do it yourself?" An amused tone infused his words.

"No, it's nothing like that. I thought about future teams and jobs. Helicopters are useful, but maybe we should get a dropship, too. It might be nice to have a dropship full of guys in power armor and anti-magic deflectors when we raid some major hideout of asshole magicals. We were lucky on the ship raid because the wizards clustered for us and Izzie was there. Otherwise, things could have gotten really out of hand."

"If you want a dropship, buy a dropship," suggested Mason with a shrug. "You can afford a small one. Although I can't fly one. You'll have to hire another pilot."

"Yeah, add another thing to the list."

"Helicopter, dropship, and guys with power armor." Hana's eyes widened. "It's like your own personal army."

Alison grimaced. "Don't call it that. You'll get used to saying that if you do. I have the AET and PDA on my side and the last thing I need is for them to have any weird ideas and start frowning at me."

"What's the big deal?" Mason asked. "Plenty of security companies have that level of equipment."

Tahir snorted. "But such firms don't also have the Dark Princess in addition to those resources." He looked around the table. "This is as good as time as any to mention that the buzz on the dark web is that everyone wants to stay out of your way, Alison. They're positively terrified that you took on the Mountain Strider and won. Some are questioning whether it's something even your father could have accomplished."

Dad and Whispy could probably have taken the thing down by themselves, but there's no reason to go into that now.

Alison nodded curtly. "Good. I'm glad assholes are afraid. It'll cut down on pointless random attacks that risk damaging my wardrobe, car, or neighborhood. I wouldn't mind if the Seattle underworld was on their best behavior for a little while. If anything, they owe me." She shook her head. "No. They owe us. It's not like that Mountain Strider would discriminate between criminals and non-criminals during its little tour of the city."

Tahir gave her a tight smile. "True enough." His smile faded. "There's another thing I should bring up now that we're all together."

Hana smiled at him. "What's that, babe?"

"I've accepted the efficiency of operating at different locations. Provided Alison gives me the equipment I request, I'll be happy to work from the Brownstone Building most of the time."

"I'll have Ava grab whatever you need, Tahir," Alison replied. "And what she can't get, I'll get, even if it means having to deal with Vincent's annoying, smirking face."

An impressed look settled over the hacker's face. "Then we'll both be pleased with the arrangement."

Mason set his fork down, his chicken and risotto already demolished but his vegetables only half-eaten. "So, you've mentioned a dropship pilot and some building security, as well as another team with magical or magical-equivalent abilities. What else are you thinking about, A? Grabbing Izzie or Lily, maybe?"

"I wish, but Izzie's still got the dark wizard garbage to worry about. Lily won't leave tomb raiding for a while, and she loves LA anyway. Harry won't leave his info network down there behind, either." Alison tapped her lips as she considered other possibilities. "But we do need a decent number of general security teams—the kind of guys we can send out for protection jobs where we don't think anyone serious will show up. Although I doubt we'll find an infomancer of Tahir's quality easily, looking for a little backup wouldn't hurt. I have to think about that."

Tahir scoffed. "Good luck. You might as well look for the Holy Grail."

Hana rolled her eyes at him. "Behave, babe."

Alison smirked. "Anyway, the more people we have with different talents, the more different jobs we can take on. Eventually, I'd like to expand to jobs all over the country, maybe even the world. That will require other transportation resources, but we'll worry about that in the future."

"Wow," Hana replied. "Your dad never went beyond Los Angeles and Vegas."

"Yeah, but his philosophy in life is Keep it Simple Stupid. Mine's, 'Find the bad guys wherever they are and kick their asses until they leave the planet.'"

The fox tilted her head. "FTBGWTAAKTAUTLTP? It doesn't quite have the same ring as KISS."

Alison laughed. "No, it doesn't."

"Don't neglect support staff," Tahir interjected. "Ava's spectacularly competent, but as the company grows, she won't be able to handle all the administrative functions herself. I also worry about using too many external contractors for things such as groundskeeping. They represent security risks."

Mason nodded. "He has a point."

Hana snapped her fingers. "I've got it. We should go all out. Dryad groundskeeper and use gargoyles as messengers."

Alison smiled down at her plate. "The School of Necessary Magic cafeteria was pixie-run."

"Oh, that would be adorable." Hana gave her a sly look. "Have you maybe reconsidered a dragon pet?"

"No, and you couldn't handle a dragon pet. Even setting aside the permits and licenses, a dragon would be too much. Dorvu was fun when I was in school, but he's also a dragon and a handful, and he's very nice for a dragon, too."

"Fine," Hana grumped and a frown settled over her face. "We'll stick with the fish."

Tahir sighed and shook his head.

"Oh, quiet, you. You know you'd love it just as much. If we can't have the dragon, then we should really focus on the pixie cafeteria."

Alison shook her head. "Pixies can be pretty scary, particularly if you ever say anything bad about their food. And we won't find that many pixies anyway in a place like Seattle. We'll probably have to settle mostly for humans." She took a deep breath. "Still, it might not hurt to bring in a few more Oricerans. Between Scott's crap and the Galbrathians, I've wondered if I can use all my newfound fame to try to do something about what they keep pushing."

Mason looked puzzled. "What do you mean?"

"It's been thirty years since the gates opened, and there are more people like me out there—children of both worlds—but there are also still a lot of people who keep to their own kind." Alison gestured around the table. "Ava's not a magical, but we all are. Maybe Brownstone Security can become a symbol of something other than powerful ass-kicking."

"Like what?"

"What magicals and non-magicals can do together. What Oricerans and humans can do together." Alison sighed and shrugged. "I don't know. Maybe it's some of my old teenage idealism coming back. Yes, there are magicals who work openly in many government agencies, and Luke's even a congressman, but I can contribute more to solving this problem than only beating down assholes who get out of hand."

Mason gave her a thoughtful nod. "Hey, I won't

complain. I worked with more than a few mixed teams when I was a bodyguard."

Hana smiled sheepishly. "Most of my friends weren't magicals when I...um, practiced the fine art of separating people from their money and things." She picked up her wine glass to take another sip.

Tahir shrugged. "Non-magical hackers have their limitations, but they aren't useless either. I wouldn't mind a team for certain types of busy work."

Warmth swept through Alison. "Thanks, guys. It means a lot. I've thought more and more about how everything's turned out since I moved here and met you all. Even if I'm...closer to some of you than others." She glanced at Mason, and he gave her a look of feigned innocence. "Anyway," she continued, "This Mountain Strider thing really made it clear."

Hana set her glass down and leaned forward, curiosity on her face. "How?"

"When I was in D.C. fighting New Veil, I had to make a choice," Alison explained. "There were a lot of options, and when I had that wish on the line, the only thing I worried about was saving people." She looked into each person's eyes in turn. "I know most of the world only sees Alison Brownstone, daughter of the Scourge of Harriken, the Dark Princess, the ass-kicker, but I've always wanted to use my power to make the world a better place. A lot of people I've met, magical and non-magical, don't understand that, or if they did, they thought I was merely self-indulgent or naïve." She shook her head. "Say what you want about me, I understand all too well about the darkness of the world. I had it shoved in my face when I was a kid, but I refused to let it consume me."

Her three companions listened with rapt attention.

Alison nodded a few times, as much as to herself as to the others. "Evil and darkness don't have to win as long as people are willing to stand up and fight them. I'm a Princess of the Shadow Forged. I have no idea what Laena thought that should mean, but if I'm supposed to be royalty, then I want to be the kind of royalty who stands up and protects the weak. I feel like all of you have your own motivation to be around me, but I also feel you understand me and that we're starting to form something truly special here—not simply friends and not only a security company. Maybe even a family."

"Evil, huh?" Hana ran her tongue along the inside of her cheek as she thought over what Alison had said. "If we're something more than a security company, maybe we need a cool nickname."

"We really don't," Tahir insisted. He sighed.

Mason chuckled quietly.

"Come on. It'll be fun." Hana snapped her fingers. "I've got one. The Dark Princess and her Justice Court. That's badass. Huh? Huh?"

The hacker scrubbed a hand over his face with an appalled expression. "Oh no."

"Yeah, I've got to agree with Tahir." Alison groaned. "That's a big no."

"The Justice League?" Hana suggested.

"I'm sure that one's already taken."

The fox furrowed her brow and concentrated. "There has to be something. The Power Friends?"

"Ah...no." Alison held up a hand. "I think Brownstone Security will work for now."

"Okay. We'll do a web survey or something in the future. Let the people decide." Hana nodded, a satisfied smile on her face.

"Sure, Hana. That's fine. For now, knowing you guys all have my back is enough. Next time some giant monster appears, I know we'll take it down." Alison slapped her hand to her forehead. "I'm such an idiot."

Mason frowned. "What's wrong, A?"

"I totally forgot to prepare a dessert!"

Hana stared at her. "Are you sure you're not evil?"

Alison laughed but didn't answer her.

The story is far from over. Alison's adventure continues in
THE BROWNSTONE EFFECT.

FREE BOOKS!

WARNING:

The Troll is now in charge.

And he's giving away free books
if you sign-up!

Join the only newsletter hosted by a Troll!

Get sneak peeks, exclusive giveaways, behind the scenes
content, and more.
PLUS you'll be notified of special **one day only fan
pricing** on new releases.

CLICK HERE

or visit: https://marthacarr.com/read-free-stories/

The story is far from over. Alison's adventure continues in
THE BROWNSTONE EFFECT.

AVAILABLE AT AMAZON RETAILERS

The New Year has barely begun but already it's gotten busy. Good news is, thinking about where to move, selling a house, buying a house, actually moving – all done. It ate up most of the year and I feel like I found hours of time just because that's behind me.

I get asked all the time just how busy is it to be a full-time author? That's followed by a sigh and the comment that there are probably less weird things going on, on a daily basis than in a corporate office.

Well...

To the first question – there's a lot of moving parts to getting a book out. Blurb, cover, editing are all just the start. Then there's the marketing. So, very busy all the time but now there's a team behind me. Shout out to Felicia, Grace and Amanda!

I took some advice this past year from a fellow author who said, 'outsource everything but the writing' and I like chatting with all of you, so I kept that too. Plus, there was Anderle saying to me, "Why are you still doing that?" There was definite 'tude in his voice. I got it. The bar was no longer, if I can do it, I should be doing it. I'm a worker bee. It took some adjustment.

Okay, on to the second question.

The more you write, the more great fans like you guys discover me, the bigger it gets, the more weird things can happen. Like this week, which frankly in all my 30 years as a writer takes the, well, mug. BIG THANK YOU to Pamela Rosen who won a troll mug for being so easygoing about a GIANT oopsy.

A simple, unadorned YTT mug that Pamela won is the start of this adventure. I ordered it – correctly – and she got the box – all excited. Opened it up, and fortunately was first met by the packing slip, which had a picture of sweet, innocent YTT.

HOWEVER, inside was a mug of a different *nature*. Seems someone in shipping mistakenly sent a mug covered in a multitude of female parts (vulva) in the shape of a heart. All different shapes and sizes like the artist did a lot of research. I still wonder what the guy in shipping was smoking or daydreaming about? Pamela reported it took her brain a few minutes to comprehend what she was looking at before she could react. I'll bet!

It's in the hands of Customer Service now and hopefully the beloved troll mug is already on its way to Pamela. Frankly, I'd take the V mug and put it at the bottom of a Goodwill box and drop it off. No receipt necessary.

So, you see what I mean? No two days are alike as an author, it's always busy and something can always take a left turn. A sense of humor is a definite requirement, apparently occasionally for a Fan or two, as well. And it's all definitely worth it every time someone writes to me to say how much they love one of the stories, how much it's made them laugh, given them a place to escape to, or taken them on an adventure. That's my goal – I write recess and love that so many of you are coming along on the ride with me. More adventures to follow (but with the right mug).

THANK YOU for not only reading this story but these *Author Notes* **as well.**

(I think I've been good with always opening with "thank you." If not, I need to edit the other *Author Notes*!)

RANDOM (*sometimes***) THOUGHTS?**

You know, I had already forgotten about the vulva mug. I 'could' say that you can't make up stuff like that, but sure we could.

We are imaginative authors.

However, I would probably have not done it because...

Who the hell thinks that someone did a mug like that? I'm 51, and I didn't think of it.

However, since then I have been to a massive (blocks large) outdoor shopping bizarre in Bangkok where you would be walking along... each stall might have something similar to the stall next to it or something totally different. It was a constant discovery.

T-shirts, t-shirts, shoes, candles, dildos, candles... Wait, what?

Yeah, that's a thing that I wasn't expecting at the market. I left for Australia so naive.

AROUND THE WORLD IN 80 DAYS

One of the interesting (at least to me) aspects of my life is the ability to work from anywhere and at any time. In the future, I hope to re-read my own *Author Notes* and remember my life as a diary entry.

Las Vegas, NV.

Back in the USA baby!

So, I'm laying down (kinda) in bed typing this to give to Lynne Stiegler

At the end of December, we went on a trip to Australia (20Books Adelaide), then to Bali for the 20Books Bali event, then Singapore, Bangkok, Phuket and then back through Bali, Australia (couple of hours) and then a four-teen hour flight to Los Angelas.

We left on the 28th of December, back on the 26th of January.

I thought since it takes so long to get over there I might as well get some research in. I can officially say that a month is too long (for me).

By the end of the trip, no matter how nice the cities, there was no place like home.

And the food.

Ok, now that I've admitted I can't handle long road trips I certainly enjoyed the cities. Out of all of them Singapore was the one that caused me to realize 'I'm not in Kansas anymore.'

As we flew in to the airport, the stewardess hands us the immigration card to fill out. As I am reading it, I turn it over to see (in bright red print) that being caught with drugs is an offense punishable by death.

It is a beautiful city. I don't do drugs, but my overactive imagination was explaining how many ways someone could sneak drugs into my bag and then I'm going to be swimming with the fish.

Sometimes, this imagination thing is way overrated.

FAN PRICING

$0.99 Saturdays (new LMBPN stuff) and $0.99 Wednesday (both LMBPN books and friends of LMBPN books.) Get great stuff from us and others at tantalizing prices.

Go ahead, I bet you can't read just one.

Sign up here: http://lmbpn.com/email/.

HOW TO MARKET FOR BOOKS YOU LOVE

Review them so others have your thoughts, tell friends and the dogs of your enemies (because who wants to talk with enemies?)... *Enough said ;-)*

Ad Aeternitatem,

Michael Anderle

OTHER SERIES IN THE ORICERAN
UNIVERSE:

SCHOOL OF NECESSARY MAGIC
SCHOOL OF NECESSARY MAGIC: RAINE CAMPBELL
ALISON BROWNSTONE
THE DANIEL CODEX SERIES
THE LEIRA CHRONICLES
I FEAR NO EVIL
THE UNBELIEVABLE MR. BROWNSTONE
REWRITING JUSTICE
THE KACY CHRONICLES
MIDWEST MAGIC CHRONICLES
SOUL STONE MAGE
THE FAIRHAVEN CHRONICLES

OTHER BOOKS BY JUDITH BERENS

OTHER BOOKS BY MARTHA CARR

JOIN THE ORICERAN UNIVERSE FAN GROUP ON
FACEBOOK!

CONNECT WITH THE AUTHORS

Martha Carr Social

Website: http://www.marthacarr.com

Facebook: https://www.facebook.com/
groups/MarthaCarrFans/

Michael Anderle Social

Michael Anderle Social
Website:
http://www.lmbpn.com

Email List:
http://lmbpn.com/email/

Facebook Here: https://www.
facebook.com/TheKurtherianGambitBooks/